THE
POTENTIALS

Adrian Woodland

For Isaac James Woodland: my hero and my world.

1

Colliery Row for Life

Dragid, the hairy giant, bellows through the letterbox again.

'Ha'way, Dan, it's tippin' down. Ye can't bush-camp forever.'

I'm in a cupboard under the stairs, jammed between the wall and the Christmas tree. I bet I can...

'Answer the door, Dan,' Dad shouts from the sweat-pit sofa. 'He'll wear the paint off.'

There's hardly any wood for the paint to wear off. This is not an unusual start to the day.

The sodden ogre steps inside and shakes off the contents of five clouds. Grinning, he hands me a different summons to the type Dad gets: I'm to attend Hatley Academy, a redbrick building of no historical significance, where any similarities between me and that wizard disappear in a puff of disposable vape. Dragrid isn't his real name. I am not the chosen one with a pass to posh school and this is not a request from a bearded warlock with a soft spot for impoverished boys: My name is Daniel Ambrose and I am a school refuser.

I don't see the point in school coz nobody uses maths in the real world. Maths and Science are a waste of time. Why would anyone want to be a doctor or a scientist with conspiracy theories knocking about like COVID and WOPPA?

"Breeding mutants with three eyes and hairy palms in there," Dad reckons. He's had the vaccine though, coz he's vulnerable and that.

Then there's History. Don't make me laugh. The only thing you can do with History is teach History and that makes no sense at all. History within History is teaching to be a teacher. It's like "Inception", but with ginger beards and tweed.

And what about Geography? I'm going nowhere, me. Hatley for life, innit?

Everything at school is a drag, except for English. Everyone can tell you're a divvy if you're not good at English. Dad reckons boys are divvies coz they don't read enough and spend all night on video games. He says that's why I'm not allowed an Xbox, but Dad's on the sick, so that'll be the real reason.

This is real life, where wizards and giants don't exist and Dads are on the sick. Nobody's the illegitimate son of Zeus and there's no magic, miracles, or superpowers to make things any less grim. In real life, it wouldn't even matter if you were a wizard or a demigod: if you're poor, you're poor. Not like in the books, where your hippy mum has plates piled high and your prankster brothers have a flying car. In real life, if there's bread with soup, you've won the lottery. Real life toughens you up and round here wizard kids wouldn't last five minutes:

"Yer a ponce, 'Arry. Giz that wand or I'll spin yer jaw."

I *do* have my own bedroom though… in a cottage on Colliery Row, a council estate in Hatley, just off the motorway between Sunderland and Durham. Hatley benefits from easy access to both cities and picturesque views of the valley and dales, but only one person on our estate owns a car and nobody's got hiking boots, coz the pub isn't far enough away to warrant the spend.

The Cock and Bull ("and Bull" has been pulled off, coz nobody likes the new manager) is across the road from ours. It opens at eleven and shuts when the neighbours leave, around nine the next morning. And a short walk from the pub, past the garden sofas, trampolines and upside-down motorbikes, is the pharmacy, which opens for two hours around nine the next morning. It's not *just* a pharmacy: Singh's Chemist is a magical place where, for three quid a month, Mr Singh sorts everyone's benefits out too. Nobody on Colliery Row is sick during pub opening hours and he has a car loan to pay for, so he's got to bolster his wages somehow.

By the time we're at the bottom of the bank, I'm being dragged along like a muddy festival tent on the way back to the car. Icy bullets batter my forehead as Dragrid tightens the headlock and we plough towards the corner shop that donates food to the local kids. By "donate", I mean, in the absence of a sober parent, the shopkeeper is "powerless to prevent the removal of his stock" by the local kids. There's no tingly-toungly-twisteroonees or chocolate toads in there, but there is a way to delay the inevitable: Speccy might have been clamming to get wiggling his wand, but I'm clinging onto the anti-ramraid bollard, calling the beefcake yanking at my hood a "dog nonce".

Around twenty minutes later, the door at the top of the corridor crashes open and I hear the familiar echo of Jackie's fake, leather boots, clip-clopping along like a prancing horse. This afternoon she's sporting a long, purple double-breasted overcoat, a paisley scarf around her neck and her hair is tied up in a ridiculous maroon velvet wrap.

'Who rubbed your lamp?'

'You'll need more than three wishes to get you out of this mess, Daniel,' she says baring her lipstick-coated teeth and sitting so close I can smell the coffee on her breath. 'I thought we'd agreed.'

'*You* thought we'd agreed, *Jackie*.'

Jackie is my dad's "special friend". After Mam left, Dad's mental health got so bad they took him to hospital and Jackie moved in to make things easier for us. There's no chance of Mam coming back while she's here. She doesn't need to be coz me and Dad are fine. Anyone can make beans on toast and there's never any mess coz Dad just sits on the sofa all day. All I had to do was wash the dishes, wipe his mouth and chuck a blanket over him. Occasionally, he cries and I don't like that.

Mr Sparks, the bald, former-military headteacher, ushers me and Jackie into the office, where the dank smell of dead skin tells me that the books lining a dozen mahogany shelves are for show and not reading. A manual entitled "Beginning Taxidermy for Beginners" lies next to two badly stuffed stoats that man an enormous lead safe behind his desk. I've met these dudes before and they remember it well, as they glare at me desperate to gorge my eyes out.

The sun beams through a gap in the curtains and particles dance around, reminding Sparky of his youth (when he had hair for dandruff). He discards his rehydrated Ramen while Jackie, the withered hag, scrunches her lips trying to look disappointed. She looks more like she's forgotten her false teeth and Sparky spots this too, coz he chokes on a regurgitated noodle.

Patting one of the infamous lever-arch files she hoards in her office, Mrs Tabel, from the pastoral team, hovers quietly in the corner. She straightens her knee-length cardigan, tips her frying pan glasses and flashes a comforting smile. Mrs Tabel is a lush woman from Jersey and she has my back, unlike Mr Sparks, who *busts* my back, reciting the school behaviour policy (again). The lecture is still dragging on half an hour later.

'This is the umpteenth time this month, Ambrose,' says Sparky, raising those thick eyebrows that I bet he wishes were on the top of his head. 'Trying to topple the kingpin? Fancy your chances as Big Frank?'

'Yer ma's Big Frank.'

'*That's* a detention.'

'Yer ma's a detention.'

'My mother is *dead*, Ambrose. She had a heart attack last week. Detention until the end of term.'

Touché.

'He's had a rough time,' says Jackie, trembling like she's sat on the washing machine. She touches my knee with her curry fingers and some bile comes up. 'He's a good lad and I'm sure he's sorry about your mother. God rest her soul.'

Oh, Jackie is a "God Botherer" determined to convert *everyone* she meets, including the dog. Dad could do with believing in *something,* mind. Maybe the tooth fairy could fetch him some paste.

'She's not *really* dead, Mrs Ambrose,' says Sparky, the lying numpty and my chair clatters against the floorboards.

'*That thing* is *not* my mam.'

'Sit down,' Sparky orders, nodding at my black eye. 'If you don't want another one of those. It was a simple mistake.'

Proper out of order that was, but I take some deep breaths when I see Mrs Tabel looking worried.

I'm heading back under the stairs tomorrow. No chance I'm coming in.

Sparky nods over for the lever-arch file while Jackie becomes noticeably anxious, craning her neck for a peek. Seeing her nosey parker routine, the head tips the file towards his chest like he's hiding homework, and she starts bricking it. I'm not surprised either — she'll be in it more than me.

I wonder how far my file goes back. What about the alien head? When I was born, my mam thought I was an alien coz my head was all squashed. Dad says the midwife took a Polaroid picture for medical research, but that must be his best attempt at a joke, coz I've heard that when you're born, everyone's head is soft and squishy and gets flattened on the way out.

Sparky's eyebrows are jumping around like he's landing a plane on his polished bonce, but the waves across his forehead aren't a sign of empathy. He's searching for evidence that I'm a loser and heading to jail like the rest of Colliery Row.

'Two years of teacher complaints,' Sparky says. 'Two years slumped on that chair like the world owes you something.'

'Anything,' I reply. 'I think you mean "*anything*".'

'The world owes you nothing, Ambrose,' says Sparky, morbidly, doubling down on his military tone. 'You earn your rewards.'

'Hard to earn rewards when everyone's trying to smash your face in.'

'Still having trouble with your friends?' he says, referencing Doug Barker.

'We're not friends,' I mumble, pointing at my black eye. 'Anymore.'

We were *proper* mates once. Thick as thieves.

Sparky rocks back on his chair and flattens his palms together like he's praying. Sucking through his fingers, so they make a whistling sound, he glances over to Mrs Tabel and then back to me.

'Interesting read, Ambrose,' he says. 'What are we going to do, eh? There is no point in excluding you again. That's exactly what you want.'

'I don't need school to get a start at the milk factory,' I say. 'You can earn almost *a hundred benk a day* at the milk factory and they pay an extra *fifty* for the night shift.'

'Mr Sparks and I think you are underachieving, Daniel,' interrupts Mrs Tabel. 'And your ambition to work in the milk factory confirms it. Fatfield is not providing the correct type of stimulation.'

'If you can't change the people around you,' says Sparky. '*Change* the people around you.'

'Chuck D?' asks Mrs Tabel and Sparky nods, impressed (but not as impressed as me).

'The hardest rapper,' he says, raising the hairy valley above his eyes. 'Mrs Tabel believes it is those around you that are preventing you from achieving your true potential. So, tomorrow you will move to Penshaw Red.'

Sweet!

Wait. What?

My rise in temperature bursts a barometer when my

cheeks flare up. I shuffle my blazer to the back of my shoulders, stiffen, thicken my accent and prepare to go ballistic.

'Nee chance. I'm not being stuck in with them plebs.'

'Will he need a new uniform?' Jackie mutters, picking at her curry fingers. 'With Keith between jobs and that.' She's properly panicking in case she has to spend her money on anything other than culturally offensive headgear and blasphemous puppy toys.

'It's a red band on the pocket, Mrs... erm... Mizz,' says Sparky, carefully. 'I'm sure we can find one in the lost-and-found.'

'I'm not gannin' in the top set man. Me dad cannet afford Penshaw.'

'Nobody pays for their education,' Sparky says, dismissively. 'Some parents contribute to the school's upkeep, but that's just coincidence.'

Absolute rubbish. Everybody knows that those parental contributions ensure a place in Privileged Penshaw. It's what winds Doug up the most. No matter how much money his dad's got, it'll make no difference: Doug Barker is as thick as two short planks. Without a parental contribution to a brain transplant, he's Fatfield for life...

'Give it a thought, Daniel,' says Mrs Tabel, standing to put a hand on my shoulder.

'No. It's non-negotiable,' instructs Sparky. 'You'll join Penshaw Red tomorrow. Then you'll have the weekend to reflect.'

Not a chance. I'm duffing tomorrow. I won't fit in with that lot. I'm Fatfield for li —

Hold your horses, Daniel Lad.

Fatfield for life? Hatley for life? Collier Row for —?

Maybe a change is *exactly* what I need.

Maybe a change will do me the world of good.

But, one thing *is* for certain — when word gets out that Daniel Ambrose, a poor kid from Colliery Row, has been moved into Penshaw Red… *Doug Barker will be livid.*

2

The Substitute and The Broken Telephone

Dad's sitting in his vest and boxers pretending to watch a home restoration program. Nobody's fooling nobody though. If he's not asleep or crying, he's watching Mam's WhatsApp status flick from nothing to online.

'She's gone, Dad,' I say.

'To see a man about a dog, Dan.' he says. 'She'll not be long.'

'Not *her*. M— dunt matter. Look, I'm going to the woods after school if you fancy it?'

'I've not been to those woods in years,' he snaps, sitting upright. 'You can't see the wood for the trees in them woods.'

'Trees *are* wood, Dad.'

'You're not listening,' Keith barks. His eyes are red raw and his veined nose peaks with a volcanic white spot. 'Mum's got a new fella, Son.'

His rant becomes erratic and he reaches forward to swig straight from a bottle. His panic starts with his arms flapping and coz he's got no core strength, he's just a wild-haired, lunatic chicken, rocking back and forth. I get to the bottle first, but he snatches at it, knocking the scab from my arm and his voice grows despondent.

'Remember the coffee shop, Dan,' he says for the millionth time (café culture makes him angry). 'I was a visionary, Son. Then *everyone* opened a cool coffee shop with unpronounceable brews that stole the tweed and suede pointy shoes.' He's proper upset and I can see his knuckles whiten. 'But they all ignored the visionary for his vision. Happens with music, venues, art, burgers, pizza, curry, sandwiches and now vegan food. Everywhere has such a wealth of limited culinary options. Just-Eat just depresses me.'

We're heading for termite territory when the door opens and Jackie comes in, dressed in a grotty pink dressing gown, pyjamas and slippers. This time she's got a Sombrero on and I have no words. She sneaks into the kitchen with a couple of shopping bags, immediately getting on my nerves.

'I'll never be good enough for your mam,' Dad says, right in front of Jackie. 'Wake up, eat breakfast, work and do the same but different stuff tomorrow. All of that for a bloody fortnight in Tenerife.' His anger escalates. 'I won't plumb mindlessly under a sink in some blood, sweat and tears profession for enough money to lie on a beach once a year. It's total madness.'

In the kitchen, Jackie puts away the food she's bought with her wages. She puts the Sombrero on the bench and sighs.

'Is that what everyone wants?' Dad continues, getting more upset. 'To bleed through life termiting? That's all we are. Termites. Highly destructive, colonising, multi-caste, reproducing and eating everything at an unsustainable rate until it's all gone. Termites. Massive, sweaty termites.' *This is getting pretty grim and I'm going to have to ring the crisis team if he doesn't shut up.*'Is that *it*? How can humans be distinguished from termites? Unpronounceable coffee names?'

'I bet termites call their coffee something easy to say, like "click-click",' says Jackie, trying to lighten the mood.

'Have you been to the shop like that?' I blurt out. It's not her job to fix Dad, it's mine.

'I'm working from home today,' Jackie says putting on a baby voice and chucking a new rubber cross at Yappy Dog. 'There ya go, Baba. Get some God in ya.'

Dad looks over to her in the kitchen and smiles. 'Oh you'll never get to Hebburn,' he sings softly, calming down and slumping back.

'In a biscuit tin,' Jackie sings in a surprisingly tuneful voice.

The sound of screeching moggies lies ahead, so rather than wait for Dragrid, I ditch Sad Sack and Mother Eraser and head out to school.

Penshaw Red's classroom is like an alternate reality. The door doesn't stick, for a start, while inside, it's full of new equipment and a fancy new Smart Board. There's no detention board on the wall like in our... Fatfield Yellow's room.

I despise that board. By the time we got to the connect activity, the teachers were marking crosses like it was bingo night and it was impossible to tell who was kicking heads or who was head-butting feet.

Class size is different too. Instead of thirty-five, there are about fifteen kids in here and they're observing me like a family of gorillas with a lost child wandering around their enclosure.

I twist the loose button on my lost-and-found blazer to

tighten it, push out my chest and mooch to an empty desk at the back, where I drag the chair feet along the tiles, flash the evils and sit.

There's no teacher yet. Fatfield Yellow would *never* be left alone. That would result in another black eye for me and broken stuff.

I take advantage of the silence and pass the time by pulling at the scab on my wrist. It comes off the knobble, releasing the pressure, but when I raise the crusty corner to my lips, my buzz is killed when the others turn towards me and express their disgust.

A kid who "shares" his dinner money with The Fatfield Four, stares over. He's wearing his parka as a cape and when I lock eyes, he turns away, tapping his face like a proper weirdo.

In front, a wiry, red-haired lad, called Oscar, gawps at my black eye as if I've got summat stupid written on my face. Technically, I *have* got summat stupid written on my face ("duck and run") but there's no need to point it out. Anyway, he's got a nerve giving it the biggun considering he wears a corrective shoe. I'm not getting lippy though, coz his cousin, a git big lad with a massive Afro Fade, cracks his knuckles waiting for an excuse to black my other eye.

Afro Gaz used to be in The Fatfield Four with me. He's proper funny and handy with his fists. He's a boxer and probably the only reason Oscar with the shoe doesn't get picked on like other kids.

'Hungry?' says Gaz, nodding at the scab.

Embarrassed, I lower my arm and think of something smart to say.

'Aye, I could scran a scabby horse.'

'Dinnet be so harsh on yersel,' he says, winking. 'Yer fyas isn't that lang.'

That's a better comeback than mine, but I play it cool and

let him think he's boring.

Down the front, a skater girl with a snapback cap sits next to a *proper* geek with comedy glasses that magnify her eyes. The skater is Molly Nell and she's a rich kid, but I don't know the geeky one. There's no time in Hatley Academy to put names to faces when you're focusing on surviving the day without a protractor stabbing. This school is a complex mix of village idiots, thugs, me, fifteen rich kids, and more idiots. That's all you need to know.

After a few minutes, I manage to stem the bleeding scab, but the flapping crust is begging to be pulled off. So, I nip the two sides together and it stings as I dig my nail into the soft lip attached to the skin. Then, just as it's ready to snap, I'm interrupted by a cough from the morning entertainment.

Dishevelled and unshaven, he couldn't look more like a substitute teacher if he tried. There is no surprise a full-time contract eludes this man. His eyes are so dull they show a spark that has long since died.

That's going in my mocks. English Language gold. Might use a colon… or a semi-colon?

'My name is Dr Angelos Urielis, Professor of Philosophy,' the subbie says, sighing and letting out a waft of gingivitis that fills the room. 'I have spent a lifetime working alongside the world's greatest thinkers. Of course, now we find ourselves here.'

Dr Life's-Gone-Wrong takes a small, silver hip-flask from the pocket of his tweed jacket and places it on the desk to drink with his mind. The other inmates look horrified (I bet their parents have him sacked) but the door opens to distract them and six embarrassed students from Hatley Junior School flop onto the floor by the window. One of them, a blushing girl with scruffy, scissor-cut hair, nips her nose and waves at Molly Nell, the skater.

'These little cherubs,' says Dr Urielis, holding out his hand as if he's dishing out tombola prizes, 'are here because of chronic underfunding. Instead of finger painting, they will be snoozing through our pre-planned lesson on —' He drops his head, 'oh, for the love of Belinda: "What is your superpower?" Really?'

This pearl of school planning has further crushed the subbie's faith in an education system willing to employ someone who looks like they live behind a dumpster. Meanwhile, the fat kid in the cape-coat leaps excitedly out of his chair and you'd think he could fly, so I'm guessing this isn't a regular topic of discussion.

Hopefully, the sight of the overfed punching the air was the final straw for the subbie, who sighs his unique brand of air-unfreshener for the second time, rubs his beard, reddens his pie-crust-coloured skin with friction burns and starts to repack his satchel. But just as things are looking up, Gaz pipes up to bring things looking down.

'It's Personal Development, Sir. Just wing it. Neebody's expecting miracles.'

Suddenly, the subbie bounds between desks as if ready to plant a left hook. Oscar, with the shoe, flinches to cover his head, while Gaz stiffens, preparing for whatever Dr Urielis is about to dish out. Even I brace and I'm used to ducking the odd clip.

'Get up,' he snaps, ready to show the room why he's on a temporary contract. 'Wind that neck in, you lanky genius. Boys and Girls, Gigantor has saved the day.'

Oh, I thought we were getting a free period.

I wasn't expecting this and neither was Afro Gaz, who towers above, looking confused, but relieved he hasn't had to flatten a teacher.

'Nee need for the lanky dig like,' he says. 'I'll tack genius though.'

'A rare compliment, String Bean,' Dr Urielis explains, with a wink. He offers his fist for a bump, showing that he's down with the kids, who leave him hanging.

As if someone's switched him on, the substitute's eyes glisten sapphire blue. 'The Egyptians tell of Horus. India's miracle workers are Attis and Krishna,' he says. 'Dionysus is Greek and Mrithra is Persian. There are so, so many miracle workers and arguably the most famous of them all is Jesus. Is turning water into wine not indeed a superpower?'

'It is on Colliery Row,' says Gaz. 'They'd be queuing round the block if ye could turn water into white cider.'

Cheeky git.

'Sounds lovely,' says Dr Urielis. 'Are superpowers and miracles the same thing?'

'T-turning water into wine isn't a superpower,' the Chinese geek with jam jar goggles dismisses. 'It is gr-grapes and yeast fermenting to con-convert sugar into alcohol.'

'Oh, we have a scientist amongst us,' mocks the subbie.

Jam Jar is a nerd with a funny bone made from binary coding and has her future planned from university to retirement.

'Ok, *Nanu-Nanu*,' the subbie continues, 'So they're not the same thing?'

What's a "Nanu"? I bet he says his views are a "generational thing" like my gran used to say. God rest her racist soul.

'No. Supernatural abilities violate the laws of nature. Moreover, they d-defy science.'

Today's "moreover" is tomorrow's "furthermore".

'Sunderland gerrin' into Europe would be a miracle,' splutters Gaz. He's canny funny.

'That's superpowers,' Oscar says punching his cousin in the arm. 'Footballers get better at footy. Thinkers think better.

People jump higher. Runners are faster.'

Chubs pulls the collar of his cape-coat over his face. At first, it seems like he's crying, but he emerges a few seconds later with his right eye closed tight, like someone's stuck a finger in a tomato. He's got this huge grin that looks more like a curvy cucumber than a smile. This is impressive considering that he's never seen a salad.

'Splendid-Man flies and he shoots fire from his left eye,' he informs the class.

I'd always thought they kept Fatfield separate from Penshaw coz we can't be trusted around anyone with dinner money, but it turns out they're doing it for *our* safety, not theirs. I owe Sparky an apology.

Molly, the skater, picks at the remains of her black nail polish and flicks bits at Jam Jar. That's proper minging, so I take my mind off it by twisting the scab-end and some torn skin leaves a frustrating, spiky bit, which I get my teeth into again.

The substitute's eyes drift, but before I'm in the firing line, Gaz slides his chair with a teeth-tingling scrape that distracts everyone and sets Chubs off, poking himself in the face again.

'Sir,' says Gaz, stooping to pick up a rolled-up mat. 'I've gorra gan dee me *thing*.'

'Oh, erm, oh… I'm sorry.'

Gaz doesn't look bothered by the subbie's disregard for diversity, as he picks up the mat and ducks out the door, laughing.

'Nee bosh, Sir. *We've* got miracles anarl, y'knar.'

While Gaz is gone, Oscar informs Urielis that *"nee bosh"* means *"no bother"* or *"no problem"* and that his cousin is from Byker, in Newcastle, "where they talk funny". Then he spends the next few minutes translating more dialect and I realise that I've leaned forward on my desk. Ok, this lesson is better than "Spot the Dog and Dodge the Missile" but only coz nobody's trying to stab me with a protractor.

A few minutes later, Gaz comes back with no mat and chewing something. Frothy saliva has seeped out of the left corner of his mouth and his eyes are massive as he bounds back to his chair.

'That was quick?' Dr Urielis says, looking surprised.

'Nee queue on a Friday, Sir. There's arnly five gan.'

'I suppose others do it at home, after school and that… less noise.'

This should be interesting. Nobody mentions religion outside of RE. Mind you, nobody discusses religion *in* RE. Nobody discusses *anything* in RE, except the authenticity of Bernie "Rat" Trapperd, a part-time "Expert Educator" who reckons he's better than teachers who've done proper training. That's just a way of saying he's got no teaching qualifications and that's why he babysits RE. He wears his baseball cap back-to-front and has a thick beard that hides a face that's been fed buckets of fishheads. Nobody likes him; he's got a hot dog van at the footy and he's a creep that infamously snitched to secure his job (hence the "Rat").

'Neebody does Yoga at home on a Friday, Man,' Gaz says. 'Ye cannet wrap yer legs around yer heed when yer full of fish and chips.'

'Yoga? I thought that was your prayer mat?'

'Gan canny, *Adolf*.' Gaz says with a wink. 'Arnly kiddin'. Dinnet follow religion like, except the Toon.'

'Oh, I've never heard of this Toon. Is that a classic club banger?'

'It's a footy team,' Oscar perks up. 'Gaz is a filthy Mag.'

'Ho'way the Lads,' Gaz says grinning and thrusting a paper bag towards the subbie. 'I dinnet do prayers nee mare. It's all a bit confusin' with me ma and that. But on Frida, I lend me da's Yoga mat to Shaz for a quarter of ket from the tuck shop and a neck on when she's done. Here, dinnet tack me jelly meerkats. They're me favourites.'

* Gaz is not a practising Muslim and he loans his dad's Yoga mat to Sharon for a kiss after school… I think.

When the laughter calms down, the subbie examines the bag's contents like he's found an abandoned suitcase at an airport. To his relief, he learns that a "quarter of ket" is a northern term for a bag of sweets — mainly jellies, with the odd sherbet saucer — and I'm wondering who's teaching who here.

Picking out a sour dummy and giving it a suck, Dr Urielis returns to his debate. 'Tho we think that thuperpowerth and miracleth are not the thame thing, do we?'

Chubs rocks forward on his chair, desperate to say something else about comics, while Urielis scans the room and I slump down towards the chewing gum stalactites that grow under my desk. What I'd give for the cupboard under the stairs, as I know it's my turn when he repeats the question louder.

'*Are superpowers and miracles the same thing*?'

His sapphire blue eyes shine as bright as stars. And, like a determined crocodile on a small mammal, with no intention of loosening his grip, his discussion hammers on my door.

'Daniel Ambrosia Custard? We can sit here for an extra few hours if you like?' he threatens, passively. I don't react. He'll be clamming for Happy Hour soon, judging by the clip of him.

'Thug Life!'

Leave me alone.

'Oi, Sweet-egg-based-dessert. Got nothing to say? Out of your depth?' *Who does this moron think he is?* 'Are superpowers and miracles the same?'

Blood races to my face with such ferocity that I feel my pores ready to spray the room like a vampire's garden sprinkler and without thinking I kick my chair back.

'*Aye, they're the same thing.* They're just made-up stories, man. They're not real.'

Gasps suck the air out of the room and everyone except Molly spins around to face me.

'False news, Ambrose,' says Dr Urielis, with an air of patronisation. 'History has proved some of these people existed.'

'So what? That doesn't mean they had magical powers.' *Brace yourself, Tweedy. Me Dad's proper into pseudo-science and has this conversation all the time when he's off his noggin.*

'But we have evidence in old scriptures. Stories passed through the ages.'

'That's not proof, man: that's just word of mouth. Nobody's interested in a bloke having a plodge in the river. But, a story about a hippie walking on water… well, that'll spread like wildfire. For a story to spread like that, it needs miracles, magic and superpowers. Stories of good versus evil. Stories of hope.'

'Hope for what?' Dr Urielis says, curiously.

'Something better… better than *this*.'

'Oh.'

'Today, if miracles or superpowers were real, they'd be all over the internet and they're not. Either, they *never* existed, or evolution's taken a step backwards, innit?'

'So you're saying that apart from getting a little better at sports or technology,' says Urielis. 'Humans have long since reached their potential and nothing magical has happened, or ever will?'

'It's just fiction to sell stories. Writers made the stories more exciting. Or it happened when they were passed across continents. What if they were translated wrong, or they got mixed up as it spread? Or people added bits to the original? It's like that game Chinese Whispers —' I spot Jam Jar and sort of apologise with my eyes. 'Err, Broken Telephone, innit?'

Slowly, Dr Urielis walks around his desk, staring at me like he's trying to work me out.

He's underestimated my intelligence: I was in Fatfield Yellow coz we're poor, not coz I'm stupid.

'Do you all know of Broken Telephone?' Dr Urielis asks the class.

Everyone except me says they do (I'm not being snarky, for once. I'd made the initial point).

'Superb. Stand up and form a line.' Urielis snaps his fingers and points to the sleeping juniors. 'You too, Little Bored Ones. The more the merrier.'

Chubs and a freckled lass with pigtails fight for the last in the queue. She's making a fuss about not standing in the middle of "smelly boys". I want to shove both in front of me coz I reckon the game will collapse before my turn, but I decide against it, coz she's a potential snitch and he'll probably rock up in a trench coat on Monday.

The mini-brawl sees Chubs in front of me. Pigtails stands smugly at the back for a few moments until a little lad, who's dribbled down his dungarees, ruins her joy by returning from the bog to stand behind. Arguably a worse scenario for her.

Down front, the soon-to-be-drunk points at the junior girl with the scissor-cut hair.

'Smiler, tell us something about yourself.'

'I have a princess doll,' she says with a shy squeak. 'I love princess dolls but my cat, Viking, chewed my old one.'

'You have a cat called Viking? That's interesting. You will tell the person behind you that Viking ate your princess doll and Moany Hawke will pass it down the line until Uhm-Pa-Pa tells *me* you want to be a Viking Princess. And then I shout it out.'

Scissor-Cut turns to the line behind her, scrunches up her face and growls. Then she curtsies and pirouettes.

'Charmed,' she squeaks at the substitute, who pinches her rosy cheek and asks if everyone is sure of the rules.

After three more explanations, the game begins and Scissor-Cut's whisper spreads right up to Chubs in front of me. The fat bodge shouts 'Viking Princess' at Urielis, much to the annoyance of everyone who *has* grasped the rules. Then, Scissor Cut goes to the back and it's the next one's turn and so on.

'A duck?' says Dr Urielis, calling out the last in the line. 'You want to be a giant duck?'

The junior, with wee down his leg, turns beetroot. 'I'd been to feed the ducks.'

He's not fed the ducks. He ate their bread.

Dr Urielis returns to his desk. Tears form under his sapphire blue eyes and he looks as if he's won an Oscar (the award, not the one with the shoe). Or he could be about to tell us that his wife wants a divorce. I've seen a teacher breakdown before and it was mint. We got a week off for "trauma" then. Sadly, neither of these is the case today as the bearded, tweed-wearing substitute inhales and addresses the room in a cracked, emotional voice:

'Princess Vikings, flying fanboys, shapeshifters, mutants, healers, and one of two robot twins from the future… I still haven't sussed that one,' he says. 'Being a substitute often requires blagging one's way through the allotted time, hoping that loosely planned lessons result in more than a tenuous link to the subject matter. But today, be it magic or miracle, fact or fiction, you've shown potential.'

And, without another word, the best teacher I've had in four years, slips some fingerless leather gloves on, claps his hands together, grins and whistles the intro to a gash eighties song. Then he punches the air on his way out of the door and he's gone.

I don't think we will forget about him.

In a proper good mood, I get to the top of the back lane and hop over the crushed takeaway boxes littering the alley. Colliery Row is such a tip and the back lane stinks with the combined pungency of garlic sauce and urine, warming in the sunshine. It's the weekend though, so I dribble an empty can to the corner shop and score an imaginary penalty against Jordan Pickford.

Over the road, Lillian-Trapperd-Cornford-Campas-Mare-Etc slips behind the distracted shopkeeper and pulls four stolen cans from her leopard-print coat.

Colliery Row's wrinkle-tanned matriarch, skilled in the art of balancing her great-grandchildren in one arm while smoking a tab *and* carrying a tin of booze in the other, furthers her attempts to win the Hatley Peace Prize by passing a can to a scruffy, bearded bloke who looks like a rubbish-dump wizard. Her next victim, no doubt. She's already got seven kids to six dads, who fetch pouches of baccy for their unwanted offspring once a month. Her unity efforts have reconciled umpteen rival ex-cons, bringing peace to a warring neighbourhood.

After Leopard-print Lil and the Wizard stumble away,

tittering into their tins and sweltering in their winter wear, I pull my hoodie strings tighter and, digging both hands deep into my trouser pockets, I click out my neck and hunch my shoulders.

Then, without looking, I step out onto the road where I'm flattened and killed by the Number 38 bus.

3

The Boy Who Died

Everything comes from nothing.
Everything begins as a black "brick" with rounded corners...
somewhere.
Nothing exists to compare it to.
The brick begins to glow.
A border of radiant violet blends to neon pink, through a spectrum
until it is outlined by pure, brilliant, white light.
It is perfect. It is beautiful.
Here, there is no sound, until there is sound.
A feint "tick", like gently pressing a rubber button.
And the brick duplicates itself, with a second brick now on top of the
first.
In the blink of an eye, the two bricks duplicate themselves.
Four, eight, sixteen, thirty-two.
In an instant (although time is nothing) the pile repeats upwards
and over.
It fans out until it is all around me.

Me.
From the very second nothing becomes something, I become aware.
I am something.
I am me.

Encased in a dome of glowing, pulsing light, my vision shifts.
A kaleidoscope of colours and geometric shapes twirl and spiral,
dragging me from within whatever this serpent-like vortex is,
toward a mosaic door at the furthest reaches of the tunnel.
Standing amidst the luminaire is a female decked in whites and
golds like I have never seen.
Incandescent in her robes, she looks at me with confusion, like I am
not meant to be here.
She smiles the softest smile and I am welcome but I have to leave.

GASP.

I am alive.

Everything hurts. My hoodie is ripped to shreds and is covered in the remains of the golf ball of blood I coughed up when I came around.

The hum of the bus engine throbs in time with a bright blue glow, as searing pain pounds me from top to toe.

Like an airport scanner, a sapphire light scrolls into my vision and down, over my face. My neck cracks and I raise my head to see tiny sapphire sparks ooze out of every pore. They coagulate over my body, which is smashed into more angles than A-level maths.

In a matter of seconds, my limbs jerk and a puddle of blood sucks back into me, while the sparks set about reorganising the mess. A hip lurches into place and an ankle flips into the socket. There are no words to describe the pain and it only gets worse as the sapphire lemmings seep over a bloody stump where my severed arm used to be.

The electro-rodents entwine into a thick, crackling rope

that squirms across the road and engulfs the sloppy bicep of my missing limb. Long-lost fingers claw along the tarmac like something out of a horror movie, as it edges towards the stump. Popping my shoulder, I reached out to give the arm a hand and it's wrenched from my grasp as the two ends reattach.

For a moment, I am silent, confused and learning to tolerate the pain, but my stillness is disrupted when the bus driver decides to reverse off my body. Of course, the bus isn't on my body in the first place, so the driver squashes me for the second time in five minutes.

This time, things seem to happen a little quicker and I'm still assembling when steel-toed boots pace cautiously towards the front wheels. The bus driver kneels to assess the mess and once he sees my mangled body, like a dropped marionette, he barfs. Some of it splashes into the re-severed arm.

He fumbles for his phone and calls the emergency services for an ambulance. Then the divvy tells them that an ambulance isn't necessary, as the body under the bus is "*definitely* dead".

'Very, very dead,' he reiterates and reports the incident to the bus depot to clarify that it wasn't his fault. He's more concerned about getting sacked than the fact he just flattened a school kid, as he flannels his excuses. Eventually, he bursts into tears and asks for a cuddle from a lady called Elaine.

I am not "very, very dead". I am very much alive and grateful for the "Step-dwellers" emerging into the sunshine. Filthy ants in stained, grey sweatpants heckle the police as they arrive soundtracking the scene with the revving of stolen mopeds. Leopard-Print Lil assures everyone that "Mamma loves her pride and joy (riders)" as the police grow weary of the ruckus, forming a barrier between Lil's many children and those on the bus.

The distraction is sufficient for me to scrape myself from under and duck low over to the bins by the corner shop. Hopefully, an inquisitive shopkeeper won't notice the alien glow of a healing teen behind his refuse, as he chucks a bag into the massive industrial canister.

I seem to have gotten away with it when he drops a second right in front of where I'm hiding and returns to his shop.

After a few minutes, a police car forms a roadblock with a Nissan Micra and more officers try to calm down the skip rats. I seize this moment to grab the rogue bin bag while several passengers offer their witness statements.

I sneak towards the back wheels while the bus driver keeps hold of Elaine's hand and nervously recalls the events. He looks as pale as a ghost.

'It was a boy,' he says. 'He was all mashed up.'

'Well, where is he then?' asks a police officer with a blonde fringe and glasses. 'Did he just disappear?'

'Probably mince now,' says another passenger. 'Bloody idiot bumped over 'im twice.'

'Moight be mashed up in them there wheel arches,' says a man with a flat cap who isn't from round here.

While nobody is looking, I stuff the rubbish bag into the wheel arch and rip open the top. Dozens of rotten apples spill out, rolling across the road towards the fringed police officer. She spots one when I'm safely back behind the bins.

'Did you pip your horn?' she asks the bus driver.

'Sorry?'

'This is looking seedy. I think I've found the victim. It's not a boy, it's an old lady.'

'Oh, God, is she dead?'

'Crumbled,' she confirms. Then, she laughs and chucks him an apple. 'Poor old Granny Smith.'

For the rest of my way home, I keep close to the walls of the back lanes and check for falling pianos and exploding planes. Dad and the lodger aren't in, but I get a canny shock when I see my reflection.

The steam from the shower fills the room. Tarmac scratches fade slowly in the clouded mirror. The scar marking the join of the reattached arm tingles with pins and needles, as it continues to vanish before my eyes.

I draw around the blurred reflection disappearing behind the steam and a blue aura glows through the haze. Droplets bounce like a million, glowing ping-pong balls, washing away the tyre marks from my forehead. The warm water soothes and the bathtub blazes brightly. Mattered skin heals and clumps of dried blood wash down the plughole.

Exhausted, I drip-dry and pull on some pyjamas. The scars are gone. No aches or pains. Only the tainted skin under my right eye and scab on my wrist remain.

My sapped energy gives way and I collapse onto the bed, my body sinking deep into the worn mattress. Pointy springs don't bother me for the first time in years. *They* come home from the pub, but I ignore the commotion.

In the liminal state of drifting, I reflect on the day — the bus driver's horror, lighting up like a lightbulb, the shopkeeper and... becoming immortal — until eventually, the deep sleep wraps comforting arms around me, dragging me into a dream world more believable than the day has been. And, as I slip under, I slur the answer to all of these questions.

"Dr Angelos Urielis...The substitute and the broken telephone."

4

Molly's Mole

Molly Nell had a mole on her right shoulder. Her dad called it her "giggle spot". Her mum said it made her unique in the world. If ever Molly needed help, she tickled the mole and it made everything better.

'Hurry, Molly. We'll be late for Dad.'

Molly skipped down the broad, wooden stairs, bouncing her fingers off the rosewood bannister. She wore her pastel-pink Ernie and Bert t-shirt, paired with navy Dickies pants, rolled-up four times because they were miles too long. She topped off the outfit with Vans trainers and a cap — Molly's favourite clothes for visiting her dad, who bought all his "little tomboy's cool stuff".

'You're finally awake,' said Molly's mum. 'Come on.'

Arriving at Hatley General Hospital, they hurried past

Ward Nine, the first ward Mr Nell had been admitted to.

When they passed the chapel, Molly took off her cap, as a mark of respect. Mr Nell would joke that the man in the chapel was the Grim Reaper, because he visited the patients before they departed. He told Molly he had seen the Grim Reaper ride the hospital lift down to Louis' Coffee Shop, where the patients wait to meet their visitors.

"Smells of death in 'ere, Mols." Mr Nell had said, flashing a mischievous grin. "Here's the Grim Reaper buying a scone."

Molly probably shouldn't have giggled, but she joined in with the joke. "Does the Grim Reaper put jam or clotted cream on first?"

"Neither, they sell so quickly... they're alway-sgone."

Mr Nell and Molly pronounced "scone" in the proper way.

Her dad called the cafe "The Departure Lounge". He and Uncle Eric fitted a door chime that played "Leaving on a Jet Plane" whenever a customer entered. Mr Nell would nip his nose and, in an absurd airport announcement voice, he would say, "Last call for strokes and heart attacks at table five. Uh-oh, there's Old Mabel away."

Even Louis found that funny and Mr Nell got his coffee for half price.

Last time Molly had asked if the Reaper put jam or cream on first, her dad said he would ask him when they met. Molly had not laughed at that joke because, that same day, the doctor told the family that the man in the chapel would visit soon and they must prepare for the worst. That's when Molly realised her father was going to the actual Departure Lounge. Her dad was going to die.

"I don't fear the Reaper," Mr Nell said to comfort his daughter, but it did not work. Molly was sure that the man in the chapel *was* the Grim Reaper after all.

Molly put her head down as she passed Ward Ten, where the staff would soon transfer her dad. Her mum buzzed Ward Eleven's buzzer and then washed her hands thoroughly with the lime-green antibacterial gel. Molly washed her hands too, as she did not want to spread germs. It didn't smell of lime at all; it smelled of clean.

The big, fat matron opened the door, asking if they were here to see Mr Nell.

'That's my dad,' said Molly, annoyed that the matron did not recognise them after six months of visiting.

Staff Nurse Gabrielle, a short lady with a haircut like a helmet, ushered the matron out of the way and greeted Molly and her mum. She often told Molly amusing stories, mostly about senior nurses scolding her for taking things to extremes.

Nurse Gabrielle made Molly and her mum feel relaxed, and she was kind to her dad — even when he messed up the sheets.

"It's not his fault," she said. 'He can't help it."

Gabrielle scrunched her lips and her tortoiseshell glasses rocked on her pointy nose. 'Matron Burgerbreath is in a right old mood, again,' she huffed.

'What did you do?' said Molly, setting Gabrielle up for her punchline.

'The "Macarena"… with Ward Eleven.'

Molly chuckled, although she probably shouldn't because Nurse Gabrielle was a professional after all. Nevertheless, she was very caring and the patients loved her.

'Well, I think it will have cheered them up,' Molly said, supportively.

'Me too,' said Nurse Gabrielle with a grin like a Cheshire

cat. 'Although, I suppose Mr Wallace did get a little overexcited.'

Molly scurried past the other rooms until she arrived at her dad's "penthouse suite" (as he called it) with the machines, the wires, and the tubes sticking into his body.

One tube was red with blood while another had clear liquid and stretched air bubbles, like the spirit level her dad had used to straighten Molly's shelves. It probably worked better than the spirit level.

"There's something wrong with this thing," Mr Nell had said. "Your books are falling down Rocky Hill."

Molly's dad sucked at fixing things.

A white tube attached to an oxygen mask was the worst. That was for when he choked.

Eventually, the doctor arrived to meet the family.

'A lolly for Molly?' he said, passing a strawberry lolly to his favourite visitor. He looked tired today and his hair dangled, unbrushed, onto his forehead like a shrubbery. It wobbled as he asked Molly to sit with her dad while he spoke privately to her mum.

Mr Nell's bloodshot eyes barely blinked as his daughter waved her hand in front of them. He looked scared as if he had spotted a monster hiding behind. Molly squeezed his hand and tickled the mole.

'What are we going to do with you, eh?' she said, because that's what her dad said whenever she was poorly. 'Let's get you all fixed up.'

Suddenly, the heart monitor beeped faster and faster. Mr Nell's body twitched and spasmed as the doctor rushed into the room.

'I need you to see your mum while we get your dad back off to sleep,' the doctor ordered, pulling at Molly's shoulders.

Molly cried out. Then, when she let go of her dad's hand, the bond broke and a tiny ruby-red spark of electricity scratched the end of her fingertips, making her jump. That was all. Just the smallest spark. It sizzled and tingled up the arm, right into the middle of the mole.

Calmly, the doctor ushered them out of the room while Nurse Gabrielle settled Mr Nell with an injection.

And the mole pulsed like a heartbeat.

Mrs Nell sobbed as they left the ward.

In Room B, Mrs Walker waved at Molly through a gap in her curtain, blowing a big, warm kiss that Molly returned with a tiny wave. Mrs Walker was a lovely lady with a yellowish face, curly, grey hair, and cheeks so sunken they looked like wishing wells. Molly wished she could make a wish in them and right now, she'd wish not to feel quite so poorly.

Next, Mr Wallace hollered, 'Chuck us a smile, Duck Egg' and offered an apple. Mr Wallace had a juicy red apple most days, which his son brought in, but Molly never took it, just in case. He wouldn't be in there if didn't give his apples away.

The mole throbbed harder and Molly burped in her mouth.

At home, the shiny fridge reminded Molly of better times.

Before Hatley Academy, Molly was home-schooled and a "Development Schedule" took pride of place. However, initial trips to the hospital led to mainstream education and put an end to strict routines.

The family spent more time having fun together and who wouldn't love less boring home-schooling. Who wouldn't love meeting new friends and drinking more milkshakes at Louis' coffee shop with Dad?

But one day, some dried ketchup on the mahogany table foretold of misery brewing. Mrs Nell, an obsessive polisher, had ignored the ketchup, raised to the size of a chocolate drop.

That day, Mr Nell had sat opposite the ominous blood button, at least three days old and stinking. Then he told Molly that he was sick. He told her that there was no time. He told her that one day soon, he would see the man in the chapel.

Molly wished that she could have the development schedule back. She no longer liked stupid mainstream education and she still cannot bare the smell of dried ketchup.

Molly came over dizzy while speaking to Nanna Nell on the old, brown phone.

Her mum sat on the sofa and wept as Molly set the table.

The mole bulged and Molly's skin turned grey.

She fed Viking the cat and gasped through crackling lungs.

She ate a mouthful of vibrant salad but couldn't finish it.

She washed the dirty dishes before coughing up in the sink.

She lay down on the wooden floor while her mum screamed for help.

She spat vomit over Ernie and Bert and then, with a jolt, Molly left her pale, dying body in a frightful mood.

Up-there Molly looked down and watched as the girl took a fit on the carpet.

'Hello, *Down-there Molly*,' she said. 'What on Earth are you doing?'

Molly twitched, just like her father when Nurse Gabrielle

had jabbed him with the needle.

The mole on her shoulder was purple and bloated. It swelled, becoming darker and shinier as it did. It grew from a mole to the size of a grape, then a bouncy ball, a tennis ball, and a melon, until finally, it looked like an enormous ruby balloon.

Up-there Molly watched the balloon twist until it detached and bobbled above Molly's head, tied to her shoulder by a short, ruby-red thread.

'Pull yourself together!' demanded *Up-there Molly* and before she could say another word, *Up-there Molly* sucked back down with an enormous gasp.

The fit stopped suddenly and Molly felt the colour return to her cheeks, like pouring her favourite blackcurrant juice into a clean, sparkling glass. She jerked upright and blurted out "holy mole" right in her hysterical mother's face. Mrs Nell promptly passed out.

Molly's mum came around moments later. Tears formed pink watercolour lines down her cheeks and she sobbed in mournful distress. Molly sucked in a breath, wriggled onto her mum's knee and reached out to clasp her hand.

'Let's get you all fixed up,' she whispered. And then the phone rang…

A tiny, ruby-red flash clicked the end of her fingertips as Mrs Nell let go of her daughter's hand to talk to Nurse Gabrielle. A spark zipped up Molly's arm, right into the centre of the mole and her heart sank to the pit of her stomach, washing her soul with sadness.

And the mole rose once more.

5

The Alien Museum

It takes about ten minutes to prise my top lip from my teeth and pick the crust off my eyelids. The morning sun has me lathered. The sheets are drenched.

Icy-cold pyjamas peel from my sweaty back and the towel on the floor from last night is rough, like sandpaper.

Jackie is wrong. Wet towels dry perfectly well on the floor.

Throughout the night, I've had vivid nightmares of buses, fractal images, and gods. I'm shattered.

Dad's in his usual spot and as soon as he hears me come in, he flips the phone and starts singing a mumbled version of "Oh, You'll Never Get to Hebburn", a parody of an old camp song from scout camp where he met Mam. Keeps him calm but has the opposite effect on me.

Jackie unpacks a shopping bag and chucks another squeaky cross for the dog. I swear it gobbles on God every other day. That mutt is going to Hell.

'Late for work,' I point out.

'Don't work Mondays, Daniel.'

'Eh?'

'You've been in bed for three days.'

'Three days?' I jump up and dig a creased shirt from the ironing-basket-that-knows-no-iron. 'Did neither of you think to check if I was alive? Three bloody days!'

'Think you're all immortal at your age, sleeping your lives away,' says Jackie, catching me off-guard. 'You'll regret it when thirty-something hits you, like me. Then it's all passed you by.'

'Thirty-something? Aye, thirty-*twenty*.'

Keith holds up his arm to intervene but decides against it when his phone buzzes. I unhook my hoodie from the nail and hide it from the two of them. It's completely shredded after the bus incident.

'I need a new hoodie,' I order. 'When you're done feeding Squeaky Jesus to Fleabag, gerriz new'un.'

'What's wrong with your *old'un*?' asks Jackie.

'Put a bit of beef on, Boi,' I say, but she's not looking cos the dog's halfway across Rainbow Bridge, choking on the chewy crucifix. 'What time is it, anyway?'

'Half eight,' says Dad, dislodging the son of God from the gob of dog.

'Crap.' I barge out of the door, yelling. 'I'm gonna be late for the WOPPA trip.'

Thirty students sing "The Wheels on the Bus Have Two Flat Tyres" for the whole of the fifteen-minute drive to WOPPA — World Organisation Planet Protection Agency, or "The Alien Museum" as the locals call it.

Shortly after the reported UFO crash in Roswell, the British government set up a task force to search the skies for the next threat to humanity's existence. Probably due to isolation, or the fact that nobody likes it up here, they chose to build WOPPA's headquarters on the outskirts of Hatley and employed almost everyone in the town.

In no time at all, WOPPA expanded into an international operation, but it never found an alien (which is bad form considering that Cletus from Ohio gets probed once a week). So, for almost thirty years they were considered a bit of a harmless joke, deemed necessary *should* Martians ever decide to use that killer death ray they [don't] have up there.

Then, sometime in the Nineties, the organisation was shut down abruptly without notice. And this is where the story gets a little blurred, depending on which side of the fence you sit: The press release says that the agency disbanded due to a lack of public funding, but the *rumours* suggest that a leaked memo led to the destruction of a fleet of yachts owned by Russian Oligarchs and not spaceships owned by little green men.

All seemed lost for international conspiracy theorists and thousands of people across the globe lost their jobs. Colliery Row changed forever and we're still bitter about it, especially after an anonymous billionaire stepped in at the eleventh hour and his takeover coincided perfectly with a successful movie about a stretchy-necked waddler and his throbbing digit.

'E.T. sent the world alien crazy,' says Mr Sparks to the bus, half of whom are vomiting jelly sweets and the other half are fighting.

'And BMX,' yelps Molly Nell, the skater girl. 'The Kuwahara E.T. remains the most iconic bike in the world. The movie didn't even credit Cardoza, Ceppie and Lee who rode in it.' She's batting away two red balloons tied to her hoodie and they're getting tangled with the wire from her old-fashioned headphones. She is deffo the class weirdo.

'I know, Molly,' says Sparky, deflating. 'You tell us every year.'

The WOPPA buildings in Los Angeles, Paris, Tokyo and Florida were renovated and transformed into enormous theme parks, with massive roller coasters, cotton candy stalls and 3D Alien Blasting enjoyed by millions worldwide.

Hatley HQ remains a dump, with most of it cordoned off. The older locals reckon it's a blot on the landscape and Dad reckons it'll all be shut down soon. The swimming pool and living quarters are earmarked for demolition, which is a shame coz it's mint fun smashing the windows.

I suppose it's only going to get worse, but I like it here. The biased info-centres and rubber aliens are crap, but it's a doss about and an easy tick in the "Daniel attended" book.

Mr Sparks double-checks the numbers, counting heads once again as we dismount into a heavy flash shower. The rain's bouncing off the tarmac and Mrs Tabel stands by the doors, panicking to get us into the building before we're drowned.

'Nice clobber, bee, tee, double-yoooo,' says Dandy Doug looking me up and down. I try to cover the rips on my hoodie.

'Aye, yer nan borrowed iz them when I left hers.'

His nan always preferred me.

'Nanny died,' he says, momentarily crestfallen.

'Oh, soz. She was a lovely lady.'

'She's not dead, *Danielle*,' Doug sneers. 'She's polishing her Rolex and laughing at your father. How is he these days? Still in the loony bin? Your mother still avoiding you?'

I'm going to kill him.

Amidst the bustle, McKenzie Hilton slips away to steal sweets in town and an old revolving door spits the rest of us into a heavy-set security guard with a scrunched-up face. His slobbering cauliflower lips spray disapproval as he ushers us through one at a time, emphasising his handheld skimming skills, mainly on the girls.

Dodge pot.

Passing through with glee, Doug Barker informs the guard that he is a mutant (he isn't). He says his Rad-amantium-fused skeleton will set off the alarm (it won't). Impressively unimpressed, Scrunch Face tells Doug to "jog on and sort yer poncey lug out".

With all three coaches now indoors, the Fatfield Fan Club barge into the foyer and gather around Doug to adore his new right-ear diamond stud. The lads at the milk factory all have their left ear done. You don't get the right one done, coz they say that means you're gay. The older lads and blokes say that like, not the younger ones, coz we don't live in the dark ages: milk production has one foot in the past... euriser.

'Av ye seen heez lug plug?' Afro Gaz whispers from behind me. 'It's got manky greenies around it.' He's super-caffeinated — twitching like he's about to smash it in the body-popping contest we had in year seven.

'I'm surprised McKenzie hasn't twocked it and flogged it for fags.'

Sensing the unwanted presence of Chubs from Penshaw Red, I take a step away from Gaz, but the fat lump moves closer and into my vision, rattling out War and Peace on his cheeks. For some bizarre reason, he's got his hair slicked back and a solitary curl is plastered to his forehead with wet-look gel. He's rocking a pair of fake glasses too.

'Hello, Daniel in the corner.'

I don't respond, so he presses some more buttons on his face.

'Hi, Daniel in the corner. I am Ralph, from the other corner.'

'Soup,' Gaz interrupts. 'Neebody calls him Ralph. Not even the teachers.'

'But today, I am Ralph Robinson, not Soup.'

I'm not getting involved in this conversation.

'Knock knock, Daniel in the corner,' he says to me.

'Weez there?' says Gaz, now doing The Robot.

'It is me. Ralph Robinson.'

'Ralph Robinson wee?' says Gaz, sighing.

Chubs raises his glasses and his eyebrow, then winks with two eyes. 'It is me, Soup.'

'Ye just said you woz Ralph,' says Gaz, seemingly contemplating his future. 'Ye like being called Soup coz—'

'I love superheroes, yes,' interrupts Soup, or Ralph or whatever he's called... the fat one. 'But my secret identity is Ralph Robinson. You will know which it is when I wear my glasses.'

'What's all this got to do with knock knock?'

'I do not like jokes. Why would anyone shout through the door in the first place? Video doorbells remove the need for knocking, which would also remove the need for humour. I like video doorbells but I am not good with humour. Humour is the mushroom of the conversation world.'

Really?

'Knock knock,' I say, without looking at either of them.

'Who is there?' Soup responds.

'Yer nan.'

'That is odd. What is she doing there?'

'Just whippin' iz up a bacon sarnie.'

'Very strange. My nanna was a vegetarian.'

'It's an egg sarnie then.'

'Very strange. My nanna is dead.'

I'm not falling for that one again.

'Aye, dead fit.'

'No. Dead from Covid. It was very sad because we were not allowed to visit the hospital while that horrible man and his rich friends squeezed ladies' bottoms at office parties.'

'I'll squeeze yer nan's hot bottom.'

'It will be hot, yes. She was cremated.'

I think, judging by the look of horror on Gaz's face, that maybe I shouldn't make any more family jokes.

'Mummy and Daddy thought I had Covid this weekend,' says Soup. 'I slept for three days in bed because it was so comfortable on my new super comfortable mattress.' He opts not to take a breath and then drifts into thought, staring through the floor. 'Did you know that a giraffe only needs two hours of sleep per day?'

This grabs my attention. Not the bit about Lord Pamplemoose lounging on his four-poster and staring out upon the wildlife park in his back garden. The bit about sleeping all weekend. Then, Gaz begins spasming so much that I wonder if we need a defibrillator.

'Heya, I've been akip all weekend like,' he says, 'and now I'm like jittery as owt. Ower much kip, I reckoned. And ower Oscar, like, he's like stoppin' in, like at ower grannie's like coz she reckons she's gorra new cat, like but I divvunt knar if that's reet coz like Oscar's olergic to moggies and ower grannie's not deed like —'

I pray for teacher intervention coz I have no idea what he just said. Good luck, Reader.

'Listen up everyone,' bellows Mr Sparks.

Prayers answered.

'Delores Nichol, Director of WOPPA,' he continues, 'will conduct today's very special tour of the museum. Say hello to Mrs Nichol.'

'Hello, Mrs Nichol,' drones everyone together, except for Doug Barker, who whispers, 'Hello, Mrs Pickled Onion.'

Delores "Dee Dee" Nichol is a shot-put-framed, American lady with a part-American, part-British accent, who dresses like a librarian from World War One. Her A-Line dresses would make excellent curtains at my dead gran's house, who also had a settee the same colour as Dee Dee's mustard tights and brown brogue shoes.

Delores has fringed, ash-blonde hair that outlines straight white teeth, except for one loose front tooth, a-la-McPhee. Dee Dee *was* my aunt until she cheated on my uncle Ken nine times and "worked" her way to the top of WOPPA. She's another "talk of the town" — like Leopard-Print Lil, but from the posh bit.

With everyone paying attention, Dee Dee introduces herself to the group, but she doesn't need to, coz she's met us every year for the last three years. She's got a script though and she won't budge.

'Good arfternoon, Chilblains,' she says. 'My, how you've grown since I last saw you all. Today we sharl keep the history of WOPPA section quite short, me Larvelies. Follow me and we'lla be looking to the stars and stripes.'

Half of the group still thinks it's hilarious when Delores slips from "A Mary Poppins" to "A Mary Cain" — that's her party trick and her own joke.

We're guided to the main hall, where soundproof dividers section the room into maze-like corridors containing rubber aliens and four push-button information centres that tell the tale of WOPPA's publicised history (without the real bits).

'Now then, Ladles and Gentleboys,' calls Mrs Nichol, regrouping the gang after we begin punching rubber aliens. 'Hatley UK has finally secured an enormous sum of investment and we have some remarkable news. We're going big! Bigger than a burger from Toby Joe's! Bigger than the belly of a Buddha after eating a burger from Toby Joe's!'

'I'm hungry,' says Soup. 'And—'

'You're always hungry, Ralphie,' says Mrs Nichol, probably thinking that a jaw-wire would do him no harm. 'Take your mind off lunch momentarily, because today I'm proud as a peacock. Wait. Are peacocks proud? Anyway, I have the scoopsicles on some marvellous news. Are you ready, Chilblains?'

It's like "Top Trumps, ADHD Edition" in here. I can say that, coz I'm right up there.

Everyone cheers and Soup sticks a pair of noise-cancelling headphones on. I'm mildly envious at the calm he must be experiencing. Then, when we're herded into the old canteen, I'm even more envious when he rams a swimmer's nose clip over his beak. It stinks in here. It's a proper weird stench like chippy grease and lemon cleaning solution.

Nobody except me seems to care about sensory overload, as rowdiness becomes mumbled curiosity, coz in the centre of the hall are a dozen long benches with cool-looking VR headsets laid across them.

The geek with the jam jars is properly staring at Soup, who's about to have a meltdown overthinking the VR goggles and his headphones. She's fashioning something from elastic bands and when Molly Nell twangs it off Soup's head, I realise she's made something to modify the headset strap.

Nerd love blossoming.

This room wasn't part of the old tour, so it's new to us all. At the back is a thick metal tube droning a deep pulsating hum that won't be annoying anyone else. It's probably a chimney.

Next to the chimney is a podium and Dee Dee steps up to tap the mic. The PA system whistles until she makes an announcement.

'Hatley children,' she says, over-egging her presenter's voice. 'Today, we are honoured to hear all about WOPPA's plans, from our very special guest.'

Doug nudges his mate and half an unbuttered ham sandwich sticks in my throat.

'Boys and Girls. We are proud to introduce *the* servant to the town, Mayor William Noggin.'

The bumbling-est man on Earth.

But at least it's not Doug's dad.

Pigeon-chested, a small twerp with an untidy blonde wig and an oversized khaki suit, heads towards the podium waving two plastic Union Jack flags. He's strangely confident, considering everyone thinks he's an idiot. Mayor Noggin has never been popular and he stumbles as voices mumble rumours overheard from parents.

'It's a wig, deffo.'

'He's pocketed the money, Grandad reckons.'

'I heard that he is at war with The Horse Botherer.'

Finally making it to the podium after several trips, Noggin spreads his arms out wide, gripping the sides, and leans over with authority, whilst speaking with none.

'Erm, yes, welcome,' he splutters through bulging lips.

Clearing his throat, he tries again.

'Welcome, erm, yes,' he bumbles, slightly less bumbling than before, avoiding eye contact with his critical crowd. 'I am Mayor William Noggin.'

Doug whispers something into his mate's ear and Norman Pratt, the lanky Hoover, snorts so hard that we're almost minus a diamond stud.

'You, Boy,' Mayor Noggin barks. 'Yes, you. Is something funny? Stand outside. I will not share this marvellous news with uneducated buffoons. Leave, or I shall have you removed forcibly.'

Mrs Tabel marches a tearful Pratt out back and Mayor Noggin continues his presentation with a noticeable smugness.

'For decades, the heart of the WOPPA organisation remained a sleeping giant,' he says. 'But after tough negotiation and thorough planning, it is my great pleasure to announce a brand-new attraction to put Hatley firmly on the map.'

'We're already on the map,' shouts Gaz, careful to raise his hand first. 'I've seen me da in his boxers on Google Earth.'

'The metaphorical map,' says Noggin, dismissively. 'Recognition.'

'Are we getting a roller coaster?' yells Doug to cheers of sheep.

'Silence!' Noggin booms into the mic. 'We are not bringing frivolous entertainment for the poor to your doorstep.'

Some people boo, while others look up "frivolous" on their phones.

'Six months ago, the Biological Energy Lab launched a satellite camera system with lenses more powerful than the Hubble telescope.'

On a screen behind the podium, a massive sphere appears. It's kinda like a planet but covered in cameras. It looks a bit like one of those knobbly gobstoppers you get for a benk.

Next to the gobstopper cameras, about half the size of it, is a picture of the International Space Station.

Bloody hell, this thing is massive.

'The Interstellar Nebular Discovery Angel is quite remarkable,' Noggin brags. 'The cameras feed millions of panoramic images to a central computer in the basement.'

'Unlike anything before,' Dee Dee adds. 'The Angel uses specialised cameras to identify undiscovered potential energy sources.'

'Indeed,' says Noggin. 'And who knows what else we could discover as we search our deepest oceans, our most remote islands and then up into the known universe and beyond.'

Naturally, everyone is impressed. Mind you, I'm immortal... so, not *everyone's* that impressed.

'It is, even now, constantly building a detailed map,' Dee Dee adds, 'We will *go boldly* where no human has ever witnessed, on Earth and into space.'

Hoshi, the Jam Jar geek from Penshaw, shakes her head at the Trekkie reference, while I'm impressed by the repaired infinitive. Mrs Tabel would be proud of me.

'The system's primary aim,' continues Mayor Noggin, half-flustered by Delores' interruption and half-embarrassed about his zoning out mid-speech, 'is to locate sustainable energy that will free humanity from an exhausted supply. This could be located on nearby planets, right in front of our eyes, or hiding in the farthest reaches, at the end of our ever-expanding universe.'

'There is no end t-to the Universe.' Hoshi spits with such force that she almost loses her glasses. 'This p-p-primitive machine will only further scientific ignorance b-b-by making assumptions. The human brain c-can't c-comprehend that, but there is no end to it. It's infinite.'

'If there is no end to it, then how is it expanding?' says Mayor Noggin, raising an eyebrow. 'Our Discovery Angels may discover the meaning of life, or prove the existence of a creator.'

Hatley Academy receive this information with mixed response. Around half of the room respond positively thinking WOPPA deserves an award for potentially locating God. The others brick it, contemplating the celestial grovelling required if they do. I consider being nice to Jackie for a moment, although, by the time I reach the pearly gates, the hinges will have rusted solid, so Jackie can get lost.

Molly Nell's not impressed (*there's a pattern here*) and punches her hand skywards.

'How do you power it?'

'With the very renewable, sustainable, *clean* energy it is searching for,' says Mayor Noggin, puffing his chest. 'Our Discovery Angels source potential Biological Energy on the journey which WOPPA scientists beam here to investigate practical Earth applications. We at WOPPA have isolated early samples for a project of our own. Take that in for a moment. Clean, abundant, sustainable energy *on Earth.*'

Mayor Noggin points to the pulsating cylinder.

'This is a state-of-the-art storage system for said energy.'

Ok, but it looks like a chimney.

The mayor pauses, basking in his glory. This is massive for Hatley and could lead to jobs for everyone... even Dad, if he sorts himself out. I was hoping he'd get Chief Candy Flosser at a theme park, but this opens even more doors. Chief Door Opener... he could be Chief Door Opener.

'What about infrastructure?' yells Molly Moodkill. 'More traffic down one access road.'

'We are negotiating infrastructure with the council,' says Noggin. 'We will be looking to accommodate an influx of tourists in and around the greenbelt areas.'

'Having processed initial images from our camera system,' interrupts Delores Nichol, nudging Mayor Noggin to avoid the topic. 'We have made great progress. We are aware of energy sources here on Earth, but each time one of two thousand headsets powers up, it will view a unique space never viewed before. *This* is our legacy. This makes *every* visitor an explorer of space never explored before. Oh, and there'sa free tea and bissqueets.'

In the corner of the room, I spot a mouse scurrying into a hole in the skirting board and the mayor coughs.

'Let us finish with an exclusive viewing. Ladies and Gentlemen, Boys and Girls… witness a demonstration of the Interstellar Nebular Discover Angel.'

Sparky and Delores Nichol shuffle us to the VR headsets and instruct everyone to put one on.

A blinding flash thrusts me deep into an outer space familiar to me. But unlike when I was dead, there are no brightly coloured kaleidoscopic visuals. Instead, there is just blackness, and for a tourist attraction, it's not got that wow factor. You'd expect an exploding planet or hurtling meteors, but there's nothing here.

Maybe if I turn around? Oh… there's the moon. Hardly exploring the further reaches of space here. The graphics are naff — it's just a pixelated circle. WOPPA's Discover Angel appears to have discovered eight-bit and I whip off the headset unimpressed.

'To move you need only to point,' hollers Delores Nichol as Year Nine stumble about, bouncing off the sharp benches and bashing into each other like the arcade game, Asteroids.

And then, as suddenly as it started, the exclusive viewing is over, with most of us having exclusively viewed nothing.

'That is enough for today, Chilblains. We hope you have enjoyed our demonstration and we look forward to seeing you again next year.'

The marvellous invention-system-thing is done. Switched off. Powered down.

I think the Greenbelt areas might be safe.

Mayor Noggin has left the room and Delores is not far behind. Over by the info centres, Mr Sparks orders everyone to buddy up and file out through the tacky gift shop for a pen and a badge.

'Do not forget the boy on the fire escape, Mr Sparks,' Soup reminds the head and I think about thumping him for it.

Filing out, Gaz has a real gripe about the graphics.

'Me Xbox is better than that crap,' he moans. 'It's not garna get very far if the moon looks like a tortilla.'

Molly and Hoshi Jam Jar are full-on arguing about the importance of scientific advancement versus a drain on local resources and misguided priorities. They sort of agree upon concerns for the loss of Greenbelt. Soup, however, reckons he's enjoyed the peacefulness of space and wants to move there one day.

...

Out by the bus, I realise that I've left my hoodie under the VR table. So, while Sparky's counting, I sneak back in — unnoticed coz Scrunch-face and co are nowhere to be seen — and follow the aroma of grease and lemon cleaning fluid through to the canteen.

It's eery in here without people. My hoodie's under the table and I stoop to pick it up. Behind the pulsating energy chimney, there's a grotesque gurgling sound and my senses suggest that I'm not welcome here.

When I hear voices, I crouch low, peeking over the desk to see Mayor Noggin enter the room, pacing the floor and shouting down his phone.

'I told you to set it further out, Barker' he snarls. 'It may as well have been in the bloody woods... I do not care that it was a *demonstration*, this is bad press.'

Doug's dad has glitched the VR system for the big launch. Berk. Ha!

'I have a *potential* problem made worse by your incompetence,' Noggin continues. 'I want to know his every movement over the last seven days. I want to know what he has watched on television, who he has contacted, what he has eaten... Every detail right down to the colour of his underpants. Do you understand? *Find me Urielis!*'

6

The Cod Delusion

Nanna Byrd worked in the North East's famous fish and chip shop, "The Cod Delusion". It sat right at the top of Colliery Row and people travelled miles for fresh, line-caught cod and chips, fried in proper dripping. Nobody could believe Cod could be so good.

After school, Oscar followed his usual routine, heading to the shop and hopping onto the counter by the cash register without being spotted. He tucked into chips soaked in biting malt vinegar. With great relief, he slipped off his corrective shoe while waiting for Nanna Byrd to finish her gruelling shift. School put lots of stress on his ankle.

Friday was Oscar's favourite day of the week and at six o'clock, he hopped from the counter, wriggled his wonky foot into the shoe, and waited for Nanna to lock the shop. The Cod Delusion reopened at seven for the evening customers, but Nanna Byrd didn't work Friday evenings — the wonders of Hatley Woods awaited and no amount of batter would get in the way of their Friday adventures.

Beneath a fallen trunk, the ground beetles scurried about their business, freaked that Oscar had removed their roof. A woodlouse wiggled its legs on its back after falling off the rotten bark, so Nanna Byrd flipped the louse and it wandered off, confused, looking for dinner. A worm slurped into a hole, like sucked spaghetti, and a spiral dirt pile curled out. Nanna Byrd pointed out a woodpecker pecking at a fallen oak's outer bark and a common-black millipede marched across the trunk.

'Look at its legs,' said Nanna Byrd. 'How does it keep those shoes on?'

'Not corrective shoes like mine, Nanna,' said Oscar, gloomily.

Nanna Byrd explained an insect with one zillion perfect legs was unlikely.

'Can you imagine how relieved he must be, after tying all of those laces, to flip over Velcro straps on a corrective milli-shoe?'

Oscar nodded and wondered if the millipede saved the corrective shoe until last, like eating a burger after finishing the fries.

'Can you smell garlic?'

Nanna Byrd explained the smell was coming from a disgruntled Garlic Snail which farts when disturbed. Oscar found it odd that snails smell of garlic and they're cooked in garlic too.

While heading downstream, Nanna Byrd hushed her boy. Quietly, the two approached a leafy mound by the waterside and Nanna pointed to the top. Oscar couldn't see anything interesting, so Nanna rustled the leaves and a common frog hopped into the stream, unaware the strong current would whip it towards a broken dam the children made camping last summer. Although they could, camouflaged frogs were fabulous at hiding to avoid hungry crocodiles. Crocodiles probably didn't live in Stickleback Stream, because they're pretty good at pretending to be logs. Oscar told Nanna to be careful lifting a log next time, just in case a crocodile popped up.

'The wildlife in Hatley Woods, and wherever crocodiles live, have it pretty sweet,' Oscar said to Nanna Byrd. 'Animals are pretty perfect, Nan.'

'Although evolution is a miracle, I think nothing is perfect. Camouflaged frogs need camouflage because they're vulnerable to predators. Necessity is the mother of invention.'

'If I was a camouflaged frog, I'd hide and do missions and stuff.'

'You'd need to hide from hungry snakes.'

Nanna Byrd pushed Oscar on a frayed rope swing and then threw small stones at annoyed Sticklebacks. The squirrels toyed with popping down for a chat, but then they thought better of it, in case the Stand-ups stole their nuts. Then, as the sun set, millions of midges arrived for a bite to eat, so Nanna Byrd sprayed peppermint and Oscar's head tingled.

On their journey home, Nanna Byrd sucked her teeth and pointed to a small man wearing a messy wig and making notes on a notepad.

'Hungry snakes,' hissed Nanna Byrd, but Oscar was not paying attention because he had spotted someone odd sneaking from tree to tree. A wild-haired man was wearing a coat covered in leaves and he followed the man with the wig. The leafy man waved at Oscar's nan before raising his finger to his lips.

Nanna Byrd whispered, 'He's a slightly weird Stand-Up but loves a battered sausage on a Friday.'

'What's a "Stand-Up", Nanna?'

'It's what animals must call us human things. We stand up on two legs, Lovely.'

'How do you know that?' giggled Oscar.

'I was told over a battered sausage.'

'Is the man a spy?'

'He speaks to animals and used to be a policeman.'

'I could be a spy if I was a camouflage frog… or an owl, or a squirrel or —'

Nanna Byrd gave Oscar another little squirt of peppermint, to shut him up.

That evening, Oscar and Nanna Byrd sat in the back garden around the log burner and Nanna read some Sherlock Holmes. Soon after, Oscar became twitchy. His wonky leg ached from sitting in the same spot, so he stretched it out, exercising a while.

At eight o'clock, just before bedtime, Nanna nipped indoors to make piping hot chocolate and feed the cat some chicken. Oscar grinned because Nanna didn't have a cat anymore, but she pretended to steal a late-night snack. Secretly, Oscar and Nanna Byrd longed for another cat. They once had a big blue-black visitor, but that got flattened by a WOPPA truck.

An owl perched on the apple tree while Oscar scraped chocolatey bits from his mug and yawned. He asked Nanna to comb through his red curls and then, on the third owl's hoot, she took his hand.

'Bedtime, Little One.'

'Isn't it funny?' Oscar said, hobbling upstairs. 'I'm a Stand-Up that can barely stand up.'

'You're a special Stand-Up,' said Nanna Bryd, turning to take Oscar's hand.

'A Standout,' he replied, glumly. '*Everyone* calls me Oscar the Shoe.'

'Everyone called a penguin I once knew, "Floppy Flipper".'

'They didn't, did they?'

But Oscar knew that they did and suddenly he wasn't glum anymore. He slid under his quilt and settled down to hear Nana Byrd's favourite bedtime story, listening as joyfully as if it were the first.

'Of every animal in the world, the owl is most observant.

The cheetah speeds and puppies play to the trumpet of the elephant.

The seal applauds the sea itself, and nimble squirrels chatter,

Of all the good done in the woods, while penguins only natter.

Of Terry.

Floppy flipper Terry.

His flipper flips and flops and flaps, it points out to the right.

And every other penguin laughs both day and night.

Terry looks down at his flop and wishes it was straight.

Until the octopus he meets, says, 'at least you don't have eight.'

Let me tell you of the thing that other penguins fear,

When out from down the depths below, the great white shark appears.

The others with their flippers straight tow a distinct line.

But Terry, with his wobbly flop, evades the shark each time.

So, when you're feeling different, think of Terry's name,
For great white sharks would eat us up,
If we were all the same.'

'I'm thinking of Terry's name, Nanna,' said Oscar, closing his eyes.

'I know.' Nanna Byrd placed a kiss on his forehead and then left the room.

'Terry, Terry, Terry, Penguins and Owls, Squirrels and Camouflage Frogs, Owls and Camouflage Penguins and Spies and missions... and sleep —'

PUFF!

7

The Necessary Flashback

The bell hasn't even finished ringing when the doors burst open, scattering shards of paint like broken glass, as a swarm of kids spill into the holidays like fizzing fireworks. The lasses sign the "Free the Fatfield Four" t-shirts that Doug's dad had made "for the craic".

I bet he's selling them

Mark Barker does nowt for nowt. Even though the term's over, he'll profit from them somehow. Let's face it, they'll all be back in isolation next year, so no biggie. Doug's hoodie is off, so they can sign his t-shirt too, and someone's drawn a willy on his back.

At least I'm not the only one who thinks it.

Desperately trying to gain order with a smile on her face, Mrs Tabel encourages everyone to disperse.

'It's been lovely having you all year,' she shouts. 'Now bugger off and enjoy the sun.'

Her plan works and the yard becomes clear of all but the curious and determined. I am both of those.

'Mrs Tabel, will Dr Urielis be back next year?' I ask.

'Doctor who?' Mrs Tabel replies.

'The subbie from Friday,' Gaz butts in. He's super-spasming and a jelly meerkat scoots across the car park. 'Scruffy beard. Pickled liver. Ginger bloke. Talks about Soccer-Teeth and Pilates.'

'Socrates and Plato,' Mrs Tabel says. 'I still don't know who you mean. I vet all of our staff and —' she hyperventilates, spluttering between phrases. 'HR will need retraining. I have never hired a substitute by the name of Mr Uri Geller...'

'Knew it,' says Gaz as Mrs Tabel panics back into school. 'Nonce.'

The Tunnel of Trees lies at the entrance to Hatley Woods (or the exit from, depending on which way you are going). Thick, bowed branches of the towering oaks form an enchanting tube of luscious greens and browns, banking left into the distance towards Stickleback Stream, which wiggles its way from wood-end to wood-end.

Dewy duff and rotting bark hovers pungent. The sun splits through tiny gaps in the trees, lasering into the dirt while crab apple branches stretch between oaks for any leftover beam. Sharp stinging nettles and thorns knot the ground around extinguished campfires where the children tell scary stories at night.

On the banks of Stickleback Stream stands Oakey Croaky, a thick, tall tree with sturdy branches. Its roots are solid, despite being bullied out of the soil by approaching sycamores, craning their necks like nosey neighbours. This survivor fights hard for the little land it has, adapting to its space with a lopsided trunk and a thick branch that touches the water when the stream rises, and doesn't when it's low.

You put yer left branch in, left branch out... Ohhhh Oakey Croaky Croaky... and so on.

This is my place. My safe space. I've played here since we moved to Hatley, building rickety tree dens and bivouacs. And, for the last two years, I've spent my time working on a fallen birch not far from Oakey Croaky. I call it "The Whittling Log" — a felled trunk etched with the initials of amorous teens, worn like badges of honour over its mossy coat. Lighting split the birch in half and the branches were perfect for my bivouac. I stripped the bark and painted every single twig. I pulled the top around until it was hidden amongst other trees and covered with ferns, so it's more of an autumn igloo — it's comfortable, dry, and a perfect hiding place from Dragrid and other morons.

Now there's a title for a book! "Dragrid and Other Morons".

Nobody comes down this way – local families prefer to play football and have barbecues in the clearings which back onto X-Park, the outdoor skate ramps at the base of Rocky Hill.

Erm... where's the hell is my Whittling Log?

Drowning in around two inches of water, that's where.

'Like the improvements, Danielle?'

This sounds awfully like my former best friend and slimy cack-bag, Douglas Barker.

It is indeed, so I might be heading to jail after all.

As I said before, Doug *used* to be my best mate. I wasn't always a loner; I've known him since we were toddlers. The Barkers lived next door to Mam and Dad back in Sunderland, back when Dad had the coffee shop and Mam worked. We did everything together when we were kids: we rode our bikes for miles, washed cars for money, played retro video games, wrote love letters to Lisa Graytass (a girl from Juniors) and spent every minute that we were allowed playing hide and seek. Oh, and Doug's the reason I'm good at English. I read so I could be cleverer than Doug's dad, who used to think he knew everything except the fact he's a dick.

But, all good things and that… I remember the day it all went wrong like it was yesterday. I was wearing salopettes and a green Parka coat with a furry hood. I splashed into slushy puddles in my Wellies and ogled the Christmas display in Fenwick's window. The lights glowed in the darkness, reflecting in patches of wet pavement where snowflakes lay. An animatronic snowman bobbed a fuzzy head at Mam, who was nursing a mulled wine and ignoring my pleas to visit Santa's grotto. Dad hurried us through every scene in the windows, telling us he needed to get set up for a Christmas performance that evening. Mam joked she was sick of hearing him play the same songs at his gigs and Dad overreacted, saying that he was sick of hearing her "full stop". Mam dragged me home while Dad left to rock the stage in a smoky dance hall and at around seven o'clock that evening, I watched her pull the old Datsun Sunny out of the detached garage for the last time.

Doug's dad got a new job and the Barkers moved up to the big houses on Larkfield Road. Dad fell to bits, lost the coffee shop, and the council stuck us on Colliery Row — all within a fortnight. He sold his car to get a sofa, but he had to pay for a removal company, so we couldn't afford a sofa. So, he sold everything else to buy a sofa for the removal company to move. The only things he didn't sell were his sound system, records, and guitar.

Later that week, we got two beds from a charity shop and some bedding. Dad used the last of his removal funds to buy us Christmas pyjamas and a notebook for my Christmas present. Next door donated a battered grandfather clock that delivered its first chime at one o'clock on Christmas Day, having missed at least a dozen previous hours. Fragmented timekeeping and Dad's self-pity resulted in a burnt turkey and tear-soaked pyjamas. Nevertheless, I tried my best to make dinner with frozen veg and a dry bird, only to see my efforts wasted on the blubbering man.

With dinner in the bin, Dad sucked on a bottle of vodka like a hungry baby sucks on milk. Dad never drinks milk, but he should, coz when the grandfather clock struck again at seven, I chucked a shovel of coal on the fire and called the Crisis Team.

On his way to the ambulance, Dad told the nurses that he couldn't "do it anymore" and that his world had "ended". He said he couldn't carry on and he wanted to sleep forever. They took the sobbing, pyjama-wearing man away while a social worker with straight, bobbed hair arrived to arrange a temporary foster placement. The first-ever splinter on our doorframe came from me slamming the door on her. I hid under the stairs for the first time too. It was pretty cool coz I was small enough to squeeze into the empty box from the Christmas tree.

I was there for over an hour, ignoring the social worker knocking, but the standoff ended when the lock clicked and a vile, witch-like woman walked in like she owned the place. Her hair was tied up into a maroon Fez and she stumbled towards me with her yellowed fingertips, crooked and warty. All I could think of was gingerbread houses and murdery stoves as she explained to the social worker that Dad had asked her to come and look after me while he was sectioned.

"I'm Dad's special friend, from the old days," she said in a high-pitched croak that sent me out of the door and straight to the telephone box at the bottom of the estate. I called Dad, begging him to get better and come home to get rid of her.

A week later, the ambulance dropped Dad back, but it was clear he wasn't better and *she* was going nowhere.

Money bought Doug posh clothes with labels on and a top-of-the-range Mountain Bike that he rode to school on sunny days. When the weather got bad, Mark Barker dropped him off in a sparkling new car that is entirely responsible for climate change.

At school, it didn't take long for the Fatfield girls, who tie their ties with the thin end at the front, to notice Doug's posh car and new clothes. Once they did, it didn't take long for the leader of The Fatfield Four, McKenzie Hilton, to notice the girls. Unsurprisingly, with his eye on a few of them, McKenzie initiated me and Doug into his gang. We replaced Josh 'Albino' Potter — a bleach-haired orphan with Sellotape on his glasses — and McKenzie's scrawny brother, who was kicked out of school after he rammed a stolen moped into a teacher's car.

The flashy life and gelled hair had everyone swarming around like sharks on chum and Doug *loved* the attention. But, despite his bling, McKenzie Hilton took a shine to *me* coz I was a Colliery lad.

Jackie moved in properly, saying that it was to help with the rent. But I know she was circling the wagons for a ready-made family. Nobody falls in love faster than someone who needs a place to live.

Accompanying the awful hag was Yappy Dog and a massive, miserable, grey cat called Gospel. Yappy Dog fetched its fleas and they bit so badly that I ripped my hands pulling up the carpet. The fighting between cat and dog became so frequent that I threw the moggie out at night and Flat Gospel earned its nickname after an incident with a WOPPA truck.

Dad never replaced the carpet, as one glass of wine on a Wednesday became a bottle of red and before long, it didn't matter which day it was.

For a while, The Fatfield Four (Dan and Doug edition) ruled the school. We were all pretty tight and I felt I belonged, despite the stealing and general havoc. But all good things and that… again… happened one day, when a little first-year picked the wrong moment to perform his entry into the schoolyard talent show.

"Your dad's an alcoholic and you've got a council house," he sang. "Your mummy couldn't stand you and your best friend is a mouse."

"You going to put up with that?" said Doug, setting off the red mist to wash the farthest cobweb of my mind. My blood pressure rose so fast that I made the snivelling, little snot-rag bleed from both nostrils and an ear with one punch. Up and back down like a billionaire's rocket, my adrenaline drained as quickly as an Audi's petrol tank in queued traffic: I didn't know the kid was one of McKenzie's many brothers until my cheeks were grated cheese down the school wall.

The constant beatings never let up and although Doug basked in the glory of his new status, he got fed up trying to protect me. In deep with the gang, he spent more time hanging out with them (stealing). He still invited me over to his *massive* house, but only for an hour or two, just in case McKenzie found out. That was until one day when Doug reckoned that McKenzie had mentioned me. Said he reckoned I was sound. Said that if I proved myself to be "one of The Fatfield Four", they'd stop kicking my head in and let me back in. I had a chance. I could be popular again.

Doug dared me to do all sorts of stupid things and brag about it. It started with binning those taxidermy weasels through the library window. Then I spat at Mrs Aubrey-Smith and spread rumours about her and the gym teacher in the broom cupboard. I did *anything* and *everything* that Doug suggested, until eventually, I was excluded from school.

So, after making a complete berk of myself, it turned out that McKenzie didn't want me back anyway and I've been looking over my shoulder ever since, except for during the pandemic, which gave my broken bones a bit of a break. I've avoided school as much as possible since then (anxiety and that), but whenever I bump into Doug and his pals, there's usually a black eye attached to my face shortly afterwards.

Not today though. I'm immortal, innit.

Lit up by the beams of sunlight, Douglas Barker, my former best friend and recent zillionaire, wears a crisp, light-blue polo shirt with a body warmer. Douglas Barker doesn't sweat unless he's forced to eat in "chain restaurants". *Oh, and he calls a body warmer a "gilet".*

'Where's the big lad?' I snarl, referring to McKenzie Hilton. 'Must be nearby if you're here.'

'Gettin' supplies,' says Doug, smugly fondling the collar of his polo. 'Petrol and matches for bivvie burning.'

Suddenly, there's a rustle in the trees that delays Doug's golf handicap from being permanently handicapped. It's Soup stumbling into the clearing and pretending a stick is a laser gun. The lump backs right into Doug, stamping on his white trainers and then grins that stupid cucumber.

'Sorry, Douglas,' he says, genuinely. 'I was defeating The Dark Dangler. He is a vicious entity from the planet XzUyzn.'

'Shut it, Fatso. You owe me five hundred quid for my Gucci's, so I'll be taking your dinner money for the rest of your fat life.'

Everyone's distracted momentarily when, in the distance, we hear the sound of a boy sobbing like his dog's just died. I recognise the tone, but I can't put my finger on it. There's no time to ponder it anyway, coz at that moment, things get nasty.

'You're not touching my bivvie,' I say, prioritising.

'Log burning later, *Danielle*.'

'Logs do not burn if you push them into the stream, Douglas,' says Soup, looking over the bank at the Whittling Log. 'You should collect dry wood and kindling instead.'

'Shut it, Special Needs.'

Now then, no matter how embarrassed you are coz a lad wearing a coat like a cape just outwitted you, you can't say that. I'm going to have to get involved.

'I can help you collect the correct kindling,' Soup continues, making the whole situation worse. 'I learned this while I was at Nutsy's Cleaver Beavers at Sandy Bay. We will need flint and some beech bark.'

'Did surmberdy say fiya? Cooked whale meat. Bloody blubbery.'

Oh, no...

Ladies and Gentlemen, I introduce to you, Logan 'Slap Heed' Noutch — aptly named coz a curly, beige mop sits so far back on his enormous, shiny forehead he looks like a lollipop dropped on the dog's rug. A boy, so unfunny that every time he opens his mouth somewhere in the world a clown dies, Slap Heed is a founder-member of The Fatfield Four, snared by McKenzie Hilton because his obscure knowledge of Geography proved beneficial to homework. He's not McKenzie's mate: he's a hairy Chupa Chup that happens to like maps.

And if he's here…

Enter Norman 'Pumpkin-Teeth' Pratt, the canned laughter. Slap Heed's best mate: a scrawny, (maybe) half-Turkish boy with teeth like someone has rammed candy cigarettes into his shrivelled gums. They're well-matched coz Pumpkin-Teeth finds Slap Heed hilarious, snorting through his elongated hoover-hole like he's choking on a testicle every time his mate opens his gob. They make the perfect couple and I'm certain they'll marry one day.

'Didn't see you in class on Friday, Danielle,' sneers Doug. 'Daddy couldn't put the bottle down?'

'I saw Daniel and so did everyone else,' interrupts Soup, and I cringe.

'Oh, that's interesting,' says Doug, with a proper smirk on. 'You and Fatty Bum Bum are bum buddies, ey?'

'Danielle and Fatty eating in a tree,' Slap Heed sings while Pumpkin-Teeth sniffs up a few midges.

I would rage, but I'm getting used to this "taking a breath" thing. Ok. Here goes.

Mercy is for the weak…Sandafloor… Sweep the leg, Danny Boy….

'Me classmates, innit.'

Crane stylee…

It takes a while for it to register, but when it does, the response smacks Doug harder than the Number 38 smacked me. The *exact* moment that Doug's heart shatters is graffitied over his face and I lap down the aftershock like a toddler on hazelnut spread.

Dumbstruck and baffled, Doug stumbles backwards into Slap Heed, who trips over Pratt's tusk sending them spiralling, face first, into a patch of nettles. Pumpkin-Teeth Pratt stands gormless, with his lower jaw sunk so far into his neck that he looks like a Hungry Hippo while his mates breakdance amongst a thousand pricks. Soup's halfway up Oakey Croaky, crawling out towards the rope swing. The commotion has set him off and he's trying to get out of the way but making the whole thing funnier by muttering "classmates" over and over.

Incensed, Dandy Doug drags himself from the stinging nettles, pinpricked and furious. He launches himself onto Oakey Croaky, which sends Soup into a state of panic that would melt the coldest heart.

'Leave him alone, Doug,' I yell, but it's too late. Doug's up on his feet at the thickest part by the trunk and Soup spins, snatches at a branch and all I see is him disappear towards the water below. It's going to hurt and he's not immortal, like me.

Behind, Slap Heed and Pumpkin-Teeth guffaw as Dandy Doug turns towards me, pointing like he's trying to stab my eye out.

'See what *you* did,' he sneers. 'Why would *anyone* want to be friends with *you*? Everything you touch turns to sh— Where are you two going?'

Well, that's unexpected: Scrambling over each other, screaming like eight-year-olds with a mouse on the loose, Slap Heed and Pumpkin-Teeth snatch and tear at the bramble to get as far away from Stickleback Stream as possible.

Dandy Doug roars angrily, but his rage is cut short and his mood swings faster than a frog in a liquidiser. With his back to me and looking down at Soup, he sneers:

'Well, well, well, seems Father may be getting that promotion after all.'

And then, he's hot on the tails of his pathetic mates, like they've pinched his trousers from the locker while I take a step towards the stream.

Oh…

I am gobsmacked and unable to move.

Oh, God, no…

'Daniel,' says Soup, hovering around a metre above the river bank. 'Why am I not wet?'

I remain as calm as ever before, but not quite as calm inside.

'Take a deep breath, Fella,' I say.

'I will but I do not see how that —'

'Soup… you're flying.'

8

Molly's Mole II

Nobody could see the shiny, rose-black balloons, which was annoying; but not as annoying as when they rubbed against Molly's head. The static made her hair stand up and it looked ridiculous, even tied through the snapback of her cap. The squeaking was the worst and it made her shudder.

Molly stormed down the stairs, faking a big smile for her parents. They had been super-happy since the doctor told them of her dad's miraculous recovery, but it was sickening. Molly's mum told the neighbours that the power of Molly's love had brought Mr Nell home fit as a fiddle. But Molly knew differently. It was the mole that saved Dad, just like the other balloon had taken away Mum's sadness. Now, they throbbed with disease and sorrow, and Molly wanted rid.

'Mum, where are the scissors?' she asked.

'Good grief, what happened to your hair?' Mrs Nell replied, cleaning the sideboard.

'I know. It won't stick down.'

'You can't cut it yourself, Petal.'

'I'll deal with the sticky-up bits later,' said Molly, holding the scissors by the pointy end. 'These are for arts and crafts.'

'You must have slept awkwardly, or it could be your shampoo. I'll get some after I finish the housework.'

Around five minutes later, Molly returned downstairs.

'Broke the scissors, Mum,' she said. It was not the first time that arts and crafts had broken household essentials.

'No worries, Lovely. Stick them in the bin. I'll get some more after I finish the housework.'

Even with the sharpest scissors, the neon threads were uncuttable, while the balloons remained unburstable, even with the pointiest pin. Molly contemplated trying the garden shears but decided that asking to borrow them may be harder to explain.

Slipping outside, Molly bounced down the long driveway, heading along the road to where some village children were kicking a football around the street. The ball rolled up to Molly's feet, so she booted it into Mr Marshall's Garden, annoying the children and probably Mr Marshall too.

'Hi, Molly,' said a shaky voice. It was Hoshi Solo-Spock on her way home from school. 'I went to X-Park, b-but you weren't there either. Are you ok?'

'Fine.'

Molly worked at the local skatepark as a first aider and she rode her bike there every Saturday and Sunday too. Her bike was one of Mr Nell's vast collection and her favourite. She helped source the parts for the 1983 Diamond Back and even chose the Mushroom grips herself.

'Can't ride today,' mumbled Molly. 'My balance off.'

'That'll b-be the b-b-balloons,' said Hoshi.

Molly dropped her Walkman cassette player sending the

batteries spinning under a car. Hoshi shook her head and wiggled her phone.

'Sealed lithium,' she said. 'Modern t-t-tech.'

'Retro is cooler."

'You know who says that?' chuckled Hoshi. 'Weirdos. Th-that's who says that.'

"How can you see my balloons?'

'They're attached t-t-to your shoulder!'

'Nobody else can see them,' said Molly, while Hoshi gave the balloons a playful flick. 'Stop that! It's annoying.'

'It's logical to love a balloon, C-Captain. Even though they're d-depleting the p-p-p-planet's helium.'

'There's no helium in these.'

Hoshi and Molly lay on the grass, in the smallest clearing of Hatley Woods, looking up at the crystal sky and cotton clouds. Molly battered the balloons away because they bobbled in front of her face and blocked the view.

'Hoshi, what if *I* can save all the good people from dying of horrible disease.'

'Like opposite Thanos?' said Hoshi. 'I think you might float away b-before you g-g-got to Newcastle.'

'Yeah, I didn't ask to be a walking birthday party.'

'Urielis and the b-broken t-telephone?'

'Yeah.'

Molly pondered the substitute and she pondered miracle workers.

'Maybe *only* certain per-people with powers c-c-can see the b-balloons,' Hoshi ponders too. 'Like, from our class. If they have p-powers t-t-too?'

'Have you got powers?'

'Maybe. I'm a little b-b-better at marbles.'

Over the crease of the valley, fire-breaks separated blankets of trees into squares of leafy chocolate. The sun beat down on Hatley Woods through wispy clouds and the trees trapped any breeze from the coast, creating a glorious sun trap. Molly and Hoshi got a Ninety-Nine from the ice cream van. They licked them as quickly as possible before any ice cream ran and the raspberry sauce stuck their fingers together, when, suddenly, a high-pitched squeal of excitement came from within the trees. It was Molly's eight-year-old cousin, Billie, sprinting up in dirty, blue dungarees.

'Mols! I love your balloons, Mols.'

'She can see them,' Molly whispered to Hoshi, who stared so wide her eyelids almost lined her spectacles.

'Here, B-Billie, g-g-get a ninety-nine.' Hoshi passed Billie some change and directed her towards the van.

'With monkey's blood?'

'Yes, with monkey's b-b-blood.'

Billie gripped the money and ran off to the Walter Whippy Van. She waved Spindy (she can't pronounce Cindy), the doll that her cat Viking had savaged beyond recognition. There were only a few flimsy strands of hair left on its head, no nose, and half a leg.

Molly followed her cousin with her eyes while Hoshi freaked out.

'I might b-b-b-b-b-be, I might be wrong b----b-but wasn't Billie a Viking?'

'Yes. So, whatever you do, keep her calm.'

Billie returned masked with raspberry sauce and Walter Whippy's ice cream. She licked her sticky fingers and grinned.

'I love Monkey's Blood, me,' she said in a half-growl, rubbing the cuff of her long-sleeved T-shirt across her chops.

"Monkey's Blood" is a nickname for the raspberry sauce that ice cream sellers squirt onto a Ninety-Nine. "A Ninety-

Nine" is a huge ice cream, with a Flake in it. A "Flake" is a chocolate stick, which crumbles and glues to clothes, looking a bit like poo if it is on the seat of the pants.

As expected, Billie's ice cream slid off the cone, onto the grass, and the little Viking growled. She stomped her feet and with her face turning as red as Monkey's Blood. She stomped again, although much harder this time and, somewhere nearby, a car alarm sounded in time with a squirrel squeaking. The noise caused Billie to look a trifle startled, while Molly gasped and grabbed at a hyperventilating Hoshi.

'Billie, come over here and chill on the comfy green grass,' Molly ordered, breathlessly. 'We can make cloud shapes in the sky.'

'No! Princess Viking is angry,' said Billie, raising her knee to huff again. Then she screamed and two mountain bikers crashed into a tree. 'Wasp!'

Billie's cheeks flushed and she ran in circles, waving her arms around her messy brown, scissor-cut mop. Immediately, Molly jumped up, but not because she was afraid of wasps.

'Calm down,' she yelped and then lowered her voice. 'It's more scared of you than you are of it, Dudeski. Come on, let's get another huge Ninety-Nine, erm, Mannnn.'

'Why are you talking weird?' said Billie, shrugging her shoulders and plonking onto the grass. 'No, I'm sticky. I need to wash my hands in Stickleback Stream. And then we can play in the woods. Hoshi can fix my Spindy, and I can play with my cat. Ok?'

'Anything you like, D-D-Dude.'

The rest of the afternoon passed without further incident as the cousins, and Hoshi, pretended to search for Old Man Isaac's missing shoe (because Billie wanted to). Hoshi hated the childish game and said she had science to do, but Molly persuaded her to join in, just in case Billie caused further damage to the surrounding areas and bikers.

As there were no lakes or rowing boats in Hatley Woods, Hoshi used her knowledge of mathematics and Origami to make a paper yacht. They sailed it down Stickleback Stream and rescued Old Man Isaac from his cursed, smelly shoe. In the story, he grew to a ripe old age, living happily ever after with the extremely large duck that now lived in the stream: the duck really lived in the stream, while Old Man Isaac, did not.

Anyway, by the end of the role-play, Molly and Hoshi had quite enjoyed themselves, but probably would not admit it.

'Fanks for today, Mols,' says Billie. 'Daddy and Lil are cooking yucky beans again, so I have to go home.' And, with that, everyone headed down the dirt track next to the stream, relieved for a ravage-free afternoon.

On the way, while Hoshi threw stones to make the sticklebacks dart and Billie picked fresh daisies, Molly hushed the pair and dragged them behind an ash tree.

'Hide,' she whispered. 'It's McKenzie.'

'Who is McKenzie?' said Billie, standing as tall as she could.

'McKenzie Hilton, the school bully. He's a nasty boy.'

'I don't like bullies,' said Billie with a stern face. 'I shall kick him in the shins.'

'No! Why don't we pick more daisies from behind that birch tree instead?'

'B-Better than p-p-picking bits of McKenzie from behind a tree,' said Hoshi, with a worried grin.

Fortunately for McKenzie, he tramped by to make fun of a small, red-haired boy. But as the boy began to get upset, the thread on Molly's sorrow balloon gave a sharp sting.

'Ouch.'

It got hotter and stung more.

'Aya!'

It got so hot that a tear formed in the corner of Molly's eye. Her face flushed, and she dropped to the ground.

'Give him the balloon, Silly,' said *Up-there Molly*, jumping clean out of Molly's body and onto the shoulder opposite the balloon. 'The sorrow one with Mum's tears inside.'

Molly said nothing, she just sat there.

'Are we having a sit down, Molly?' said Billie, while Hoshi grabbed her phone to ring an ambulance.

'Don't you think he deserves it? He's a bad, bad boy,' continued an impatient *Up-there Molly*. 'What are you waiting for? Pluck the balloon.'

And, without another word, *Up-there Molly* sucked back into Molly, who yawned and rubbed her eyes.

'Let's get *you* all fixed up,' she said, menacingly, and tugged at the thread of Mrs Nell's balloon.

POP!

The balloon burst, and a ruby-red balloon-shaped mist hung in the air. It spun around, faster and faster, whooshing and darting across the path and straight into McKenzie's ear. The lad coughed and his eyes widened. He clasped his hands to his head and, just as it had happened to Molly only days before, he exploded into tears, letting out a ground-shaking, mournful sob. The boy with glasses looked so confused, but not knowing what to do, the kind soul put his arm around McKenzie's shoulder to comfort him.

'It stung,' said Molly taking Billie's hand and heading out of The Tunnel of Trees, past the weeping bully.

'The wasp?' said Billie, looking around in panic.

'I must give them away. I take bad from good and give to

bad.'

'Like opposite Robin Hood?' said Hoshi.

'Yes,' said Molly, staring up at the sky. 'I am justice.'

Billie pretended to boohoo like a baby while pointing at McKenzie and three of his friends who had just run up. She wiped away her pretend tears and gave her cousin the best grin she could with two bottom teeth missing.

All the while, Hoshi lagged behind, wondering.

What if the other balloon stung too? If it did, then somebody could be in big, big trouble.

9

The Ginger Seagull

'Calm down,' I say, shushing Soup.

'I cannot come down, Daniel,' Soup squeaks, flustered. He flaps and his legs kick like a Cossack dancer, mid-squat.

'I said "calm down", not "come down".'

'I cannot calm down *or* come down, Daniel, as I am not familiar with the physics of human flight.'

'You'll have to do *something*, coz the more you kick, the higher you go.'

Sure enough, Soup has launched himself way above the branch he slipped off and now he's snatching for the rope swing.

'It's fine, Fella. You're flying, just like Splendid-Man.'

'Daniel.' Soup folds his arms. 'Splendid-Man is not real.'

'What did you learn about flying from Splendid-Man comics?'

'Only a scientific journal on the theory of human flight is *actually* a scientific journal on the theory of human flight,

Daniel. Comics are comics.'

'Oh, for God's sake. Hold on. I'm coming.'

Bouncing up the tree with excessive-immortality-confidence, I'm along the branch without major incident and it's an easy reach to grab the shoulder of Soup's t-shirt. But, when I pull him towards me, he snatches at the branch and this casserole of disaster gets much worse when he tries to swing his legs up. His belly is in the way, so they float high above his head and now he's completely upside down, screaming like an axeman is on the loose. The spare change in his pocket bounces off my head.

'It is not working, Daniel.'

'It will,' I say, grabbing at his belt to pull his legs over the branch. This fails miserably too, coz his frantic flapping drags me off Oakey Croaky and then we're both dangling in mid-air.

'Daniel, you are pulling my shorts down,' says Soup, snatching to save his pants.

'If we fall you better not land on my face!'

'Aye aye,' says Gaz. 'What's gannin' on here like?'

Two things happen at the same time, and they're both equally terrifying. Emerging from a puff of leaves is Gaz, and he's wearing nothing but a pair of Speedos. At that exact moment, Soup tells me that I might not be the only one with undiagnosed ADHD.

'Look, Daniel, there is a ginger seagull. I have never seen one of those before.'

And we're off.

Seemingly, with a skill he didn't have two bloody minutes ago, Soup whips us up above the trees, looping a full three-sixty in hot pursuit of the oddest seagull I've ever seen. It has a ginger head and instead of grey wings, it has ginger —

Ohhhhh, craaaaap!

Soup accelerates and I cling desperately to his belt. He skims over the dip, following the gull, and up above the chocolate block trees. He's punched his hand out like a superhero and we're speeding low over the tips, twisting around like space-fighters, while he ignores my screams to stop. My fingers are not having fun at all and my belly feels like we're in a speeding car on country roads. Then, all of a sudden, we're stationary again and I have no doubt we look like two flies "attached" (*"doing it"*) and I'm the dangling receiver.

Where was I…. Oh, yes. Other than that, the seagull's a pretty normal northern seagull. It's massive from stolen battered sausage and chips and threatening like it wants to batter heads for stolen sausage and chips. And, of course, like every other vermin bird around here, it's got a deformed leg —

Ohhhhh, craaaaap!

The flying butterball splits the branches, as the seagull emerges from the greenery engaging us in a high-speed sky dance. Then, we're ripping apart the air, spinning like a drill bit until Soup whips up, abruptly bringing us to a hover that causes me to almost slip out of his shorts.

Get your mind out of the gutter.

This momentary lapse allows me to pull my legs up, but I've not thought this through at all. Now I'm on his back, upside down with my face level with his backside and this is the worst day of my life.

'Do *not* fart!' I shout.

Ohhhhh, craaaaap, agaaaain!

The cold bites like a thousand hungry piranha when Soup increases his speed, ascending the valley after the seagull. At double the height of the trees and up the side of the valley, we are so high that WOPPA and the hospital are in view between his butt cheeks. I see a valley within a valley.

Meta Cracks.

The tango continues for a while and it's not so bad when he's horizontal coz he's built like a mattress. But when he shifts angles, I have no idea where the world begins and the sky ends.

Suddenly, I'm overcome with a familiar dizziness. We're so high that even the gull bails on us. I'm hollering to stop, but he's wandered a million miles away in his head and I know we're in trouble when sparks attack my lungs. Everything's spinning, including us... down towards the trees. One of us is headed for a painful short-term death and the other is going to —

It appears that the other is going to be just fine, coz at the last second, Soup snaps into life and jolts back up, ripping my fingers from his clothing, separating the docile fly from its host.

The first of many branches tear my skin and then I'm gone.

I feel pulled from my body, blasting through the geometrics of numerous dimensions until I'm spat out, right next to the ankles of a female entity.
She smiles, drenching me with a warm, loving glow that tells me, without words, that I am safe and welcome.
Her headdress is hair, golden blonde and cut sharp into a fringe. Entranced, I feel myself floating amongst a multitude of emotions until she nods over for me to observe something in the distance.
Four other entities dance in front of me.
They are jesters, their black and red jester hats ring out as they... they mock me.
One of them holds his middle finger up and grins.

The other three pull faces and then the female entity waves goodbye.

'Definitely immortal,' says Soup to naked Gaz, who has the seagull on his shoulder, and both are gobsmacked by the healing process.

'What do you mean, "definitely immortal?'

'You are not invincible or invulnerable. You are immortal like Dead-Fool.'

'Who?'

'After a diagnosis of severe constipation,' he says, in a movie trailer voice. 'Wayne Williams is injected with the Power-Patroller Serum. Hideously disfigured, but immortal, "the Goon with the Gob", dons his mask to repair a failing movie empire... He is good, but he says rude words, so Mummy doesn't let me watch the films.'

I creak my bones, take a deep breath and spew bile onto Chubby Soup's school shoes.

'Not to worry,' Soup says, patting me on the back. 'Better out than in. That is what Mr Sparks said to me when I was poorly on his briefcase.'

'You hoyed up a lung on Sparky's satchel?'

'Mushrooms. I am not good with mushrooms. Daddy says they are athlete's foot and I should not eat his special ones. I often ask why athletes have mushroom feet, but Daddy never answers me. Maybe I should check the internet for it? What do you think?'

He is as stupid as he looks, is what I think.

'You're quiet,' I say to Gaz, who promptly passes out, sending the seagull into the trees for an unexpected trip.

The top of the whittling log is a bit muddy but drying much better now our little fire is going. Gaz and I repair as much of the bivouac as possible, while Soup digs up a hidden Tupperware box full of brownies he's "borrowed" from his dad's secret stash.

Once we've got things nearly back to normal, we tuck into the cakes but they're quite rich, so we only manage half of one each. Gaz still hasn't said anything but he's no longer twitching like mad either. I'm pretty mellow too, while Soup's stumbled off to hide behind a bush for ten minutes preparing to show us his "secret surprise".

Oh, good Lord. If anyone comes into the clearing right now, they're gonna take one look at Speedo Gaz, then Soup, and I'm going to prison.

Hiding his six rolls of blubber, Soup's hero stance lacks the confidence of his hands-on-hip idol. It's a look everyone is familiar with, but not quite like this. I don't know which of the images will haunt my nightmares the most — Gaz in his duds, or Soup in a red footy top, red leggings and green wellies doing the Can Can, trying to cover himself with his knees like he's keeping up a footy. The yellow cape is not much bigger than a tea towel, probably from a toddler's fancy dress outfit and it's fastened with a Velcro tab that turns his face a bit purple.

At least I can't die laughing.

'It is my *Soup*-er-suit, Daniel Fella,' Soup says. 'Perhaps I would not have fallen from the sky if I had worn this.'

He looks like a Jelly Baby.

'You'd have bounced.'

'Heya,' says Gaz, eventually. 'Looka. Like, ye've both got stuff glowin' around ye. Like when a fire has blurred air and that.'

'An aura,' I say watching Soup stir his fingers like he's got hands in treacle.

'My mummy mentions auras a lot, Fella,' he says, nodding and observing the glow. 'She likes crystals and bongos, Fella.'

With his palms flattened Soup pinches his fingers together

and, within the aura, amber sparks dart like sticklebacks in the stream. I do the same, observing sapphire sparks dancing around.

'This is mental,' says Gaz. 'I've got gerld ones anarl.'

'Erm… why are you naked?' I ask, coz somebody probably should.

'Lang story,' says Gaz. 'But I reckon its got summat to dee with that Urielis blerk.'

I nod and decide not to push this further.

'I know a lot about superpowers,' says Soup. 'Almost every power has a weakness, but from my evaluations, it seems that Dr Urielis has given us powers that are all weakness and no super. I am afraid of heights and Daniel's life is terrible.'

'Erm, cheers,' I say. 'It's not that bad.'

'It is now,' says Soup. 'Now you will enjoy many lifetimes of watching everyone and everything you love die, possibly thousands of times over until the planet dies.'

Class. Nice one.

'Then the planet *will* die,' Soup continues. 'And that will not be pleasant. But not as unpleasant as when Earth explodes, jettisoning you towards the sun, where you will be unable to breathe, dying over and over, burning as you get closer. Until you eventually become conscious ash, floating through space for around a trillion years, until nothing is left except you and one lonely Red Dwarf on its last breath.'

I don't think he took a breath.

'Oh so you're not an expert on the theory of Human flight, but you're a bloody boffin when it comes to immortality? What if I'm only immortal for a few deaths? Like, temporarily immortal.'

Soup ponders for a moment.

'Temporary immortality would be a paradox, Fella. You could not be immortal if you were only temporarily immortal. Although you could be pseudo-immortal, Fella. That is not as bad.'

'What's that?' I ask and immediately regret it.

'A pseudo immortal regenerates from a single cell but can die by complete annihilation of cellular structures. To find that out, you would need to find someone with super-strength to throw you into the Sun. Was there a super-strength Broken Telephone in detention?'

'*Nobody's chucking anyone into the sun.*'

'Then you will just have to be patient, Fella. I think you must accept that it will be a long, long time until you get to Heaven.'

'I don't believe in all of that rubbish.'

'You did not believe in magic and miracles,' Soup says. 'And now you do.'

Naturally, there's a short break from the debate because I am scared while Soup is plotting complete annihilation of my cellular structure and Gaz is just off his chops.

'We're garna have to have a plan,' he says eventually. 'Poncey and the ugly bunch are garna grass us to anyone and ivryone as soon as they can. Then we're garna end up strapped to a scientist's table while they poke us... and I'm not garna let that happen.'

'You mean Douglas and his friends are going to tell someone and then we are going to be tested on by scientists, Fella?' says Soup.

'Aye, so we need to find that subbie and get him to switch us back.'

'But I quite like flying now,' says Soup. 'Just above the trees and not far though.'

'You're afraid of heights,' I say. 'Splendid-Man doesn't just fly around the tops of the woods. You might as well not bother.'

'But it is fun.'

'Until someone sees you and you get poked by scientists.'

'You are right, Daniel.' Soup stutters in panic. 'We must find Dr Urielis immediately.'

'We dinnet even knar where to start looking for him,' says Gaz despondantly.

'We could try Holy Island,' says Soup.

Well, well, well. He is cleverer than he looks after all. We've done a bit about Lindisfarne in history; it's popular with tourists coz of the monks and Vikings and religious stuff. Cliched perhaps, but Holy Island is a likely hideout for supernatural power-givers obsessed with religion and history.

'Right, what you doing tomorrow?' I say, with urgency. 'Let's get the metro and get this Urielis bodgie to reverse the powers.'

'Do not be silly, Daniel,' says Soup. 'We cannot get the metro to Holy Island. It is a tidal island and therefore is only accessible when the tide is out. Also, Mummy would not let me get on the metro because of the noise and the statistical likelihood of a train crash.'

'Ok, then we'll fly there.'

'From here?' Soup shrieks and starts prodding holes in his face. 'No, no, no. It is too far and I fell out of the sky.'

'Heya, dinnet worry about that, Man,' says Gaz. 'I knar someone who'll sort ye a *proper* super-suit.'

10

Molly's Mole III

Saturday night television was a family event. Viking the cat curled up on the sofa, hoping for some scraps of Molly's mum's special sandwiches — the best sandwiches in the world. Mrs Nell pre-cooked the weekend roast, cut two thick slices from the crispiest part and laid them between homemade bread, dipped in gravy. These were served up with glasses of ice-cold lemonade.

'I prefer Chicken Ping,' said Molly's dad, wiping gravy from his moustache with a napkin.

'What's that?' said Molly's mum, suspiciously.

'Chicken nuked in the microwave!'

'Hilarious,' Molly, lied.

Molly's mum pulled her ears back to hide her brand-new laugh lines. 'Do you think I need a facelift like Lil?'

'No, just a decent haircut,' said Molly's dad. 'Hide your ancient features.'

'Right, come here.'

Molly's mum jumped across the sofa to batter him with the nearest cushion, but Molly deliberately ignored the play-fighting and yawned at the talent show. She had other things on her mind: things like Billie. Saturday nights weren't the same without her since Aunty Helen passed away and this Saturday was yet another evening missing the little viking princess.

After the squawk-fest talent show finished, it was time for *Ultra-Sound Guys* — Molly's mum's favourite hospital drama. When Billie was there, she loved a bit of blood and guts with Mrs Nell. Molly and her dad would go and play cards because they thought it was rubbish. Tonight though, the opening credits, featuring white coats, stethoscopes and kissing, were interrupted by Hatley's very own hospital drama in the form of a newsflash.

Neville: Good evening, Heather. Ready for a story of rebel behaviour in the small town of Hatley?

Heather: Yes, Neville. Four pensioners are leaving a trail of devastation after embarking on a Hollywood-style road trip. CCTV footage shows two of the group "borrowing" the purple minibus from their hospice. The gang collected two further members from Hatley General Hospital before breaking into WOPPA's abandoned swimming pool and hosting an impromptu glow party.

Neville: Police have released the names of the "Outlaw Oldies" and are asking the public for any information which leads to their apprehension.

Heather: Reggie Wallace, Charlie Fairweather, Mavis Walker, and gang leader Margret Nell are not to be approached, under any circumstances. They are armed — with walking sticks — and not that dangerous!

Neville: They're certainly making the most of their twilight years, don't you think, Heather?

Heather: They might not be here for a long time, but they're up for a good one, Nev. Maybe you should take a leaf. Anyway, in response, Dee Dee Nichol from WOPPA has announced the reopening of WOPPA's pool! Come on oldies, be more outlaw...

Molly could not hide her grin as four shiny new balloons danced around her head on ruby-red threads.

'Can Billie come next week, Mum?' she asked, trying to distract her parents from the television.

'I can ask, Darling, but I've not been able to get hold of Eric.'

Eric was an awful human, but also Billie's dad. When the doctor diagnosed Aunty Helen, Eric left her the very next day. Molly's dad called him a coward and Mrs Nell even swore.

Poor Billie.

Aunt Stacy and Uncle Alex looked after Billie for a while, until Eric insisted on taking his daughter back. The real reason for his change of heart wasn't because he cares; he had chosen beer and cigarettes over his family before and only agreed to Billie coming home for the Child Benefit money — more fags, more booze.

Now, Eric lived with his new, much older wife, Lillian (or 'Leopard-Print Lil', as Molly's dad called her). Lillian made the local papers after bragging that her brain operation was a free facelift paid for by the NHS. Fortunately, the operation was a success, but the plastic surgery was not. Mr Nell unkindly, although accurately, likened her to a chamois leather.

'I'm off to do my homework,' said Molly to her parents, who were slow-dancing to soppy music. During the school holidays, Molly had no homework, but they would never notice. There had been a lot of this smooching since her dad's recovery and mum's constant positivity.

The lovebirds locked eyes in silence, so Molly sighed and headed straight outside.

'Frog guts!' she yelled.

'Yes, Darling, love you too.'

Sometimes, Molly forgot the balloons were even there and she was quite fond of all except the painful one. Her dad's balloon was dangerous, so she tied a blue ribbon around that thread, just to avoid any mistakes. The other balloons would come in handy though because both Eric and Lil could do with a dicky tummy or a dodgy knee.

Many friendly people lived on Colliery Row, or the "Dark Side" as the villagers called it. But it had a terrible reputation thanks to a few scumbags whose behaviour made the townsfolk suffer. Eric was one of the scumbags and his bungalow sat in the centre of the street.

Loosely hanging from cracked paint, an old, yellowed doorbell hung with a spider's web in the crevice and the butt-end of a mutilated wasp cocooned within. Molly banged on the blistered, maroon door instead of ringing the bell to allow the wasp its dignity.

Eric and Lil were home but nobody answered her knocking. Ghostly shadows glided behind grimy windows and every knock saw a silhouette ignoring her. Then, Billie screamed.

Uh-oh, was she on the warpath?

Had she turned into Princess Viking?

Was she enormous and muscly, but pretty and dainty?

Eric and Lil probably deserved it — they certainly deserved something — but maybe not disembowelment by a darling psychopath.

Someone needed help, although at that point Molly wasn't sure who, so she tried the handle, just as one silhouette moved closer to the door.

'I can't have her,' screamed a voice. It was Aunt Stacy. What was she doing there? She had given Billie over to Eric already.

Enough was enough. Poor Billie shouldn't have to hear that sort of thing.

'Open this door at once.' Molly banged the door hard and yelled through the letterbox. 'I'm calling the police!'

Still nobody answered.

'Step aside, Mols,' said a nervous voice from behind. 'I g-got this.'

A short, skinny, mysterious figure stood, dressed head to foot in black, with a tattered face-mask from the pandemic covering their mouth. Thick glasses steamed up under a hood that was pulled forward over their head. The sports-shop ninja took a hero-like stance with hands on hips.

'Do you have super-strength?' asked Molly.

'B-better,' said the ninja, focusing a gaze on the door. 'Watch.'

Slowly, Ninja raised an arm and spread wide their fingers, shuffling their feet apart to improve balance. They dropped their chin, revealing a furrowed brow below the hood. A low hum radiated from beneath the mask and eyes glowed behind the foggy specs. It looked like the ninja was channelling some potent energy. But, after a while, the anticipation became unbearable, as Molly braced for something incredible and nothing much happened, other than the occasional grunt and a flicker of Colliery Row's streetlights.

Perhaps she was channelling some potent energy in the wrong places?

After a while, Molly wondered if the radiated hum was just the ninja's stomach rumbling. 'Erm, Ninja, are you planning on getting us in there, or have you had an accident?'

'Shhhhhh, I'm c-concentrating.'

Oh God, was she actually going in her pants?

Molly covered her mouth and nose with her sleeve, trying not to gip, but then Eric's handle began to shake and a faint grinding sound saw one brass screw ping to the floor.

'Is that it?' Molly said. 'Twenty minutes for that? Hoshi, hurry. Billie's in trouble.'

'Ah, man,' said Hoshi the ninja. 'How c-c-could you t-tell it's me?'

'It's your school hoodie,' said Molly, pointing. 'With your initials on it.'

Hoshi Solo-Spock was Hatley Academy's quietest geek and moderator of "The Peer-e-Oddic Squad"— a global think tank of science nerds who anonymously trolled celebrity scientists online and had nightmares about social interaction with anyone outside of a motherboard. Despite "The Peer-ee-Odds" (which is barely shorter than the full name) lack of sunlight, they were no meagre force to be ignored. These pizza-eaters were as smart as a Saville Row suit and the science world feared them. Professor Brian Cox took down his social media and not because of his surname. Hoshi had disproved over seventy per cent of the professor's doctorate, even though she agreed with his theories. Brutal keyboard warriors who enjoyed it. They would happily disprove anything Einstein or Hawking popped out but could not see the point because "they're already on the secret island". There were a fair few crackpot conspiracy theorists amongst The Peer-ee-Odds.

'You haven't done this before, have you?' said Molly, folding her arms and tapping her foot.

Hoshi's face blushed above the mask, but she refocused for another few minutes until the last screw dropped to the doorstep. Molly could not be bothered to wait for Hoshi to wiggle the handle, so she yanked it off and booted the door.

Down the dark, junk-hoarded corridor that smelt of cat wee, the adults argued. Molly stormed forward, into the kitchen, with her balloons dragging behind.

'Where is Billie?' she shouted. 'I demand to see Billie.'

Uncle Eric was drunk. His beer had spilt over his white shirt and his fat, hairy belly showed through like, erm… a fat, hairy belly. Hoshi gagged behind the mask and gagged again at the smell of the gag.

Lil was dressed in fake animal fur, as usual, and smoked a long cigarette, which smelled like a future corpse, while Aunt Stacy stood by the table with steam ejecting from her ears.

'How did you get in here?' she snapped, purple with rage.

'Where… is… Billie?' snarled Molly. 'Billie? Billie?'

'Who is this angry little elf then?' said Eric, squinting to focus on Molly.

'Shut it, Eric,' snapped Stacy. 'Molly, it's ok. Billie's fine. She's showing us her dolly.'

'Molly, the jolly little dolly. I knew a dolly called Molly

once,' sang Eric into a beer.

Lil said nothing that made any sense.

Under the table, Billie sat on the greasy kitchen floor, holding Spindy tight to her cheek. Her face was as grubby as a miner and her clothes were dirty and torn.

Molly clenched her fists.

'Ninja.'

Hoshi looked over her shoulder.

'You, Stupid,' Molly said with a growl. 'Get Billie and I'll deal with them.'

'Oh, I am Mind Melt. I like that name.'

'Shut up, Hoshi. Get Billie.'

The balloons bounced off each other, fizzing and full of charge. Hoshi stooped to help Billie from under the table as Eric and Lil canoodled on the kitchen bench. Stacy scolded the heroes, snatching at Hoshi's shoulder, giving Billie just enough time to bolt past, but the little girl yelped as Stacy's long nail scratched her cheek accidentally.

Molly grabbed her cousin and Billie buried her head into her tummy. Crouched by the table, Hoshi focused hard and Stacy's painted fingernail snapped. She flushed and spun to glare at Molly.

'Billie is frightened and scruffy,' Molly screamed. 'How dare you? You're supposed to be looking after her. You shouldn't be allowed to look after anyone!'

Molly's hand reached across for a thread... and she plucked.

POP!

Clutching her belly, Stacy slapped her other hand onto the kitchen table, bending double in pain. Molly dragged Billie through the door and they dashed down the path into the estate. Hoshi Solo-Spock followed close behind.

They dodged armchairs in the street and families fighting, never looking back. They jumped over dog poo and litter, pushing on through clouds of barbecue smoke. Molly held Billie's hand tightly and they ran so fast their lungs burned.

Then,from out of nowhere, two scrawny youths in grey track bottoms and hooded Puffas stepped out on the trio, shouting abuse. The biggest, Del Collins lashed out with a fist, catching Hoshi on the cheek. She squealed, her eyes watered, and she squinted to look for her lost glasses.

Molly stopped dead in her tracks. Her face became solemn as she stared up through her brow with one fist clenched. Her cheeks were as red as ketchup while Del Collins and Owain Hilton barged forward with angry threats. And then…

POP!

POP!

…the half-brothers crumpled to the floor.

Molly, Hoshi and Billie sprinted past the school into the Tunnel of Trees, eventually stopping to catch their breath.

'We'll be safe now, Billie,' Molly spluttered.

'Hold up a minute,' said Hoshi, removing her mask and hood. 'Billie, will you walk ahead with Spindy so the g-g-grown-ups can t-talk?'

Billie shrugged and let go of Molly's hand. She gave Spindy a tight squeeze before skipping down the path.

'Come on, Spindy,' she whispered. 'Our heroes want to kissy-kissy.'

With a concerned look, Hoshi pointed. The static from the remaining balloons tugged at Molly's hair and the threads glowed much brighter. The thread from the death balloon shone brightest.

'What did you d-do?' Hoshi said, quivering.

'It's just a couple of creaky knees.' Molly twanged the death balloon playfully. 'See, this one is the bad one. It's still here.'

'You're not the law. You c-can't just der-dish out balloons.'

'Oh, Hoshi,' said Molly. 'I sort of *can*.'

'You've g-got to think carefully.'

'And you've got to shut up… or you're next,' said Molly. 'Only joking! Let's go.'

She turned and jogged away to catch up with Billie, who was knelt by Stickleback Stream, modelling a hammer from twigs and a rock.

Returning to the Nell home, the heroes' welcome they expected did not come, as Molly's dad fumed with rage.

'You've let Mum and I down,' he said. 'Worse still, you've let yourself down.'

Hoshi could not resist a balloon joke, which no one found funny, so she excused herself and went home.

Mrs Nell dunked Billie in a bath, while Mr Nell ordered Molly to her room, where she paced backwards and forwards, screaming inside. She threw some clothes onto her bed. Hoshi had looked the part in her outfit and Molly wanted to wear something that represented her own power. Light and shade — saving good people and punishing those who deserve it. Like lightning ripping through the darkness with devastating consequences.

Black Jeans were a must with Doc Martens. Molly was sure she had a high-neck, black track top with a white tick on the shoulder, folded somewhere at the bottom of her wardrobe. She picked the logo with a pin to shape a lightning strike and cut the fingers from her leather gloves with the new kitchen scissors. Then Molly painted her nails with black varnish. Finally, she used her mum's eyeliner to draw a straight line across her cheek, where Billie was scratched, as a reminder of her cause. The outfit was complete.

'Justice,' she growled. 'I *am* Justice.'

Her heart raced and beat harder than ever before.

She marched past the bathroom with raised shoulders and clenched fists, stomping down the stairs and straight out of the back door, ignoring calls from her parents, who wouldn't understand.

She disappeared towards the fading light, to put things right.

First, she would visit Eric and Lil.

And then into the night…

When the bad guys come out to fight.

11

Super-Suit

'Here ye gan. I telt her ye're gannin' for lessons. She proper fancies ye like…'

Dear Ralph,

Please find attached an equipment list for Scuba. May I recommend a YouTube tutorial "Scubin' with Ruben". He is very thorough.

1. Scuba mask. Colour - black. Snug fit. Water and airtight, tinted polycarbonate screen. Speciality deep-water mask with added pressure protection and visibility.

2. Youth's XL wetsuit and gloves (5mm). Colour - black/no logo. Comfort-Fit. Easy to put on unaided. Thick and flexible for warmth at cold temperatures and ease of movement. Protects against cuts and tears (Kevlar weave). Kevlar-soled wet socks.

Additional - Goalie gloves and a packet of wet tissue to

clean splattered bugs from the mask.

3. Buoyancy Compensating Device. Colour - black. Snug fit. Gas pockets allow stability at varying depths. Utility pouches big enough to store junior-sized fins.

4. Diving Regulator. Colour - black. Low profile, sturdy mouthpiece and flexible hose.

5. Aluminium Scuba Tank. Colour - black. Lightweight. Normal Air Composition.

Totally cool.

6. Fins/flippers. Colour - black, lightweight.

Look daft.

The tanks have enough oxygen for one hour and only use the mouthpiece when breathing becomes difficult.

Wear the flippers and you can move faster with less energy. This can give up to another hour of oxygen.

You will be warm and can "swim" for about five hours.

Be Careful,
Hoshi

'Perleeeeeeeeeeeeeaaaaassssseeeeeee, Mummy.'

'No.'

'I promise I will stick at it this time."

'It'll be like the Karate thing, Carol. He'll be wearing them as pyjamas in a week.'

'Karate was a waste of money, Ralphie.

'I super-duper promise that I will practice. Daniel Fella will make sure I get there all safely. Scuba Lessons are twice a week, in the evening and this means you will get the night to yourself.'

'Say what?'

'The whole night to yourself.'

'Ordered. They'll be here Saturday.'

12

Sandy Bay

A country track, walled with carboniferous sandstone (*check me out!*), lies perpendicular to the mouth of The Tunnel of Trees. It bends and narrows to the right, barely wide enough for a family car, then broadens around farmer's outbuildings into Hatley Village. I came here with Mam and Dad when I was younger, but I doubt I'll get a wave from someone who recognises me. More likely these nosey parkers twitching their curtains will call the police.

At the top of the village, The Ivy House stands next to two normal houses. Ironically, The Ivy is a sandstone pub with no ivy, while the two thatched houses next door are covered in the stuff. One of them, the house with a neatly trimmed lawn, is home to the Robinsons — Soup's family.

'Ambrose,' Soup's dad says in a deep, accepting voice. He has dried egg down his shirt, of which I'm not surprised.

'Daniel Ambrose.'

'Aye... I mean, yes, Sir.'

'Going to stand there all day, or are you coming inside?'

Mr Robinson scratches the egg from his shirt with his thumbnail. 'Banjo sandwich,' he says, with a wink. 'How's Keith? Not seen him or Jackie for decades. Lovely couple.'

He must mean Mam, but I let it slide. I don't know if my social skills are up to small talk, so I nod and squeeze past.

Inside the hallway, the air conditioning catches my throat. Soup's house is immense. The doorways are wide and the rooms look huge. Everything's immaculate, with pictures of the Robinsons smiling and doing stuff together lining the corridor walls between the dark wooden beams spanning floor to ceiling. Above the kitchen door, the same framed photo of the Scout and Guides dominates their wall as does ours, but theirs is four times bigger (like everything else in this house including the occupants).

I peek into the living room at the biggest television I've ever seen. Below, a new Xbox sits in the cabinet. All around, dozens of smiling faces are frame-mounted and hung straight. Hopefully, Soup drew them when he was a toddler and they're not by a proper artist. Tacky silver, wooden lettering spells "Live, Laugh, Love" on the mantelpiece and a teak cross hangs above the open fire. So, Soup's a God botherer too, but I'm not sure his God is the traditional one like Jackie's. I imagine his God is a purple bloke on a golden steed with a magic axe and a burger, or something.

'Come through,' says Mrs Robinson, a squat lady with a cucumber smile just like Soup's. She ushers me away from the living room and into the kitchen, where I'm welcomed with an awkward hug. Then, Mrs Robinson forces me to drink some juice and rams a handful of chocolate cookies into my hands. There's no wonder Soup's the size of a house end and I hope this isn't a Robinson tradition or I'm bolting out of the front door.

'Ralphie's had a bit of an episode with the cat,' Mr Robinson says, pointing up the stairs. 'Carol will sort it. She's good at that stuff.'

But, from the look of it, the tabby cat is fine, although externally, it's unsurprisingly the shape of a hot-air balloon. So, internally, its arteries probably aren't fine. If it's alive, then it's asleep by the kitchen entrance and seemingly unfazed by an encounter that has seen Soup come off worse. I wonder if they've had a scrap for leftover chicken?

Mrs Robinson heads upstairs and around halfway up, I hear her sing, 'Listen to this, too good to miss, trala lala la la'. Then she either farts or the stairs need sorting. This has to be a private joke amongst the family. They're farters, for sure. I bet they cock a leg whenever someone comes down.

'You know about our Ralphie, then?' Mr Robinson says, unimpressed. He folds his newspaper and spends about twenty minutes listing off behaviours associated with Autism. It's stuff we've learned about in school, but, although Soup's a teenager, it's clear that his dad feels overwhelmed. I cram a biscuit in my mouth and nod a lot so I don't tell him about my ADHD coz he'd explode.

Eventually, Soup comes down wearing a green Incredulous Bulk t-shirt and matching joggers. His cheeks are raw, so he's been programming face drums again. It's probably the wardrobe change that's caused the meltdown. In the short time I've been forced to know him, he's been a heavily greased politician to Jelly Baby and now a frog. They're all cringe.

I bet the cat was winding him up.

'Mummy, Daddy,' says Soup, sitting without looking at any of us. 'This is my friend, Daniel, Fella.'

Jesus. Still?

I palm off some cookies from my pockets and he rams them down his gob like a hypochondriac pops tablets.

'What have you boys planned for the holidays?' says Mrs Robinson, between sips of tea.

'Not a lot,' I say.

'Probably sleeping all day,' says Mr Robinson from behind his newspaper. 'In my day, we never slept. I was a milkman. Five o'clock starts.'

'Milk Man is the worst superhero,' says Soup, pondering possibilities. 'Would milk shoot from his wrists? Good for hot drinks, but not Big Boss endgames.'

…

'Your dad wasn't a milkman, an astronaut, a scientist or SAS,' says Mrs Robinson, rolling her eyes. 'He's never seen the other side of eight o'clock.'

'I was so,' grumps Mr Robinson, leaning around the newspaper and winking again. He's hoping we'll bond before Soup hits puberty and starts hating his parents.

I could be the thin son he never had.

'You know what?' says Mrs Robinson, dusting her apron. 'The church fayre is Sunday, so we mustn't touch my baking. Who fancies —'

'Fish and Chips,' bellow Soup and his dad.

I'm not a fish fan. It's too fishy. I normally get sausage. Although I do like a mince pie and chips in a buttered bun. The best sandwich ever.

'Martin, ring Jackie and we'll take Daniel to Sandy Bay for the weekend.'

'I can't,' I blurt out. 'I'm busy this weekend.'

I know I'm only thirteen, but shouldn't they consult *me* before they ask my dad's unwanted girlfriend if I can go somewhere with them? Technically, this is kidnapping.

'Sandy Bay is in Newbiggin, Daniel, Fella,' says Soup. 'The Northumberland coast is lovely and there are very wonderful places, such as… *Holy Island*.'

Ahhhhhhh.

'Sorry, I forgot. It's next weekend I'm busy.'

Dad sounded pleased to see the back of me and I can't help feeling rejected. Since Mam left, he's always wanted me around. He pretends that he wants me to go to school, but I know he prefers it when I'm home. I hope the microwave burns their tea and they choke on whatever wine they're slurping. I feel better when I see Mrs Robinson looking properly chuffed with herself, though. She's canny.

'Well, that's settled,' she says. 'Ralphie, go pack some clothes while I knock up some sandwiches for the journey. Daniel, Jackie is packing you an overnight'

While Soup's off up the fart-stairs faster than he can fly (Mr Robinson cocked his leg), the reasons for the family rotundness become clear. Hot-knifing butter onto crusty bread, Mrs Robinson makes a mountain of sandwiches for a forty-five-minute journey to get fish and chips. When both parents eat one, I establish that she's made sandwiches to make more sandwiches, to get fish and chips. It's like "Inception" in Greggs and I fear for our cholesterol levels.

By the way, as soon as the cat heard "Sandy Bay" it bounced out of the room in relief. I bet it's desperate for a few days fasting.

'How was your last day at school?' Mr Robinson says, spitting crumbs.

'WOPPA,' I say, wiping crumbs from my face.

'That bloody alien thing is a cover, I'm telling you it's a mutant farm. One day we'll have three eyes and hairy palms.'

He might be right. Mark Barker could be a mutant, for sure.

'It's a shame your redundancy didn't happen earlier,' says Mrs Robinson, buttering more bread. 'Now go shave your hands before we leave.'

Mrs Robinson is the funny one.

Around an hour later, the Robinson family car is full to bursting with half the kitchen, several suitcases, and Mr Robinson's fishing equipment. I squeeze into the back, where I am greeted by a plastic box filled with wriggly maggots and Soup's face matching his ghastly green outfit.

'Mummy, do we need to take the entire house?' Soup looks nervously at the maggots like they're going to jump out at him. 'It is two nights and these horrid maggots could go in the back.'

'It's just the essentials, Ralphie. You need your special cheese toasties, don't you?'

They need salad, not more bread.

'I'm with the boy on this,' Mr Robinson says. 'I can't fit my drill in.'

'Why do you need the drill?' asks Mrs Robinson. 'Fitting a new shelf in the bar?'

Definitely the funny one.

It takes a while to get out of Hatley Village coz there's a black van blocking the road up to Larkfield. Now they've built the big houses up top, Mark Barker, the posh car parker, is planning minimum impact vehicle infrastructure.

"Thou shalt not dare pass my mansion in a Honda, Peasant."

Moron.

We stop by the embarrassment that I call home and I rush in before the Robinsons follow. Yappy Dog has a chewy rubber nail while Dad has had too much bread and wine (pizza and Special Brew). As usual, his phone is face down, so he's been checking Mam's status. I don't want him sectioned again. He's telling Jackie stories of personal failure again but she's not listening coz there's a history documentary on the telly. Jackie loves a bit of history to go alongside her religious obsession. This is ironic, coz if she'd existed back then, they'd be dunking her in a pond.

After she's given me my backpack, Jackie tells me to have a great time and that she'd love a holiday.

'I'll save up for a one-way ticket to anywhere except here,' I respond eagerly, but sadly, she doesn't react.

For the majority of the forty-five-minute journey, I try to explain humour to Soup with some "Yer Da's a Liability" jokes:

'Yer da head-butted the bloke in the hardware shop,' I say. 'Because he asked him if he wanted "decking or flooring"'

'Daddy, violence is not the answer to DIY,' Soup snaps and taps his face, so, I try again.

'Yer da's an Egyptian taxi driver. Calls himself "Toot 'n' Come Oot".' Unfortunately, this leads to a thirty-minute dissection and confirmation that Mr Robinson is neither Egyptian nor a taxi driver.

The adult Robinsons are buckled by my comedy skills though.

Quick maths — a forty-five-minute journey, plus three toilet stops, one petrol fill, a "snack emergency" and a box of spilt maggots, equals two hours to get to Newbiggin by Sea. I could have walked here faster.

We drive past Sandy Bay to head into Newbiggin where

some new-build houses look proper posh. Dad reckons they're likely falling to bits as they're being sold coz the materials are cheap. He says politicians give out contracts for backhanders and he's probably not wrong, coz they're scumbags.

After the new-builds, poverty rears its ugly head until we get to a canny little town centre with a strip of shops, a few pubs and a few takeaways. But before we get to the unnecessary chip shop, we visit a bloke whose house is decorated with old spirit bottles and pirate memorabilia. This colourful display of poor taste and alcoholism could well explain the man's summer teeth — some are yellow, some are black, and some are missing.

While Mr Robinson chats to Summer Teeth, the man's sister-wife comes out with a cup of tea for Mrs Robinson. Mrs Robinson proceeds to tip it out as soon a Sister-Wife is distracted. Finally, Summer Teeth hands Mr Robinson a box of brownies and we drive to a chip shop called "Clem's".

I have no idea why I find that so funny.

Anyway, although I'm not hungry, the sea air melts into the smell of fish and chips and my belly rumbles unexpectedly. What kind of trickery is this? Even though I've pouched two sandwiches and a sausage roll, I'm starving.

I concede and order mince pie, chips with a little salt, plenty of vinegar, and a buttered roll.

I'm "one of them" now.

Next door to the chippy, an arcade rattles with the sound of Push Penny machines and Mrs Robinson gives us a handful of coins while they wait for the gargantuan order to fry in lard. The neon lights, high-pitched bells and beeps are Soup's worst nightmare and he's trying to prod the back of his heed through his cheeks. But when I point out the Splendid-Man toys in the grabber machine, he calms.

Five benk down and there's still no Splendid-Man.

Later, blazing barbecues settle to white coals while I scrape the last of the gravy from the paper my food was wrapped in. The smell of charring sausages and broiled burgers mingles with the scent of citronella candles as the outdoorsy folk enjoy their holiday adventures. Adults think that getting drunk and shouting at children while attempting to wash the dishes with a bean-covered sponge is an "adventure" and this makes me wonder if I ever want to grow up.

Oh, hang on. I'm never growing up. Ha!

With a full belly and barbecued nostrils, I watch darkness arrive outside our static caravan. Everyone enjoyed their Clem's (hahaha) and we listen to the distant thumping of the clubhouse, while over the cliffs the waves chop against the rocks and sea spray wets my cheeks. Then, Mr Robinson lights the log burner and cracks open his first beer of the day. The fire takes hold and Mrs Robinson pours a large glass of wine. Soup gazes into the pit and he's thinking about flying because his hands waft around like he has butterflies on his fingertips. Hypnotic ripples of air pulse towards the flickering flames and he occasionally claps his hands to blast a cheeky fireball at me. I'm not a bloody marshmallow, but it's dangerously funny.

About an hour later, Mr Robinson's in a topper mood and treats us to drinks at the club. We're allowed full sugar OoGoo Joose, which sets the sparks off in my belly and transforms Soup into a hyper-lunatic. Mr Robinson finds this funnier than his wife, who scolds Soup for drinking "blue stuff" and her husband for "being a tool". In response, Mr Robinson downs a few more beers to "make the weekend pass quicker" and embarks on a lager-fuelled rant about "that ridiculous rat". He means Nutsy the Squirrel, the camp mascot, and, as another drink disappears, Mr Robinson notifies nearby holidaymakers of the park ranger's shorts being "too tight to be around children". Soup reckons by Sunday the park staff will have removed his dad from the bar at least twice.

And then…Soup gets up for the talent show to perform his version of *my* "Yer Da's a Liability" jokes.

'Your daddy likes the man in the hardware superstore,' he mumbles into the mic. 'They got a taxi to Egypt to lay some flooring in a pyramid.'

…

He didn't win.

After that embarrassment, Mrs Robinson has a ball at the post-talent show "Dance Like a Nutter" disco. She's had a fair bit of wine and keeps trying to drag her "special boys" up to dance. I'm not one of her special boys, but she treats me like I am and it feels weird.

'Come on, Daniel. I'm on me Holidayyyss,' she squeaks until I give in.

Soup masks his hatred of dancing for half of the "Macarena", digging his heels into the sticky carpet as his mam tries to get him up. But something's gotten hold of me and it's not just Mrs Robinson. Unwittingly, I'm pulling shapes like never before. I've… I've… I've let go. So much so that all the smiling and singing gets a couple of lasses my age up dancing with me too. I even drop the Australian Dinosaur from the Olympics and they love it.

But, I love OoGoo Joose more.

And just when things couldn't get any more class, my electro-popping becomes contagious when the DJ plays The

Sugarhill Gang. With a restricted shuffle of the shoes, Soup slides next to me and the lasses. But when the opening barres to the "Cha-Cha Slide" kick in, suddenly, he's lost in expressive dance and in no time, we're all bopping away like there's nothing better in the world. Even Mr Robinson gets up for "Johnny B. Goode".

Afterwards, we all walk under the moonlight back to the van and they jibe me about a sneaky kiss from Megan. I am not a kisser and teller but I'm blushing, for sure.

Feels good, doesn't it?

Like, yeah, but I wish this was Mam and Dad.

Like, I wish this was my family.

Like, the way it was.

13

Molly's Mole IV

'Where the hell have you been?' barked Molly's dad. 'Have you seen the time?'

'Out. I'm not talking to you. I'm going to bed.'

'You'll do as I say. Get in the front room now.'

'*I am not talking to you.*'

'It's not an option, Molly. Get in.' Mr Nell held the top of Molly's arm and marched her through. She took a sharp breath as she saw Aunt Stacy sitting next to her mum on the sofa.

Molly was made to stand by the television, which meant a lecture was coming, but she had no intention of listening to her dad's lawyer routine, or the sofa jury either. She put her Walkman headphones over her head and pressed play. The split foam covers tore as her dad ripped them off and a tinny, piercing rendition of The Cure's "Pictures of You" played on the wooden floor. Only one balloon remained — the death balloon. The neon thread burned deep into her skin and the knotted ribbon scorched brown from the heat.

'Aunt Stacy told us about what happened and I'm embarrassed Molly,' said Mr Nell.

'I…' stumbles Molly.

'You'll speak when you're spoken to. You'll have your opportunity to defend yourself when I'm good and ready to let you.'

'Fine.' Molly folded her arms and stared at the open door.

'I can't describe how bloody angry I am right now.'

'Go easy. I'm sure she was trying to help,' said Aunt Stacy.

'No, Stacy. Don't make excuses for her. She's out of order.'

'Billie was in trouble,' growled Molly. 'She was dirty and scared and I saved her.'

'You saved nobody. You behaved like an irrational, angry teenager,' said Mr Nell sternly. 'Your stupidity made things worse for your cousin.'

'I heard her say to Billie that she wanted nothing to do with her,' snapped Molly, pushing her fingers into the pockets of her jeans.

'That's not what I said, Molly,' said Stacy, calmly.

'I heard exactly what you said, *Stacy.*'

'That is your aunt you are talking to,' snapped Mr Nell. 'Have some respect!'

'Respect? Like she showed Billie when she abandoned her? Is that respect?'

'You heard half a conversation with Eric.'

'I heard enough.'

'Aunt Stacy was at Eric's fetching Billie here.'

'What?'

'You heard me.' Mr Nell folded his arms and paced the floor, just like stories of winning in court.

'I care for Billie dearly and I would never harm her.' Aunt Stacy looked grey, with yellowed eyes. 'I was there to protect her.'

'Your cousin will be just fine, Sweetheart,' chirped Molly's mum, bobbing her head to the advert music on the television. Molly's dad snatched the controller, to turn down the volume, while Molly stared at the emerald rug on the floor. The mole scorched her skin and the balloon tap-tapped her on the head.

'Billie needs stability, love and care,' Stacy said. 'Uncle Alex and I wanted Billie, but, well, we have some big changes coming, not least at work. Your Mum and Dad suggested Billie live with you guys.'

'I contacted Children's Services and went to court to safeguard Billie,' said Mr Nell. 'But these things take time. We didn't tell you in case you got your hopes up and the court didn't grant custody. That's why Stacy was at Eric's.'

'I was delivering the court order,' said Stacy. 'I had a doctor's appointment, so I dropped in on the way home. You know me, I cherish any opportunity to let Eric know what I think of him.'

'But I heard you say, "I don't want her",' Molly protested.

'I said, "I can't have her" and I really can't now. Eric's such a — well, I'm glad you showed up later or you would have heard much worse.'

Molly took a sharp, fluttered breath between guilty sobs. Mr Nell said that Billie would live with the Nells until Eric completed rehab for alcohol abuse and proved himself as a responsible parent. He had agreed to the judge's order, making wild promises a sober person would never agree to. Eric's slurred assurances meant Billie was safe and Eric would only get his daughter back with major life changes. After Molly's visit, Eric and Lil had been sober for a couple of hours and they were seemingly confused and deeply regretful. For the first time in ages, Molly felt the heat of her scarlet face instead of the death balloon's sting.

'What do you have to say to Aunt Stacy?' said Mrs Nell, reaching for the television remote again.

'Sorry, Aunt Stacy.'

Stacy held out her hands for her niece. 'You're a wonderful role model to Billie and you'll be a fantastic role model to another little Nell —' Stacy rubbed her belly and Molly's heart sank.

Heather: We interrupt this programme for a news flash.

Neville: Yes, Heather, an urgent public health announcement follows…

The newsflash distracted everyone in the room, except Molly, because her mind raced like a comic book fight scene. Bam! Thud! It processed everything. She could make this all better. Yes, she could fix everyone. She would carry the balloons and give them to a dying insect. The contents could be taken back. Yes, she would take them back.

Sliding over to her aunt, Molly put an arm around her and snuggled into her body. She reached out and held her aunt's hand, wishing hard to take back the balloon that she burst.

'Let's get you all fixed up,' she thought, bracing herself for the spark.

Nothing happened.

She tried again, speaking the words. 'Let's get you all fixed up.'

Still nothing.

'That won't work, Molly,' said *Up-there Molly*. 'Once gone, always gone.'

Molly sat wounded when the newsflash began …

Heather: Two teenagers are on life support in Hatley General

Hospital, after contracting a mystery virus that attacks the liver and kidneys. Parents are advised to isolate children for twenty-four hours until scientists know more.

Neville: And concerns have been raised for a missing Hatley teen. More on this later.

Molly sobbed into her aunt's shirt as her family remained glued to the television for the final news flash. A robbery had been committed by the Outlaw Oldies. Molly dipped her head. She was to blame for everything and the death balloon thudded relentlessly against her head. The sizzling thread fried her skin.

Later, Mr Nell knocked on the bedroom door and peeked around. Opening it quietly as he could, he approached Molly who sat on the side of her bed with her head in her hands. Dried, salty tears tightened her pink cheeks. Her dad knelt next to her and stroked her hair gently.

'I'm sorry, Dad. I didn't mean to hurt anyone.'

'I know.'

'Have you ever done something bad and not been able to fix it?' said Molly.

'Your shelves.'

'I'm being serious.'

'I know, Sweetheart. I have made mistakes, yes and I learned from them. Sometimes you've just got to hold your hands up and say you're sorry. People forgive eventually.'

'I was angry,' said Molly.

'You're thirteen years old,' said her dad, teasing. 'Been there, done that. Get some sleep, we'll go to Louis' tomorrow.'

'But you don't understand. I've done something *te*rrible.'

'Molly.' Mr Nell moved his daughter's hair from her face and lifted her wet chin with his finger. 'I know about the mole.'

14

The Hattening of Flatley Woods

'What's the delay?' said the Stand-Up with the white, floppy wig.

'Paperwork,' said the female.

'I want that place levelled.'

'For roads, obviously,' said the female. Her face suggested that she was less than pleased with the male Stand-Up.

'I want that place turned upside down so there is not one worm with a place to hide. Get it. Get its eyes.'

'For roads, remember. Roads.'

'Whatever,' said the mop-headed Stand-Up. 'Line up the machinery while we wait for that useless councillor.'

'Alright,' said the female. 'You need to meet Barker by the school in twenty minutes.'

'I expect to be ploughing the trees in thirty.'

'For roads.'

In extreme panic and with little option, the mouse called

upon the fly for help. Mrs Mouse would be dropping the new additions to the family any moment and hormones clouded everyone's judgement, so priorities lay at home.

Determined to help, the fly buzzed up to the rooftop car park to see the last of twelve dirty, yellow diggers lining up next to the jets on the helipad. The flattening of Hatley Woods was about to commence and the fly must seek out the legendary squirrel.

THE MESSAGE:

'Superfly,' buzzed **the Bluebottle** and it dusted down its pristine wings.

Flies are generally unaware of comic books but take great pride in their appearance.

Soon after, the fly landed beside a **vegetarian spider** and sought help.

'Your worldwide web can reach the bird far quicker than I can fly,' it buzzed, and the spider agreed, discarding a Beyond-Wasp sandwich to wiggle and jiggle and tickle off to the nearest tree.

After flashing webbing from branch to branch like swinging between New York skyscrapers, the spider collapsed, exhausted, next to a bird and gasped for further assistance.

'How absurd,' said **the crow**. 'I shall fly as fast and far as I can.'

Taking the most direct route, the crow passed over the hospital and to Hatley Village, where, outside of an ivy-covered house, it noticed **the ghost of a big, flat cat**, licking its paws. Surprisingly, this crow feared the darkness of the woods far more than the ghost of a big, flat cat would, so it landed on the bird feeder and begged for help.

'Fancy that,' said the spirit moggy. 'Yes, I can help, but I am too flat to run to the woods. As it happens, I know **an agile dog** that is due a walk though.'

The ghost of a big, flat cat wobbled through the farmer's field behind The Ivy, into the stable where the shocked dog was tied.

'You've put on weight,' said the dog to the cat-napparation. 'Lengthways on.'

'Got three different owners,' said the ghost of a cat, smugly.

'What a hog,' said Killer, under his breath. 'My leash will only let me get into the next field, but I'll ask for help there.'

Through the hedgerow, the German Shepherd approached **Milky, the Jersey cow**. She was chewing on grass and was surprised to see the dog.

'I need you to tell the legendary squirrel that the animals of Hatley Woods are in danger,' said the dog.

'I don't know how,' replied Milky. 'But the horse will.'

'Ned's dead,' woofed Killer abruptly, and all seemed to be lost until the fly buzzed by, with his energy replenished.

'So, you could have done this all by yourself?' said Killer. 'Why didn't you?'

'I don't know why,' said the blue bottle. 'Then I remembered that I know **an old lady**, who knows **a squirrel**.'

The pigeon was the first to see the fly arrive and she cut short a conversation about "The Hounds of the Baskerville" to find the legendary squirrel. Unfortunately, the newcomer spoke a language foreign to others, but her wing gestures were sufficient to get the message across and eventually, she found the half-red, half-grey squirrel deep in debate.

Several angry Red Squirrels disagreed with the updated clause in the "Treaty of Stickleback Stream". They had been driven out of their homes by their grey counterparts and remained convinced of extinction if they did not fight for survival.

'But the world has enough space for all creatures,' said Jeremy, the half-red, half-grey squirrel. 'Why can't we all get along?'

'Selfish creatures want all the nuts to themselves,' chattered Red Leader. 'Regardless of the suffering of others.'

Jeremy reasoned not all grey squirrels were the same and that some greys understood the plight of the reds, but it did little good as the squabbling continued. Most greys refused to show any empathy. Instead, they blamed mutant genes for red fur and sang patriotic songs, despite not being a native species themselves.

It was all bonkers and each year, lots of nuts went to waste. If everyone shared, then squirrels would prosper as a species.

The pigeon skidded on two legs, down a narrow mudslide which she had been making with cautious mini skids for the last few minutes. Her frantic pointing in every direction grabbed the attention of everyone and the fly told his tale.

THE PLAN:

The Bats figured they'd get the blame; they get the blame for everything, the bats.

'They *must* not destroy our home,' said Jeremy to the others. 'The Stand-Ups will regret it when there are no trees to give them oxygen and they fall to a more serious bat virus.'

'I'm right here you know,' said the hurt bat.

The hedgehogs, who had waited a whole winter for some warmth, followed the gull's instructions and rolled into balls.

'Tumbleweeds,' mocked **the old badger**, as the hogs

passed by with leaves collecting on their spikes.

'FTM,' said a Mackem hog.

Most of the woodland creatures seemed keen to find a safe place nearby, except **the rabbits and hares**, who were determined to embark on some "Watership Down" style road trip to the Angel of the North.

PUFF!

Jeremy pointed out that a real-life mission of such extremes would undoubtedly end in carnage and ten fat Rottweilers. Naivety would scupper any chance of reaching The Angel of the North — a popular tourist destination for Real-Ale-drinking-rabbit-pie-eaters. The animals of Hatley Woods should remain **animals of Hatley Woods**, if they could find somewhere safe… somewhere that Noggin could not plough. Somewhere deep in the corner — Of course! **Haunted Hatley**, home to **the Horse Botherer**.

THE MISSION:

PUFF!

The ginger gull suggested everyone pack.

The rabbits bolted for the safety of the fenced football pitches, sealing the entrance, and burrowing once inside. The stoats and the weasels, who often murder rabbits, begged for sanctuary and forgiveness, but the thumping kick of the hares barred them.

After brief discussion, and much to their disapproval, the hares were outvoted because, as everyone knows, rabbits are conscientious creatures. So the stoats and weasels were given a set of rules they must promise to follow.

Rule 1: Help to burrow.

Rule 2: Don't murder the rabbits.

Unsurprisingly, the rules were ignored because stoats and weasels are deceitful beasts and ruthless killers.

The bugs, the ants, and the rather dopey wood pigeon dug faster and lower on the banks of Stickleback Stream.

Patricia La Pidgin spent a lot of time discussing 'alternative uses for a modern statue in a city centre' with the **ladybirds**, who couldn't understand a word and wondered why the pigeon seemed to think she was part of the family. Patricia identified all lady*birds* as birds and subsequently identified herself as an insect. It was very confusing for all involved, but most weren't offended.

Even **the worms**, who had few belongings, grabbed their belongings because **The Council for Critters** had issued three punchy taglines, so the worms would understand and vote accordingly.

"Get your stuff out. Get the heck out. Don't freak The Horse Botherer out".

And, just like that, the floor of Hatley Woods rumbled. The animals were on the move.

Everyone did as they were told, hastening their actions. Jeremy skipped branch to branch, chatting instructions. Patricia La Pidgin fashioned a secure shoebox trunk for her jewellery, preventing a magpie from stealing her "shiny stuffs".

'Arr, geyt yer beaks erf my shiny sterfs,' she warned. 'Oive gert sharp beaks too.'

Ground animals wove between bramble and parting thorns, while dock leaves and ferns fell, mapping out a route. The ants and bugs were quite proud, but the slugs and snails, being pulled along by **fat frogs** and **a giant duck**, were most chuffed. Their slimy trail glistened in the sun, keeping the smallest, weaker animals on track.

Half a mile away, the leaf-ball hedgehogs broke disguise and spiked the tyres on the councillor's car. That would be three hours until the roadside assistance would arrive. It was a good job the ginger gull had explained about roadside assistance. A paperwork delay would bring about dusk and another twelve hours of safety for the animals of Hatley Woods.

"Safety" directed the stoats while the weasels waited in a burrowed lair. Jeremy spotted the carnivorous ploy and launched a chestnut off one stoat's brow, sending him spinning.

PUFF!

A mongoose flashed a menacing stare, so the stoats feigned apology while the weasels nursed the injured stoat.

PUFF!

Thousands of the woodland wildlife dug and climbed and flew until they were all crammed into the dark, eerie corner of the woods. Only a family of field mice had not made it, perishing to a hound, along with two weasels and a stoat that fought valiantly, seeking redemption.

Haunted Hatley lay off-track from Stickleback Stream, where The Horse Botherer had made his home. The Stand-Ups said he lost his mind eating a horse's brain and, in a rage, murdered his family (his own family, not the horse's). These were nonsense stories, concocted to keep children away from the old bunkers. Stories that the animals of Hatley Woods ignored as they escaped the destruction of their homeland, awakening the landowner with the commotion.

'Who goes there?' boomed two loudspeakers attached to a twisted tree.

The animals chattered with nervous energy and a fern-covered bunker door swung open. Jeremy shushed everyone as a tall, skinny Stand-Up stepped into the light. He was dressed in a brightly coloured Hawaiian shirt, flared purple corduroys and leather sandals, with dirty, white socks.

Bearded, with long, dark hair, standing utterly upright, the Horse Botherer's mop had a grey streak running right through the middle and he looked like he had just seen the most terrifying thing anyone had ever seen.

'I thought I heard a party,' said the Horse Botherer, 'and here we are.'

'The Stand-Up is making stupid noises,' said the badger. 'He's a bloody idiot.'

'Don't be rude, Badger,' said the Horse Botherer. 'Now then, what brings you all here?'

'Oi thinks eeza troyin' to communicado,' said Patricia La Pidgin. 'We animools joost need a safa place to get our families safe.'

'What was that?' said the man. 'Yes, Patricia, your family is more than welcome to stay for a while. I'm loving the improved accent. Hello there Mister Squirrel, you're new to these parts. We have an abundance of greys, but I've not seen a half-red, half-grey squirrel before.'

'I get that a lot.'

'Oh…' said the man, solemnly. 'You can't be here. The others are welcome, but you must leave **Potential**.'

Every ant, bug, bird, and frog looked at Jeremy, confused.

'He doesn't want me here,' said Jeremy. 'I'm not one of you.'

Patricia La Pidgin nodded, patting the squirrel on the back. 'Ve're arl prood of you, boot you must be garning,' she said.

Reassured, Jeremy skipped branches and perched on his oak.

PUFF!

High in the trees, the ginger gull looked down on a furious

Mayor William Noggin arguing with Mark Barker at the gates of Hatley Academy.

'Call WOPPA HQ and shut off the digger engines,' ordered Noggin, more authoritative than the last time he and the ginger gull had met. 'Stop them now.'

The seagull sighed with relief. Perhaps the mayor was staging a demonstration?

'Four tyres?' Noggin snarled. 'No more delays. Pick that bloody councillor up first thing tomorrow and get the paperwork signed. Then, plough this monstrosity into the ground. Find it. I want its eyes!'

Perhaps he was not staging a demonstration after all.

Stand-Up Mark Barker fired finger guns and winked.

'Infrasthructure,' he said, heading to his car. 'Roadsh and reshtaurants.'

As Mark Barker drove off, Mayor Noggin folded the paperwork without breaking eye contact with the seagull. After a short fumble with the locks — which would have been easier to do if he had just looked — Noggin placed the paperwork into his briefcase.

The Stand-up blinked and turned away momentarily. He opened his car door and placed the briefcase onto the back seat and for a second, the ginger gull thought to attack. But he had been hasty before — Noggin may look like easy prey, but there was something more to him than fat lips and a wig. Of course, there was: he was trying to stare out a gull and everybody knows they're the most difficult animals to beat in a staring competition.

Tomorrow would see the flattening of Hatley Woods continue. The loss of wildlife would be catastrophic and the evacuation itself would cause inevitable interaction with Stand-ups, some of whom would be kind, some of whom would be trappy and killy. It was not going to end well and now that the paperwork was in place, it could not be stopped.

'It can be stopped, you know,' shouted Noggin. 'You can stop it. You, up there.'

'Corrrrr.'

'You can pretend all you like, but I know *exactly* what you are... I just want to borrow them. Study them. You can have them back.'

'Cawwww.'

'Don't say I didn't warn you. Your friends will pay the price.' He answered his phone, listened and then hung up. 'You have twenty minutes,' he said, grinning. 'We have one.'

And with that, Mayor William Noggin slid his miniature frame into the vast leather seat and slammed his car door, driving off with a screech and pollution of burnt rubber.

A low, droning hum cut through the sounds of swaying sycamores and then **Oscar, a shapeshifter stuck in the animal kingdom**, began his next mission.

15

Holy Island

The next morning, rain streams relentlessly over the caravan windows and I avoid frustration by steaming up the plastic to draw offensive works of art for the kids opposite.

As tempers begin to fray, Mr Robinson battles a hangover by bullying the television aerial, so he can watch the cricket. In turn, Mrs Robinson attempts to murder two kids with buttered pastry, until mercifully, the British weather flips and the sun burns through a wispy layer of cloud. Soup's on his feet before the last drop hits the grass.

'Can we go to the Nutsack Comedy Giveaway? I love comedy now. I might be a comedian.'

'Jimmy Can't' I say, winking at his dad.

Instant regret. His dad's probably Googling "adoption regulations".

'You're bloody obsessed with that rat,' Mr Robinson says, adjusting the TV aerial to get reception.

'They're squirrels, Mr Robinson,' I say. 'Nutsy's Crew.' He

knows, but he's topping up his levels with a beer and a brownie, so he's getting lippy.

'Nutjobs more like. Take a twenty from my wallet and don't come back drowned. Give me a hand, Carol. I can't see the ball.'

'Yes, Boys, enjoy yourselves.' Mrs Robinson pushes us both out of the door. 'I'm going to wiggle Dad's aerial.'

Weird…

The lock clicks shut and the curtains are ripped closed as soon as we're clear. Soup sneaks around the back of the caravan and asks me to help pull the tent bag from underneath. I wondered where he'd put the scuba stuff.

Well played, Soup. They didn't suspect a thing.

We grab a handle each and carry the suit down a stony path towards the b—

Oh. My. God. I've just realised… No, please, wipe that thought. Oh. God. No.

'Daniel, I do not love comedy. That was a white lie and you must not tell *anyone*. We are going to Holy Island.'

'Really? Now?'

'Yes. I am ready Daniel, Fella.'

'I know, Fella. That's why I came.'

A delicate mist conceals the end of the sands, but a dusty ray zaps a hole in the translucent sky, pointing over dozens of dunes out to sea. Coarse, grey-green marram grass whips at my legs as we navigate the sandy tracks to a tiny pebbled cove.

I step carefully over the seaweed-covered rocks and clamber out onto the sand. The caravans on the cliffs above look over the water but below, the secluded cove hides us from tourists, who probably avoid it anyway because of the pebbly sand.

'Right,' I say. 'Have you practised the breathing techniques?'

'I learned everything from "Scubin' with Ruben."'

Scubin' with Ruben? We're dead.

Undeterred, I unpack the wetsuit and equipment onto the sand. Soup is wearing shorts and pulls off his hoodie to reveal a white vest, like a mini-Mr Robinson but without the dried egg.

I pour powder over Soup's head, which unsettles him, but he tells me Ruben reckons it's necessary. He steps into the shoes and when he pushes his arms into the rubber wetsuit, it pops over him with a little effort. I pull the ballie over his powdered head and his chubby cheeks bulge out of the side of the rubber, like muffin tops.

'Mmmmffff,' he says. 'Mmmmmmmpphfffff.'

'Take the mouthpiece out.'

'I look silly. Super-Soup would not wear a rubber suit. This is not my chosen apparel.'

I pull on my swimming goggles and fasten the straps of an empty rucksack around my chest, so Soup has something decent to hold on to.

'Don't drop me this time. Keep low and keep hold.'

'You look silly too, Fella,' he says. 'I feel better now. Ok. Ha'way, Fella.' And with that, Super-Soup grabs my rucksack and we shoot up the cliff, corkscrewing through the air and out over the water.

The North-East has never appeared so glorious to me. Blasts of air cut my throat like Vicks VapoRub, cleansing lungs that are used to the complacency of Colliery Row's coal-flavoured skies. The sea looks so massive up here and I feel free. Free of barriers and thought. Free of troubles. Life becomes more three-dimensional as the entire world opens up to me as we zoom towards Druridge Bay.

Soup's singing Splendid-Man's anthemic horn-section hook as we tear apart the menthol sky. Unexplainable aerodynamics keep my legs in line with my body. I'm weightless coz Soup's only got the rucksack in one hand. He's punched the other in front like his hero and I fly like I'm diving into the deep end.

This is amazing.

We dip and rise at my command. I've memorised the route, flying high where people termite or oldies walk dogs. We are a dot in the skies. Flippers propel us forward with heavy torque. Over the greenbelt land, towards Lindisfarne — Holy Island.

Ten minutes or so later, we slow and I look over my shoulder like I'm catching a breath swimming crawl. Soup's spat out the regulator and pulled a Wet Wipe from the elasticised wristband of his goalie glove to wipe a splattered comrade from his mask.

He's mastered this.

'What's happening?' I say, dangling.

'Look, Fella,' he says, shocked. 'The ginger seagull.'

Sure enough, out in front, with wings spread gloriously, the gull pounds the air. My body stiffens and I shout a warning to be careful, but Soup's not listening. He's got the regulator back in and it's a sign that we're about to "wander off" again. He rises with the bird along the coast, past Druridge Bay. The shores are packed with dog walkers and the waves are high, enticing surfers who stretch out their limbs. We remain distant and constant, stretching out ours too. Then, as we near Amble, Soup pulls us higher and with a swift kick, we're far out to sea. Like a drone, I scan the ocean below, looking for sharks and I see a pod of dolphins. Runny Paint. I've seen him on the news. Everything is legendary until everything turns to chod.

BANG!

Powerful wings slash me as the seabird lets out an almighty screech, delivering a hefty thud to my chin. Immediately, another swift blow forces a startled Soup downwards and we thrash around blindly with the ginger gull attacking from all sides. Left and then right, thumping and screaming, it claws at Soup's wetsuit and the straps of my rucksack.

Soup's grasping at his mask and I search desperately for the assailant.

Why is the bird attacking? Has Soup hidden chips in his suit?

Another attack sees the gull's razor claws grab at my jeans and it twists easily on its deformed leg, dislocating its limb. The dive-bombing bird pounds and forces us downwards, but Soup pushes and kicks, rocketing us back up to the sky while shaking loose the gull.

Over the water, the onslaught continues until, as suddenly as it began, the seagull isn't attacking me anymore: the rucksack has snapped and I'm falling, tantalisingly close to our destination. Tantalisingly close to Holy Island. Tantalisingly close to Urielis.

On the drop, I flip to see Soup, high above, lashing around in mid-air, still fighting with the beast. A black shadow of approaching clouds blots their battle from view... and I hit the water.

Oh, God. I hit the water *really, really* hard.

16

Molly's Mole V

On Sunday morning, Molly and her dad sat in Louis' Coffee Shop. Molly wore a pink Ernie and Bert T-shirt and navy cargo pants (rolled up three times because she had grown over the summer). She finished the outfit with a blue skate cap — no ticked track-top today, no black.

Mr Nell sipped a latte while Molly stirred her strawberry shake. She put her finger over the top of the straw and lifted a vial of pink milk from the glass, while the Grim Reaper did his rounds.

'They're all sgone,' said Molly's dad.

'How did you know?' said Molly, ignoring him to release the milk from the straw.

Mr Nell paused.

'*Up-there Dad* saw the spark shoot up your arm, Mols.'

'I thought you were going to…' Molly stared into the bottom of her shake, 'depart.'

'I did. But the disease sucked from me and Gabriel sedated

me before I could speak.'

'Gabrielle, you mean.'

'Whatever.'

It was always noisy in Louis', with the droning conversation and clinking of cups. More customers entered and the door chimed "Leaving on a Jet Plane" continuously. Molly blew bubbles, gurgling the last of her shake, deliberately not looking up.

'I have a superpower.'

'I know,' said Molly's dad. 'I bet it doesn't feel super at the moment?'

'No, the opposite.' Molly bent her straw and looked at Mr Nell. 'Can you see my balloon?'

'Balloon?'

'Never mind.'

'Come on. What balloon?'

Molly spilt about her power and the mole. Mr Nell looked thoughtful and Molly waited for him to interrupt with something funny because that's how he always handled serious things. He never did what he was doing now — staring distantly and saying nothing.

'It's not the only balloon I've had,' Molly broke the silence.

'Is that the terrible thing you can't fix?'

'Terrible things.'

'You'll get it right soon enough. Making mistakes is part of growing up. We can't learn from perfect.'

The two sat silently for a few minutes longer and Molly scanned the coffee shop. Mr Wallace sat across the floor from them with his red apple next to a scone. He stared blankly, at the empty seat opposite.

'It burns me, Dad.'

'The balloon?'

Molly nodded. 'I think it's deflating.'

'Like Lil's face?'

'It's not funny, Dad. It used to be full and shiny.'

'What do you think that means?'

'I think I have to give it away,' said Molly. 'Look.' She stretched the neck of her T-shirt and from the mole, grey, dead skin crept across her shoulder and down her arm. Dark veins threaded like a map of a tube station, pulsing with her racing heart.

'Oh God, you poor thing.' Mr Nell gripped her hand, tilting his head. 'The disease, it's going back into you,' he said with waterlogged eyes.

'I tried to give it to a moth, but it didn't work.'

'I hate moths.'

'Am I going to depart?'

'No. I won't let you,' said Molly's dad, standing and leaning over the table. He kissed Molly gently on her Vans cap. 'Give me a minute and I'll get myself another drink. Want one?'

'No. No, thank you.'

Molly looked out of Louis' giant window, which was great for people-watching. All types of people headed into the hospital reception and others wandered by.

Opposite the cafe, a poster for the WOPPA swimming pool's failed reopening, featuring the Outlaw Oldies, was being torn down by council workers. "Be More Outlaw", it read. But the pool closed yesterday. The robbery and subsequent arrests put an end to any short-lived support for the gang and WOPPA's ability to capitalise on it. The balloon burned intensely and Molly wheezed with fluid-filled lungs. She glanced across at her dad chatting to Louis and stirring his coffee thoughtfully. When Mr Nell caught her eye, he headed back over and smiled.

'Here you go, I got you one anyway.' He passed Molly an

extra-large, malted butterscotch shake.

'Daddy, what am I going to do?'

'You're going to listen and trust me. Ok?'

'Erm, ok,' said Molly.

'You'll give the balloon back to me.'

'What? No.' Molly covered her mouth, coughed, and splattered blood.

'I won't take no for an answer.' Mr Nell spoke calmly. His tone was as gentle as Molly could remember. 'My Baby Girl, my Molly. The day you were born was my first time in Louis'. I have such fond memories of us together, sitting and waiting for you to fill a nappy.'

Molly wiped her mouth with the sleeve of her T-shirt and Mr Nell took her hands.

'I know I make light of things, Molly,' he continued. 'But I don't just call this the "Departure Lounge" for silly jokes. Just like an airport, people come here to see their loved ones depart.'

Molly's vision blurred but she listened as well as she could, grinding her gritted teeth.

'That's sad, Daddy.'.

'Only for those staying here, Lambchop. They have a head full of questions and concerns. *Will the journey be smooth? How will we cope after they've gone?* But, you see, it's different for those on the journey out because they've come to terms with their situation and are prepared for the inevitability of their departure. Hell, some of them even look forward to it.'

'I doubt they're really that excited about it,' Molly said as blood trickled from her ear.

'Maybe not all, but many do. They've packed their cases, double-checked their tickets and arrived at the Departure Lounge knowing that they're travelling to a new destination.'

'Heaven?'

'If Heaven brings them peace, then that's fine with me. But

even if there's nothing, then they won't know differently. We knew nothing before we're born and we won't when we're gone.'

'If there's nothing, that's easier because in Heaven they'll miss everyone.'

'That's probably why some prefer to believe,' Mr Nell said. 'Either way, the tickets are booked and it's a one-way trip.'

'I understand. They're ready for the journey away.'

'They've filled the fridge and left some money on the kitchen unit. By that, I mean they're confident the people they leave behind will be ok — just in case that simile is lost on your teenage self.'

'It's a metaphor, Daddy.'

Mr Nell winked and the door chimed with Nurse Gabrielle walking in backwards. She pirouetted and blinked twice, before waving to Molly enthusiastically on her way to the counter.

'Had you filled the fridge? Were your bags packed?' Molly asked.

'No, not even close. I was terminal before I'd finished treatment. I wasn't prepared. I hadn't filled the fridge and my money was still in my wallet. Before I knew it, I was lying on that hospital bed and it was too late. He was coming for me.'

'The Grim Reaper? Were you scared of him?'

'I don't fear the Reaper, Molly, but I did fear leaving you behind. Whenever I closed my eyes, I saw my broken-hearted little girl standing alone in a terrifying world and I hated the disease and I despised myself.' Mr Nell took a sip of his coffee. 'Then, suddenly, it wasn't over for me. I was given a miracle of unexpected, precious time to appreciate my family through grateful eyes. You were that miracle. My level-headed, brave, caring, and intelligent young lady making brave and bold decisions. You've grown into the most responsible girl I could have possibly wished for and that's why I'm ready… because you're ready.'

Molly dipped her head. 'I'm not, Dad. I made bad choices.'

'No, you did not,' said Mr Nell. 'You made decisions based on your morals. Your power doesn't define you. Strength and compassion lie within Molly Nell, not Molly's Mole. You are the full fridge and the money on the kitchen bench, all rolled into one. I know that you'll look after Mum and Billie for me after I'm gone. You can do this… you are going to give *me* the balloon.'

Molly shook her head pitifully. She could taste rusty blood at the back of her throat and *Up-There Molly* exhaled, preparing to bid farewell.

'Please Daddy, no.' Molly's throat crackled and her tears spilled.

'My beautiful girl. It's time. The Grim Reaper has finished his scone and I see him approaching.'

Molly tried to resist, but Mr Nell guided his daughter's hand across a tear-soaked Ernie and Bert and up to her shoulder. He stared deep into her yellowing eyes, curling his huge fingers over hers and closing them around the ruby thread.

'What are we going to do with you, eh?' he said.

'Daddy… No…'

'Let's get you all fixed up.

17

Lights are Blinding

*Again, I blast through the geometrics into a space occupied by
twisting pillars of data. The female entity nods towards three jesters
but I am transfixed on her mosaic face. A smashed plate with ever-
changing information on each shard.*
'Welcome back, Daniel,' she says, softly.
Three jesters mock and dance, while a fourth curls in a ball.
Smashed-Plate-Face speaks without speaking.
'A billion stories bring her joy, of quests assigned to girl and boy.
Four will set you on a path where choices lead to aftermath.
A journey lies ahead, torrential…
To mould a hero from Potential.'

Gasp.

The lights are blinding. Identifying the figures towering
above is impossible. But this is all very familiar. Blurred
aliens point and move slowly around me. The smallest alien
has wings. She is an angel and I am in Heaven.

That's unexpected. I told Soup I might be temporarily immortal. I was right for once. It can't be Heaven though. There are quite a few reasons why I can't be in Heaven…

A hand rests on my shoulder. I recognise the click of an elongated nail against whatever I'm wearing. I'm not in Heaven unless God is Jackie sitting in a brown leather chair beside a dangling oxygen mask. I'm in the hospital and seemingly *permanently* immortal.

With a raspberry-coloured beret tipped to one side, she looks like she's smuggling pilots out of Calais. That'll be us off the Dubois' Christmas list. There's only gonna be three cards on the mantelpiece this year. It's unsettling to me, to see Jackie crying, especially considering they're not sad tears. They're tears of relief, underlined by a smile that reflects the hospital lights reflect off polished, lipstick-free teeth.

A short, lady nurse says something, but my ears ring so loud I don't catch it. Jackie is mouthing my name as she holds my shoulder and this cardboard hurl tray on my chest is wasted thanks to that dental hygienist. She looks different. She looks clean.

Eventually, the tinnitus fades away, to be replaced by the whooshing of my heart, which seems to have relocated to my left temple. My head's bloody killing.

'Daniel,' Jackie whispers, above the whistling. 'I'm so glad you're back. It's a miracle.'

Back from where? What's she on about? Why am I in a hospital? I'm bloody immortal.

'Where's Soup?'

Yanking the oxygen monitor from my index finger, I ask the question again, but judging by the expression on her drooping jowls, there's bad news ahead. I've got some catching up to do, but she's avoiding the answer, so I ask louder:

'Where is Soup? Where is Ralph Robinson?'

'You need to rest,' she replies, her manky digits padding my sweaty forehead. 'Get some sleep and we'll —'

'I'm fine. Where's Soup?'

The door swings open and a woman wearing a black business suit enters.

'Well, if you're fine, I'd like to ask you a few questions,' she says, sternly. Her dark hair is cut short with purple streaks running through the longer strands. A tideline borders her face, where she's slapped her make-up on with a trowel, highlighting two enormous, swollen, stressed veins throbbing visibly at the side of her forehead.

Purple Strain introduces herself as "the investigating officer for the case of a missing child".

What?

'Missing child?' I feel a sickness in my stomach that rises to my chest. That spew tray might come in handy after all, as the officer turns around to Jackie and nods to the door.

'Do you mind?' she says. The nurse and Jackie leave, pulling the curtain around my bed on the way out. The door clicks shut. The officer sits back. And then she continues.

'I'm here to talk to you about Ralph.'

'Where is he?'

Thoughts race through my head but they're about as clear as the bus accident.

'That's what we're trying to figure out,' she says opening a notepad.

The officer tells me that I was found unconscious at Sandy Bay and I spiral into confusion. How? I was almost at Holy Island with Soup and the ginger gull when—

I'd better not mention the bird.

'We went swimming in the sea,' I lie.

'And Ralph got into trouble?'

I need to say something to appease her suspicion.

'We went swimming, but the waves were massive. We got the bus to Druridge Bay. I told him not to go out there. It's not my fault.'

'Druridge Bay? Not possible. You're mistaken. Tell me about Ralph. Describe his character.'

'He taps on his face when he gets stressed.'

'And you were friends?'

'Not really. I don't have any friends.'

'Strangers don't go on holiday together.'

She's looking at me with suspicion and I'm uncomfortable with it.

'We weren't str —.'

'How close were you then?'

'Not —.'

'Anything in common? Got any interests you share?'

'Dunno. Didn't know him well,' I splutter. 'He never listens. He's off in his head all the time.'

'What about Scuba? That's an odd hobby to share.'

'Soup did Scuba, I didn't.'

She's too fast. I'm stumbling.

'Ralph's parents say his scuba suit is missing,' she says, putting pen to paper. 'They say you wrote the list of scuba equipment. Did you encourage Ralph to do Scuba?'

'No. Yes. No. No, that was Hoshi.'

The officer says the organisation is keeping an open mind while examining potential leads and then she blasts me with doubly intense questioning.

'Did you consider Ralph's vulnerability when you encouraged an inexperienced diver to go solo?'

'I didn't —'

'Where's the suit?'

'I don't know.'

'Did you take the suit?'

'What? No.'

She's staring like she's trying to read my mind, not believing a word I'm saying. My sparks are there, at the corner of my eyes like floaters and they're in my throat too, fighting the swelling lump.

'It's worth a lot of money.'

'I didn't take the suit.'

'Considering your circumstances, would that money help?'

'That's enough!'

The pull-curtain surrounding the bed whips round and Jackie muscles in with her arms crossed.

'He's told you what he knows, now get lost,' she snaps. 'Leave the lad alone, or I'll make a complaint.'

The officer grimaces, scribbling another note. She tries to continue her interrogation but Jackie's having none of it.

'Arfter you, Occifer,' she says, sarcastically, then sneers. 'Get out.'

Fumbling in her pocket, the officer pulls out a card and asks me to get in touch. As she's pushed out of the door with threats of legal action, she almost loses her balance.

'We'll need to speak to you formally,' she says with her lips tight. Then, she says something weird, craning her neck. 'It can be stopped, you know.'

I pick up the card while Jackie slams the door.

'Coppers, eh?' she says. 'Don't let them get to you. If they thought you'd done something wrong, they'd have you down the station.'

'That was no copper,' I say. 'That was WOPPA.'

Sometime later, I wake to a darkened room and Jackie snoring. At the bottom of the bed, my big toe glows blue. I'm assuming the sparks are finishing their job, but I can't help but wonder why it's taken so long. The protractor scab on my wrist still hasn't healed either, nor has the black eye, but they happened before Urielis. Whatever, immortality doesn't make any sense at all.

She's so knackered that Jackie looks like a melted crisp packet and it's time we went home. So, disturbing her nap with a cough, I ask her to leave while I get dressed, but she insists on waiting for the doctor to sign me off. Then we argue for a while until she gives in.

I'm not sure how long I've been here, my clothes have dried, so I put them on and search for my trainers. They're not here so, sock-footed, I open the door and interrupt Jackie chit-chatting to the nurse.

'Good morning, Daniel,' the nurse says, polishing her glasses on her sleeve. 'You're free to go.'

'Can't find me trainers.'

'They were soaked and ruined,' Jackie says. 'Check the box by the bed.'

I bet she's borrowed a pair of Dad's crappy Nicks ones. Like everything else he's got, they're a counterfeit version of the real thing. I add emphasis to "everything else he's got" so Jackie knows I mean her too. My subtleness has the desired effect coz, with tears in her eyes, she nods for me to go back inside.

'Under the bed,' she says, sniffling.

Cry baby.

'I'm off for a brew,' says the nurse. 'Come on, Honey, you look like you could do with a Louis"

There's a branded courier box on the floor and a pink plastic bag next to it. Jackie scratched her name off the address labels and wrote mine in marker pen and the sent dates are from the day of the WOPPA trip.

With my keys, I split the parcel tape and open the packaging to reveal a shoebox. I give it a good shake and when it falls onto the bed, I almost choke at the label on the side. It's the exact trainers I've been drooling over for months.

I bet she got the wrong colour...

But they're not the wrong colour — they're red and white. Three stripes, not four like the cheap ones.

Unreal.

I love them more than anything.

Momentarily feeling like a normal kid on Christmas morning, my teeth tear open the pink plastic to reveal a navy pullover hoodie. It's got a kangaroo pocket, it's baggy and looks pure mint. But not as mint as the second clear bag containing a pair of Levi jeans.

They cost fortunes!

Impatiently, I bite off the tags, whip off my old stuff and pull on the new jeans. They fit like they were designed especially for me and I look purely belter.

'The picture had a skater with turn-ups,' says Jackie, arriving at the doorway. 'I got you longer ones, so you could do that.'

Once I've sat on the bed and folded up the hems twice, the light blue contrasts the red Adidas and I'm gobsmacked.

'Thanks,' I say, surprising both myself and Jackie.

'I got the large hoodie because the reviews said to size up.'

'Yeah. It's alright.'

It's not alright — it's amazing. Best hoodie I've ever owned.

'Right, I'm off,' I say. 'Ta, errr... Jackie.'

'No, you are bloody not, you're coming home to eat. You've not touched a thing since yesterday.'

'Yesterday?'

'It's Sunday morning, but I'll forgive you for sleeping as long this time.'

I can't believe I've been out for a whole day. Why didn't my sparks fix me straight away?

'I'll get soup.' I push past and spring towards the lift in my new trainers. 'Thanks for the clobber.' Not that type of soup though. I'm off to Northumberland... to find Soup.'

The lift doors close as Jackie totters on heels to catch me up. Silver lettering marks the different hospital floors and I hit the "G" button for the ground floor exit by the coffee shop.

The descent takes forever and I replay the Holy Island events. I'm certain the ginger gull was from Hatley Woods, but why was that same bird in Northumberland? More importantly, why did it attack us? How did I end up at Sandy Bay? Did the strong current bring me back? Or was it Soup who brought me back?

It can't have been the current. It's miles away. Where on Earth is he?

On the ground floor, I step out into a busy foyer. Stragglers from last night's drunken accidents limp and moan like zombies, while visitors arrive to see hospitalised family members. Leopard-Print Lil is with Del and Owain, McKenzie's brothers. It looks like they've been in a ward coz they're both carrying bags — unless they've been robbing the old ladies, which is also possible.

The Skip Rats pass Louis' coffee shop, so I hold back to pretend I'm checking the floor plans. The last thing I want is a scrap right now.

Molly Nell sits in Louis' Coffee Shop window. She's with a man who could be her dad and he's wrapping his hand around hers, moving up to her balloon thread. They're both crying and Molly's a deathly grey. Her head keeps nodding like she's dropping in and out of consciousness. Something's wrong and I feel a weird spark inside.

I leg it into Louis' and crash through the doors to a speedy, out-of-tune version of "Leaving on a Jet Plane".

'Woah there camel,' I say, skidding to a halt beside the booth. 'Anyone order an immortal?'

18

The Search

Caked mud covered the car park of Hatley Academy. **Mr Sparks** kicked some from the heel of his shoe while he and **Mrs Aubrey-Sanders** listened to police officers making animated gestures or pointing at maps.

Delores Nichol tried her best to sort the parents and children into smaller groups, but she was nowhere near as proficient outside her role at The Alien Museum.

As they awaited the announcement, increased tension amongst resident Stand-Ups bordered on rioting. Eventually, chaotic ranching got everyone organised and silence fell over the crowd when **Stand-Up Noggin** drew attention by faffing on with a microphone. Once the screeching feedback was sorted, Mayor Noggin stepped up to speak.

'Delores shall, erm, distribute search packs containing a torch, map and designated zone markings,' he said. '**Robinson** has wandered off before and in the absence of any solid evidence, we will erm, focus our search between Tynemouth and Sandy Bay Caravan Park.'

'Areas of prime interest are the beaches surrounding the caravan park and up the coast,' added Dee Dee. 'A specialist team has volunteered to cover the shores while divers search further out to sea.'

The microphone crackled as Mayor Noggin wiggled the lead and the crowd was distracted by seven Stand-Ups on two-wheelers.

'Ah, **Team Alpha** has arrived,' said Noggin who greeted the seven mountain bikers. 'An elite force, headed up by WOPPA's latest addition to the senior management.'

The ginger gull recognised the latecomers as those least likely to find the flying one. A short while ago, these younger Stand-Ups took dinner money from weaker youngsters. The flying one was often a victim, although he would happily give them dinner money, in case they needed it more. These Stand-Ups were the stoats and weasels of their species but the flying one would make an excellent gull.

After climbing from the van, **Heather** and **Neville**, from the local news, made a beeline for the incessant nuisance, **Mark Barker**. Team Alpha's leader was dressed in expensive hiking equipment, just like his son, **Douglas**.

'My shon, Douglash,' Barker spouted with one hand on his chest like he was delivering a philosophy about the meaning of existence. 'With hish determination, driven by friendship, has gathered impeccable shtudents of Hatley Academy, and grand acquaintanshes of Rolf Robertshon, to shearch tireleshly until the boy ish found, dead or alive.'

'Cor,' cawed the gull.

'Evidence suggests that Ralph got into trouble while swimming,' Stand-Up Noggin intervened. 'But we cannot rule out surrounding areas. The Robinson family notes that Ralph does, when stressed, seek areas of familiarity. Therefore, Team Alpha and WOPPA diving team will focus their search on Sandy Bay and Newbiggin, while those of you gathered before me will spread down the coast towards the restaurants and ice cream shops of Tynemouth, as illustrated on your maps. Searching will begin at daylight tomorrow.'

19

Molly's Legacy

Molly Nell had a mole on her right shoulder. It was just a mole and she tried not to think about it.

'Hurry, Sweetheart,' said Molly's mum. 'We'll be late for Nan.'

Carefully, Molly walked down the dark, wooden stairs, holding the rail gently. She wore a pretty, pastel-blue dress with daisies printed on it. The outfit was accessorised with shiny, black shoes and white, daisy ankle socks — Molly's favourite clothes for visiting her nan in prison.

She said nothing to the guards and they said nothing to her, either. They made no eye contact as they examined the documents that her mum handed over.

The chief guard told everyone to place their belongings in the locker behind them. Molly slid her MP3 player and headphones into her turquoise handbag and popped it in amongst her parents' stuff. Her dad locked the door and placed the key in a trough under the guard's window. The guard took the key and buzzed a buzzer.

The hand sanitiser stations were drained of antibacterial gel, so the family walked straight through the first door which clunked shut behind them. Then, everyone waited between doors until a buzzer sounded for the second barrier to open.

Inside, a guard made Mr Nell remove his belt while everyone else removed their shoes. Molly tiptoed through a security scanner, so as not to get her pristine socks grubby on the grey, painted concrete floor.

Nanna Nell sat in the centre of a room filled with conversation, tears, shouting, and the aroma of weak coffee. The inmates wore dark blue shirts and matching trousers and lounged around on brightly coloured sofas, which were torn and graffitied. Nanna Nell wore a cardigan and sat at a plastic table.

'Hello, My Lamb,' she said. Her eyes were so close to spilling over that they looked sore. Her lips creased as she did her best to keep her dignity. She reached for Molly's hand, but Molly hugged her, much to the disapproval of the guards.

'How is everyone?' said Nanna Nell.

Everyone said that they were doing well, but missing Nanna Nell loads. Molly's dad said that he was worried about her and hoped she would be out soon.

Nanna Nell chortled and squeezed Molly.

'Out? Why would I want that, Dear? It's better than the nursing home. I have a scream with some of the inmates.'

Pawthornton Prison was a low-risk Category D prison,

meaning most of the prisoners were not a risk to the public. It was not an overcrowded prison, with about one hundred people "detained". The inmates had keys to their cells and jobs in the building. Others had employment in the towns next to Hatley. One or two even worked for the Offender Volunteer Program at WOPPA, preparing food in non-public-facing roles.

Nanna Nell — or Big Marge as the other prisoners called her — didn't have a job because the staff reckoned she was too old and sick.

'They think I'm crazy,' she said. 'They keep saying we robbed a cake shop.'

'Mum,' said Molly's dad. 'You did rob the cake shop and you are very poorly.'

Molly stayed silent.

'The doctor says my memory is dodgy, but I remember it like yesterday. It wasn't a bloody robbery, it was a borrowy. It's a bloody good job we're not still on the run, too, coz we'd smash more than the WOPPA pool. Capitalist scum.'

The balloon did that. The balloon changed Nanna Nell. No! Stop! Balloons and moles were a mistake and people got hurt. Molly just wanted to forget about them, so she stared at her pretty shoes.

A man came over to their table and asked Big Marge for a cigarette. Nanna Nell lifted her shirt slightly, revealing several packets tucked into her waistband. After slipping her some money, Nanna Nell passed him a packet and he kissed her on the cheek.

'She's a lively one, this one,' he said with a broad, toothless smile. 'Got the run of the place already.'

Mr Wallace and his son sat at a table and chairs opposite. Molly's dad looked over and waved, but they didn't see him.

Molly noticed that Mr Wallace had a tattoo on his knuckles, but he was not the type of person to get a tattoo.

The balloons had ruined everything…. No!

Many smiles and tears later, Molly said goodbye to Nanna Nell and on the way out, Mr Wallace ignored Duck Egg.

The mole ruined everything… No!

An officer walked them back through the maze of security doors, while the prisoners picked up their deliveries and hugged their visitors.

'She's looking well, isn't she?' Molly's mum took her phone from the locker and dusted it off.

'Big Marge, eh?' said Mr Nell. 'Queen of contraband.'

On the way to the car, Mr and Mrs Nell chuckled, although they shouldn't really. Nanna Nell was in prison because…

No!

Molly would not think about the balloons.

Every Saturday afternoon, Molly was allowed to go shopping with her new friends, but she must be home by four. On her way back from the mall, she stopped at a little flower shop, where she bought lilies and small cards with "I'm sorry" written inside. On the envelope, Molly wrote "Del" and "Owain", then headed to the hospital. She walked discreetly behind someone into Louis' coffee shop and through to the hospital reception. When the receptionist wasn't looking Molly placed the flowers on the counter and ran outside, straight home.

It was the only time of the week that her heart raced.

On Saturday evening, after a sober Eric and Lil dropped Billie back home, the family curled up on the sofa. They watched the rubbish acts on the talent show and Molly wrestled with the mole's taunting. Everyone had her mum's best sandwiches, except Molly who had some cereal, as she no longer ate meat.

Billie watched Ultra-Sound Guys with Molly's mum, while Molly and her dad played cards in the kitchen. Molly won two games and her dad won one. Then, Molly went to bed but she did not sleep too well because her heart was empty.

On Sunday, Molly had nut roast for lunch, then did some self-study and went to bed, but she did not sleep too well because the mole wanted more.

On Monday, Mr Nell dropped her off at school and picked her up from flute practice.

She did her homework and had another broken night's sleep because she was not tired.

On Tuesday, she did the same.

On Wednesday, the same…

'Wanna go to X-Park?' said Mr Nell. 'I've fitted the Dia Compes to the Diamond Back.'

'No, Dad. I might fall.'

On Thursday, she lay on her bed, staring at the ceiling. Eventually, she drifted into a deep sleep and floated up and out of her sleeping body.

Up-there Molly looked down, with her hands on her hips. She watched as Molly cuddled a big pink teddy bear.

'What on Earth are you doing, Molly? You cannot just forget about us.'

Molly, of course, was doing nothing, except dozing.

'Well, that's just brilliant. You're doing nothing now and nothing earlier and nothing the day before. We have work to do.'

Nothing happened.

'Pull yourself together, Molly!' said *Up-there Molly*. And, before she said another word, *Up-there Molly* sucked back into Molly with an enormous gasp.

Molly dreamt of balloons and moles and scones and the Grim Reaper.

20

Termites

In the absence of any official statement, the residents of Colliery Row have become judge, jury and executioner. It's seriously dystopian. Mass hysteria has turned the place into a riot zone, with local anger directed mostly at emergency services and social workers. Bricks have been thrown, and windows smashed around my home. It's pandemonium and every time I look out of the VELUX, someone's fighting or chucking stuff at the pigs. The garages have all been broken into. Ours has too, but there's nowt in it since Mam left, so Keith's not bothered.

Outside of Colliery Row, people are pointing fingers at me. It's public knowledge now that I was with Soup before he disappeared and the press is fuelling rumours that my neglect is responsible. I feel like a bloody bat. They get the blame for everything, the bats. It's hardly my fault though. I'm not his bloody babysitter.

Keith's buckling under the pressure, with his anxiety and paranoia worsening. It's only a matter of time before he's back in hospital and I can't help thinking maybe it's a good idea to keep him away from succubus journalists.

Down at the station, the police interviewed me five times. I keep telling them we were swimming and got into trouble, but that seems to reinforce their suspicions coz the Scuba suit is still missing. It's too late for me to say that we were messing around and I definitely can't tell them we were flying and attacked by a ginger seagull. I reckon they're gonna nick me soon and search the house. Increasingly senior cops interrogate me each time and they're not beating around the bush anymore. They're direct and sometimes pretty mean. Sparky's like a pussy cat by comparison.

The WOPPA officer hasn't been back, but I told the police about her. I said she interviewed me illegally, but the police tell me this is a normal procedure during early investigations. They outsource information gathering to save money and time. This seems proper dodgy to me.

The black van has moved from Larkfield and now it's parked along the road from us. I've not seen anyone come or go from it. I rang the emergency services to tell them I thought a paedo was flashing children, but no police turned up. There's a WOPPA decal on the rear panel, so maybe they outsource vans too.

THUMP!

My fist buries into the punch bag and it swings, creaking on the open beam above. Another punch makes it hiss like a purple-faced child unable to hold its breath one second longer. Not a punched, purple-faced child, but one that is holding its breath like children often do. I've stopped punching children; I'm a changed lad.

A third right hook splits the leather, spilling sand onto the living room floor, causing Keith to slur something aggressive. Any response will escalate quickly, so I ignore him, snapping a line of thick silver tape to stem the flow and repair the split. Sweat trickles from the back of my curly locks and down between my shoulders, soaking into my t-shirt. I feel better after having had some exercise.

Behind the Christmas decorations is an unused dustpan and brush which I use to sweep the sand into the bin. We've still got no carpet, just bare wood boards with raised nails. When I unhook the punch bag to put it back upstairs, the door clicks open and Jackie fetches the shopping in. She's duffed the turban, thank God, but she's wearing some sort of Sombrero that will probably upset the Mexican family who owns the takeaway van.

Lunch is served on the knee, in front of the telly, as usual. The unidentifiable slop on this plate looks like spaghetti and smells of Chinese spices. After further inspection, I deduce that it is spaghetti, with mince and sweet and sour sauce. Still, I'm marginally impressed Jackie has deviated from microwave masterpieces and used a pan for once. But, regardless of the method, it's disgusting, so I move the mush around into small piles until it looks like I've scranned some and the rest goes in the bin. Finally, I deliberately pouch a bag of crisps in front of her.

About three crisps in, while Keith's pretending not to be stalking Mam, Jackie hushes everyone to turn up the telly. We all stop what we're doing when a news bulletin sets my heart pounding. It's a picture of Soup with a footer flashing "Breaking News".

Neville: Good afternoon. After the recent mysterious goings-on in Hatley, we're awaiting an update on the missing teenager, Ralph Robinson.

Heather: Hopefully, Mayor William Noggin will have some good news for once. The past few years have been terrible.

Neville: They have, Heather. The divorce was troublesome and costly.

Heather: Was she worth it? Here we go. Mayor Noggin will address the locals at Hatley Academy.

The camera pans around to the crowd gathered outside of school and Mark Barker is standing with a cardboard box. It's getting dark when Mayor Noggin steps out of Hatley Academy to flashing cameras and rumbles of the crowd.

The school headmaster follows Noggin to the podium and the folk of Hatley fall silent. Mayor Noggin acknowledges Mr and Mrs Robinson, who approach the stage from a nearby car. Mr Robinson helps his frail wife up the steps. His eyes have dark bags underneath and he looks unlike the man I met, although not too dissimilar to the hungover version.

'Er… right… good evening, Everyone,' bumbles Mayor Noggin. 'Thank you for coming. As you know, WOPPA has funded a… erm… massive, massive search for Ralph Robinson in clusters around Tynemouth and Sandy Bay. Hundreds of you have given up your precious time to aid our local law enforcement.'

Sparky puts his arm around Mrs Tabel, who is in floods of tears and above Noggin's head, up on the school rooftop, the silhouette of a huge seagull settles to overlook the performance.

'I'm afraid to announce that this morning,' Noggin says,

solemnly. 'Team Alpha made a grim discovery whilst diving by the wind turbines off Sandy Bay Caravan Park.'

Dread overcomes me, dragging my soul out through my soles, as Mark Barker places the box on the floor and removes two clear plastic bags.

'As you can see,' Noggin continues. 'Team Alpha recovered two goalkeeping gloves. These are items bought for Ralph's recent hobby. Divers have also recovered burst oxygen tanks and other Scuba necessities.'

Water brims along my lower eyelids, forced out by the wave of anxiety that started in my belly, but tiny shocks won't let me cry. I can't believe I'm watching them hold up Soup's stuff and I drop to my knees, right up at the television. They're definitely his goalie gloves.

Oh, no. Please.

'After running DNA tests on the items,' Noggin says. 'We confirm they belong to Ralph Robinson. We believe Ralph has attempted a solo dive, with minimal experience, and succumbed to overwhelming currents. Unfortunately, we have no option but to call off our search and pronounce Ralph Robinson missing, presumed dead.'

Time freezes. The entire world forms this narrow tunnel around my face, but nothing's moving. For what seems like forever, I'm frozen in a world I don't want to be part of.

He can't be dead! I — I —

I kick over the coffee table, smashing my leg off the arm of the sofa and I bound into enough space to rage. Louder, I roar, lashing my arms as if the punch bag is still hanging. Harder, I fight with nothing, thrashing wildly, the air whistling past my knuckles. Enraged, I imagine the ginger gull and I lash out.

Keith's yelling at me and trying to calm me, but I'm too far gone.

'Pack it in. You'll hurt someone.'

'Aaaarrrgh!'

The gull fills my head and I'm smashing my fists at it. Punching and fighting to stop him. Completely immersed in this looping scene, my blows cause no damage. The bird beats its wings, savaging Soup while I try to stop it, but the more punches I throw, the more it attacks him. I feel sea spray, wet on my knuckles and splashing my cheeks, as the hallucination becomes very real.

Suddenly, the gull turns towards me, morphing like a shapeshifter into Dr Urielis, the substitute. Enormous wings, like an angel of darkness, cast Soup to one side, turning to me with wanton aggression. Its wings beat harder and I feel their flow drag me towards the beast. I continue to punch and kick, but it's useless as the wings engulf my body, restraining me with their tight embrace.

He's dead!

'It's not your fault,' says Jackie. My head jolts me back into reality and I snatch my shoulders away, but as I look angrily towards her, I drain like a sink of dishwater.

She's refusing to look up, covering her face with her hair and in the absence of ridiculous headgear, it's clear she's losing some of her long, dark locks. The skin on her head is almost translucent and when I order her to brush aside her fringe, she reveals a split tomato where her lip used to be.

Electric butterflies swell inside me, like a sonic boom, filling my body and bursting out of my mouth. It wasn't Urielis' wings wrapped around me, it was Jackie's arms.

I did this to her.

Her face is swollen. I can barely see the bloodshot eyeball.

She's hurt badly. My fists are clenched so tight I can feel bones under the muscles.

I did this.

'I was just trying to keep you safe and —'

'You should have left me alone,' I scream. 'I am *not* your son. I am *nothing* to you. You are *not* my mam!'

'Daniel. Stop it,' snaps Keith, but he cowers as I lurch towards him.

'I *hate* you. Both of you. This is all *your* fault. If you'd let me live with Mam, Soup would still be alive.'

Jackie's crying and I look between the two of them as they shake with fear. They're both terrified, staring at my blood-soaked, glowing knuckles, so I snatch Dad's phone, burst out of the front door into the evening rain and sprint to Hatley Woods... to hide.

The next morning, after broken sleep in the bivouac, I get a bus and hop the metro to Sunderland. I watch the buildings blur until I get off at St Peter's and I'm just about dried off by the time I cross the road to Wearmouth Bridge where I grip the green metal.

The pressure pain of the flesh on the top of the fingertips pushes against my nails, like a loose tooth rocking back and forth in the gum socket. I cannot feel the cold, dewy metal against the sides of the fingers, although I should. I cannot feel the tiny volcanoes of burst, blistered paint bubbles or the roughness of the rusted metal in between those sharp edges.

The glimmer of morning sunlight splashes onto the sea in front and the river ripples as it flows, distorting the sun's torch-like projection. Pulsating curves, glowing musical waveforms, drift below me, under me, towards the investment area and Cultural Quater.

Waveforms: patterns created by waves. I've never thought of that before.

'Big Tesco' towers in view amidst a one-way system from hell and countless closed shops. The darkness of prehistoric industry pumps black smoke into the air while tyres on the muddy riverbanks mark out crab pots and shopping trolley handles, visible from the murky dirt that sucks them down.

Termites termite, so I get a shufty on across the bridge, towards the beach where the flats stand nearby. Ten minutes later, I arrive at the bottom of Sea View Apartments.
It's a block of flats — they're fooling nobody.

The security door has an entry code system, but when one termite leaves, I slip in before it closes. The lady looks at me like I'm on the rob but I think the fact my clothes are new *and* decent gives her the impression I'm no chav, so she smiles back.

The lift stinks of urine. It's proper grim. I remember work experience in an old people's home and even their bogs didn't smell this bad. By the time I'm on the third floor, my guts are churning and I'm gasping after holding my breath for as long as I can.

Eventually, the lift opens and I spill out into a graffiti-covered hall that doesn't smell much better. Someone needs to take the rubbish out coz this place makes Colliery Row look like Mayfair. Number five's door is repaired with plywood where the bottom has been kicked in, but I'm going to ignore this. I had expectations, but maybe the bar was set a bit high.

Anxiety rushes over me, so much so that my sparks are chaotic, fighting adrenaline to keep my heart rate steady as I ring the buzzer and wait for what seems like forever. I've fantasised about this moment for so long that my belly flutters and my breathing becomes shallow. Escaping the pointing fingers for the acceptant arms that will erase the past. Maybe we'll both start afresh. My faded memories will soon be replaced by happier ones. We've got a long time to make newer, better ones.

Finally, the door clicks open and a skinny woman in a stained, green t-shirt stands in front of me, with a cigarette hanging from her mouth. Deep wrinkles line her forehead like trenches and the bags under her eyes show years of broken sleep. They're worry lines. I can't let myself think they're excess.

She's as thin as a pencil, with no muscle build, having never seen a gym that's for sure. Her shoulders are so slumped her torso is around her knees. Her arms are lined with raised, blue veins that disappear into a collage of faded tattoos. Jackie and Dad have tattoos, but not like hers. These look like they've been drawn by Soup.

'Danny,' she says, and my heart bursts.
I've waited so long to hear her voice.
'Courtney Amb — Patterson? Mam?'
Joy, sadness, and regret bathe deep in her emerald eyes. Joy to see me, sadness for the missed years, regret for everything. Everything I've ever wanted stands before me. It arrives slowly, deadened by shock, but when she lights her dumper end and sucks the last puffs of smoke before it stains her chipped nails, I see love.

'You'd better come in,' she slurs, stumbling, steadying herself against the split door frame. 'I've missed you. Have you missed me?'
A ball of emotion swells inside my chest; the love I've

desperately needed stands before me and flicks her tab. She steps aside for me to enter her home. My new home. Our home.

My heart bleeds for the lost years and from the look of her, she needs my help just as much as I need hers. She's desperate for my love. She —

Woah there camel, gan canny, you sound like Dad.

A sticky, mosaic-patterned carpet runs down the hallway. Some patches are so worn that it's shiny and black like run-over chewy. To the right is a small kitchen, with a pan encrusted with burnt bean juice and teabags are splattered along the benches.

I can do that. I'm good at cleaning. Jackie does it after work, but Mam's probably just got a stressful job, so I get that it's difficult. A bit of bleach won't do the front room any harm, once I've tidied up the ashtrays and knickers. And I'm sure I can break down some of the boxes on the settee. She'll be so proud of me and life will be easier for her. Teamwork. If Keith hadn't been such a loser, then he could have done this. It would have worked fine, coz he is never going to get a proper job, so he could keep the house clean and gig on a weekend. Win-win.

'Take a seat,' Mum says, lighting another dumper. 'I'll just be a tick.'

Toe-pegging a cricket bat on the floor, she swears, then shrugs it off and opens the bedroom door just enough to slip inside without me seeing. That's alright, it's her haven. I'm not going to make her tidy her room.

I wonder where I'll sleep? Maybe we could get bunks until we've got somewhere bigger.

While I wait for Mam to put on a pretty dress, I flatten a couple of empty boxes, labelled "kitchen" and "front room", and slip them between the settee and a radiator under the triple-paned window. She might be a while coz Mam has stuck the radio on in the bedroom. I can hear the presenter talking in a deep voice. Maybe it's a podcast coz a woman is talking too?

An hour later and I've sorted the front room right out. All the empty boxes are flattened and now that the floor's cleared, the cricket bat looks sort of decorative, rested by her bedroom door. Once I've got some paint on that chipboard panel, it'll look great.

There must be an electrical issue in the kitchen, coz I've boxed up two knackered kettles. I'll get that seen to, but I reckon we'll have to speak to the doctor about her smoking. I've swept hundreds of tab ends into a bin bag that I found in a drawer full of needles. Mam must be diabetic. That's sad and I'm annoyed that Keith never mentioned it.

Once I'm finished in the kitchen, there's only the bathroom to do. The tiles and bath are coated with limescale, but there's a full bottle of Viakal in the towel basket, so that'll shift once it's had time to soak. I'll have to pick up some black mould remover later, but I'll need some coin coz I spent my last getting the bus.

Finally, while the chemicals get to work in the bathroom, I get a chance to park myself on the couch. The telly's old, but Mam's got a dodgy Firestick, so I scroll for something decent to watch and find one of those "I relocated abroad" shows, where rich people find a better life in the sun.

It's a bit like me; I found a better life in the Sun-derland.

21

The Arnly One of Iz Left

Gareth Swift's Glossary of Geordie Gobbledygook.
Hyem: Home. *Dar*: Dad. *Nee*: No. *Iz*: Me. *Reet*: Right *Dee*:
Do. *Ower*: To, or Over. *Howldin'*: Holding. *Naff that*: (any
expletive) that. *Scrappin'*: Scrapping. *Knacking*: Defeating.
Cloutin': Punching. *Bodgie*: Bloke, Gadgie, Fella. *Hoicks*:
Launch
Heesel: Himself. *Bassa*: Shortened "bar steward". *Mush*: Face.
Also, mate. *Heez*: His. *Fatha*: Father/Dar. *Borstin'*: Bursting.
Telt: Told. *A Geek*: A Look/Observe. *Wass*: Big. *Knar*: Know.
Hooses: Houses. *Doddle*: Simple. *Fower*: Four. *Summit*:
Something. *Anarl*: Also. *Gorra*: Got a. *Wheez*: Who is. *Mar*:
Mother. *Necking On*: Kissing. *Wrekkie*: Play area, where youths
drink beer. *Bairns*: Bairnes/Children. *Hoyed*: Throw. *Moggie*:
Cat. *Ho'way*: Newcastle version of Ha'way… or Come on. *Berk*:
Fool/Dafty/Idiot. *Nowt*: Nothing. *Garna*: Going to. *Heed*:
Head. *Bonk*: Rubbish. *Intee*: Into. *Geet or Git*: Very e.g. Geet
Big or Git Big.

Good luck…

On me way **hyem** through Hatley Woods, me and me **dar** peg it from birch zombies. I find a mega zombie-blaster what looks propa like a stick and Brian, me dar, tells **iz** to sneak behind the trees and not to snap **nee** twigs.

Spotting two enormous, infected zombies, I charge **reet** in. Me dar tells iz that I **dee** this when we're gaming **ower** much. He's much better at the stealth stuff. Anyhows, Brian's **howldin'** iz back, whisperin' 'dinnet, Gaz', but **naff that** like. I'm reet in amongst it, **scrappin'**.

There's a proper epic, drawn-out struggle and I'm git proper **knacking** all the oak and birch zombies that's surroundin' iz. I'm moss-deep in **cloutin'** branches when this geet big **bodgie** owerpowers iz and I crumple down onto the floor, beggin' for me life, like. But at the last minute, like, Brian, me dar, **hoicks heesel** reet into the **bassa** and buries heez blade reet in its bark mush.

I'm proper ower the moon that me **fatha** has saved iz and I jump up to hug the little fella, but he's gawpin' at iz like I've trodden in dog muck.

'Gaz, Man,' he reckons an'eez **borstin'** heez eyeballs at me arm. 'I **telt** ye to be stealthy, Man.'

I have **a geek** down and I start to shake like I'm knockin' out a peanut turd.

'Soz, Fatha,' I say, geekin' at the **wass**, bleedin' bite on me forearm.

'Yer infected,' says Brian steppin' away from iz. 'Ya've got about five minutes before yer undeed.'

'Ye'll 'av to kill iz.'

'I cannet dee it, Son,' says Brian, dramatically clutching heez hands to 'eez heart. 'I love ya too much.'

'We have nee choice,' I shout, angrily. 'Dee it.'

'Wait,' he shouts at iz. 'Yey should'a turned.'

'I'm immune,' I say, bubblin' tears onto the bloody wound. 'What shall we dee about it?'

'I **knar** of a commune,' says Brian. 'I'll get ya there safe as **hooses**.'

'What's this place called?'

*Self-explanatory.

'The Saulty Cow,' he says, pickin' up eez bag. 'Burt Ends and a salt beef bagel?'

'The best smoker since Fag-Ash Joe down the Legion!'

Brian puts heez arm rund me shoulder, which cannet be a **doddle** coz I'm aboot **fower** inches taller than 'im, and we mooch through The Tunnel of Trees, to our car up by the back lane.

'There's **summit** I need to tell ya,' says Brian.

'Aye, me **anarl**. Yay first.'

'I've **gorra** lass and that.'

'Really?' I says, suspiciously. '**Wheez** daft enough to date yey?'

'Ye knar, Ara?'

'Hoshi's **mar**?' I'm all actin' surprised, like, but I've knarn the two of them's been **necking on** ower the **wrekkie**. I seen them. Like **bairns** on a first date. I nearly **hoyed** me tea up.

'Aye,' me dar says. 'Ye alreet about it?'

I nods, like, and I'm grinning like the Cheddar **Moggie**.

'**Ho'way** then,' me dar gans on. 'What's youwer crack?'

'I'm a teleporter.'

'I'm ower the moon for ya,' says me dar and I must look a

bit confused, so he gans on. 'Gettin' a part-time job and that.'

'A teleporter, ya git **berk**,' I says. 'Norra *telly* porter, Man. As in, I can git gan places without walkin'.

Brian's said **nowt** on the way to the supermarket. He's **garna** pick up a few tinnies and I'm after that new pop what tastes like watered down sick but has a flashy bottle. I can see that he's git desperate to say summat, but then he checks he'sel and gans all shtum again.

When we gets near the doors, he's back on form, Lad, coz he stops iz and lifts heez hand up like he's stoppin' traffic.

'Pffffsssssshhhhhhhhtttttt,' he says, pretendin' he's used heez mind to open the automatic doors.

I dinnet laugh, like, I just says, 'I knar I've upset ya, Dar. Soz.'

'Is that what's happened to the Robinson lad?'

'I reckon.'

'Ye'll need a costume and a name, like. Incognito but summat that's not copyright infringement.'

'Eh?'

'Just dinnet nick someone else's idea.'

Brian "umms and ahs" all the way around the supermarket. I order the Saulty Cow for half past, but it tacks iz fower times before I get it reet. Me **heeds** proper battered about a name for me secret identity. Me dar's deein' heez best, but he's come up with nowt yet.

'Gorrit. Coz yer brave and ya zip all ower, ye could be called Bold! Two in One!'

'I dinnar like,' I says, not convinced. 'Sounds **bonk**.'

'Flash,' he gans.

'Ho'way, that's been done. Copyright defringement.'

'The Fairy?'

'Ah man, yer reading the bottles on the cleanin' shelf!' I sigh and he gives iz a "gotcha" shove and I stumble **intee** a little lass, wheez bouncin' about in a trackie and cap. She's got a **geet** big box of washin' powder in her mitts and she's squealin' like she's dropped the tickle lottery.

'Well, this gets whites as white as angel's under-crackers,' the mentalist squeaks, smilin' ower at me and me dar. Then, she looks back ower her shoulder at these bodgies in suits and gans, 'Careful though, there's folk about looking for stubborn stains.'

The lady chucks the box ower to iz and then skips off down the aisle, towards the tills.

'I've gorrit,' Brian blurts out. He's pointin' at the box like it's got gold in it. 'Gaz Ultra.'

I'm just garna rip the lid off and tip it ower him when the owlder lass, what the nutter in the cap was talkin' about, starts shoutin' at iz.

'Gareth Swift?' She's all dressed in a black suit an' there's two massoove gadgies either side of her. 'Brian Swift? Gareth Swift? You need to come with us.'

I look at me dar coz I dinnet fancy our chances against these bassas. Brian's lookin' back at iz weird an' gans,

'Nee chance. Ho'way Gaz Ultra. Let's gan.'

ZAP!

PhzzZAP!

'Clean-up on aisle three.'

22

Three Course Special

Mam's diabetes isn't managed well. She doesn't eat properly at all, except for every couple of days when she takes two plates of food into her room and balances it out with a handful of needles for her insulin.

Local news is filled with tributes to Soup and updates on the riots, but there's nowt on there about me being missing. Keith's not blocked his phone and Jackie's not rung to see if I'm ok. They must be having a ball without me.

With the house shabby, but clean, I'm sure Mam will be proper happy when she's well enough. No wonder it was so minging, with her being off sick. Sometimes you've got to put your health first and I'm just glad she's getting the rest she needs.

It's cool that she listens to podcasts. Clever people listen to podcasts. It's the same couple every day and, although I can't hear what they're saying, they laugh and argue a lot, so it must be quite a show. Sometimes, I press my face to her door, just to check on her, coz there's a weird smell of vinegar coming from the room. It's pungent, like the Viakal, so maybe she's spilt a bottle or something. I get that she's exhausted, so I'll sort it when she's better.

Maybe I can cook for both of us? Can't be worse than Jackie's efforts. I'll need to get some shopping in though, coz I've done the last of the packet macaroni in and there's only two ramen left.

In the shower, my sparks heal the flea bites around my ankles. I've had the window open to air the place out coz the vinegar smell stung my nostrils. She hasn't got a washing machine, but I washed the towels and my underwear in a sink of hot water and washing up liquid. I'll need to get some more of that too.

If I was looking in on this situation, I'd probably think it was a bit crap. But to be honest, it's been the making of me. Looking after Mam is way more important than school and it's teaching me life lessons. I only wish I had my pen and jotter to pass the time. Instead, I sit in my shorts and watch the telly, waiting for another tick to explode when I get a bite. It's best at night, proper lights the room up.

Halfway through *Ultra-Sound Guys*, Mam opens the bedroom door and looks around. Her eyes widen when she sees what I've done and I reckon she must be feeling better, coz she's not noticed before.

'Fancy cooking ush shum scran?' she says, slurring off the insulin.

'There's not much in, *Mam*,' I say, trying not to stress her. 'I can go to the shops though.'

'Mint,' she says, leaving me a bit speechless when she

shuts the door and sticks the podcast on. I've got no money and there's none in the flat. I've cleaned every nook and cranny, so there's no option but to knock on.

'Mam,' I whisper, but there's no answer. 'Mam,' I say louder and I hear a thud in the room.

A few seconds later she opens the door, just enough to push her head through like her room's giving birth to her.

'Aye?' she says.

'I've, erm, I'm sorry… I'll need some money.'

'Ah, me giro's not due til Thursday, like,' Mam says, with glassy eyes. 'If ye gan down to Mr Dhillon's there's nee mirrors or cameras by the bread section.'

'What? I — I can't!'

'Dinny worry,' Mam says. 'I'll square him up on Thursda.'

The door closes gently and she turns on a proper laughing fit podcast. I'll have to get her some proper food and definitely chocolate. Diabetics need chocolate and milk, or so I've heard. I'm going to have to channel my inner Fatfield.

A nip-nose lift journey spills me out into the fresh heat of the coast and I top up my oxygen. Down by the harbour, the sun casts a bright white glow over the sea. If Soup were here now, he'd lend me a tenner and I reckon his folks would know what food Mam needs.

Mr Dhillon's is across the road, by what used to be the National Glass Centre. It's Saturday and I only know this coz there's a sea of red and white footy shirts heading up from the beach towards the Stadium of Light. Loads of kids are with their parents, all donned in kits. It's a class sight.

Once I've pushed through the crowds, I arrive at the door of the shop, with a bit of a plan. First, I'll pick a pack of tomato soup from the shelf and I'll tear the seam at the back.

If I hold the bag by one handle, the ramen should weigh the bag down and it should open just enough for me to shake two soup tins into it.

With the starter sorted, I'll shake my head at the inadequacy of my potential purchase and put the other two tins back, facing the front of the shelf so it looks like it's still four.

Next, I'll need bread. Brown, coz it's got to be less carbs for Mam. This time, I'll slip two sleeves of buns off the shelf, turn away from the counter, and drop one in the bag. It's going to make some noise, so I'll cough. Then, I'll make sure I'm in view of the shopkeeper when I put the other back on the shelf.

At this point, there's a possibility I could be rumbled, so I'll have to overact searching for the right recipe. Maybe I'll ask the shopkeeper if he's got some herbs or spices that they definitely won't have. If it looks like he's onto me, then I'll just peg it.

Planning probably wasn't a good idea; I can hear my heart thumping the living daylights out of my head: I've got a carrier bag from the kitchen and washed the teabag juice out of it. I stuck the last of the ramen inside, so it doesn't look empty when I walk in. Looks like I've been shopping along at the garage.

The summer afternoon is stifling and I'm drenched with sweat. None of the footy fans care coz everyone's in the same boat, so I'm hoping a few come into the shop with me for a bottle of fizzy or a few cans. It'll be easier if it's busy.

Beetroot red and dripping, I pull unsuccessfully on the heavy shop door. I'm sure they've got it the wrong way around. Surely, if you've got bags of purchased goods, the door should push as you leave the shop, but here, they've forced me to draw attention to myself before I've even stepped inside.

The till, and Mr Dhillon, are to my right as I enter sheepishly, obviously breaking the law. Anxiety races through my body and I can hear that my heart has almost broken through my skull as I begin walking across the heavily worn carpet that trails in the direction of the bakery aisle.

At the end, four shelves are packed with bread and my stomach rumbles at the sight of the first decent food I've seen in days. Opposite, two shelves are lined with soup and I notice that there are no four packs of tomato. Lentil or chicken are the only options. I reckon I'll get chicken coz that's a decent meal on its own if I have to run.

Four footy lads come into the shop and the bell is loud enough to disguise the ripping of the cardboard pack. They head to the beer section and I drop one of the handles amongst their conversation. Bonus — Mr Dhillon has gone to help them. I've got a clear run, so, as quickly as possible, I drop the two tins into the bag and as Mr Dhillon is still helping the lads look for some fancy real ale, I stuff some pasta in and a head of broccoli.

Getting confident to cocky, I snatch some pasta sauce from next to the soup and some tinned ham too, but as I turn back to the bread, my face flushes at the sight of the shopkeeper returning to his till and his eyes are on me.

Pretending to read the label on a different pasta sauce, I squat to look for cheese sauce. Then I turn to Mr Dhillon and raise my voice.

'Do you have any Star Anise?' I ask and to my horror, he opens his countertop and comes down the aisle towards me. Swiftly, and clearly, I put the sauce back and grab the other handle of the carrier bag to hide my loot.

'I do not think we have that, my friend,' he says, relieving my panic slightly by pulling small jars of herbs from a shelf.

'No, definitely not. I have the new yellow OoGoo Joose in. Many like the OoGoo. All the boys buy.'

'No thank you,' I say. 'I want to make something special for my mam. She's not well at the moment.'

My politeness seems to have done the trick, coz Mr Dhillon tells me I'm a good son and turns back to the counter, where the footy lads buy beer and vapes.

I still need chocolate and bread to complete my shifty shop, so I turn my back and stuff a pack of buns into the bag. Then, with a nifty slip, I drop two big bars of Fruit and Nut on top. We're eating like royalty tonight.

But just as I head down the aisle, a ghostly apparition of Soup, dressed in seaweed laden wetsuit blocks my escape, guilting me into lawfulness.

Oh, Christ. I see dead people.

'Would Splendi-Man approve?' Paranormal Soup whispers with *the* most judgemental tone imaginable.

*Shut up. You're not real and neither is he. You're dead. I killed you.*I'm here to feed my sick mam. I'm not a thief. This is a necessity. A good thing. I *am* going to do this. I'm not listening to anyone else preaching to me. I've had enough of that from Cracky Jackie. I am *not* a stooge, a patsy, or a loser; I'm immortal, for God's sake!

Sounds of the sea whoosh through my head, as I battle to force dead Soup from my conscience. Sweating and fighting back tears, this beetroot boy goes for it. Riddled with guilt, but determined, I turn towards the exit, worrying that I'm probably going to slip on the puddle of sweat at my feet. *It might be sweat. I could have wet myself. I'm numb and not entirely sure.*

Instead of slipping, I pause and inhale deeply. Just in case I haven't made it obvious enough that I'm a villain, I make a bolt for the exit where, through the fortress door, the sunlight shadows the silhouettes of Sunderland fans.

'But, Daniel Fella, stealing is wrong. It is worse than mushrooms.'

Shut up, Soup.

The beer lads have finished their purchase and it's getting tense, so I begin to process my options. Should I use the noise of them leaving as a chance to drop the bag and walk out empty-handed? Should I say "oops, something fell into my bag", loud enough for Mr Dhillon to hear? Then I could put everything back. Should I just push the button and release the ejector seat and disappear from this Earth?

No chance. I am immortal. I am a god.

With a swivel, I beeline straight towards Heaven's gate, remembering to pull, not push. No longer anxious. I am going to do it. That's what I'm thinking as I make haste towards the door, as fast as my legs can carry me, not looking back.

I am going to make it. I can smell the sea and —

The blood drains from my face, down my body, out through my toes, seeping through the floor and straight to the pit that I wish I was buried in, as the hand clamps down on my shoulder.

'Not so fast young man.'

23

Always to Love, Never to Leave

Donned in a black security uniform with a peaked hat, the guard towers above me, refusing to release his grip.

Security. It's match day.

No thoughts are racing, no panic, no reasoning,... no anything. I don't *feel* anything because everything is gone, seeping through the floorboards, digging frantically towards the Earth's molten core. I drop my eyes to the floor, followed shortly after by the bag so I can lift my hands for the cuffs to be applied.

'No need for that' he says with disappointment I have only heard once before from Mr Hunter when I pretended Yappy Dog had eaten my homework.

So deep into the worn carpet that I can smell shoes, I succumb to the security man's applied pressure and follow him towards the counter. I'm the stand-out-crap-float at a summer parade as four lads, a security guard and a disappointed Dhillon line up to shake their heads in disapproval. I must have given them a proper show.

This shame is bad enough, but then it gets much, much worse when a jobsworth PC bursts in through the backwards door, desperate to ship me off to Guantanamo Bay.

'What have we got here then?' he questions with a stereotyped "evenin' all" twang. It's patronising, terrifying, annoying and deserved coz I'm a criminal, heading for incarceration.

In Mr Dhillon's brightly lit, anti-theft box, the security guard asks me to place the bag on the counter. Magician-like, he opens it, but instead of a rabbit from a hat, he pulls out my first meal for ages, placing the items one by one on the table. Observing each item with an unnecessary scrutinisation of labels, the guard and policeman tut a lot.

'How did this get in here?'

I shrug.

'You stole it, didn't you.'

I nod ashamedly.

The rest of the two-way discussion between authorities sounds something like the teacher speaking to Charlie Brown — trumpeting nonsense preventing me from going home and locking myself away for a lifetime. And then, unprotested decisions soon make it obvious that I'm not going home and I'm snapped out of my funk by the guard insisting on my arrest and cautioning "down at the station".

What? Technically, I haven't stolen anything. "Technically" I was around a metre from the door, inside the building, so "technically", I was taking some food for a wander around the shop.

This won't stick. No way will I get time for this.

Sunlight shrinks my pupils as Mr Dhillon pulls the heavy shop door and I move from the dim light to the street outside, transitioning between the scene of the crime and the armoured van. I scrunch my face up like the vile criminal that I am when they frog-march me to the awaiting police van, which has mounted the pedestrian area to await my arrival.

Three officers clear a path for my departure and this whole thing is spiralling into madness. It's only a bag of shopping… Yeah, I stole it, but there's no justifying this. The severity of my situation is sprawled across pavements in the form of hundreds of laughing footy fans. No longer silhouettes, these are real people. Mocking me, disgusted and angry. Hateful people and… Mrs Tabel in a Sunderland strip. My stony expression cracks and a solitary tear makes it past the sparks to trickle down my face.

Bunting cobwebs of Cellar Spiders line the dark, damp police van. Awaiting my fate, I sit on the rugged, woollen sheet that lies crumpled on a single, sprung bench. Alone with my spiralling thoughts, I ponder the theft, the arrest, the cold loneliness, while a flickering bulb strobes: I am a criminal. I am a lawbreaker locked in a box with bad language on the wall. I am ashamed, not only for the crime, but for becoming part of an elite group of creative writers reading the musings of the unwashed. Despite this, it is impossible to cry. The image of Mrs Tabel looking like she wanted to drag me away from the police, disbelieving of the situation, breaks my heart. I want to punch the van wall, like in the films, but bloody knuckles will make me look more like a convict than I already do. If I must go to see a judge in court, then I want to look as innocent as possible. What if I get life? Christ, that's gonna be a long lock-up.

I just wanted to make Mam some decent food. Get a grip, Daniel. You nicked a bag of shopping. You didn't murder the cashier on the way out.

An eternity later, the heavy door opens and an officer directs me out of the cube (it's more of a cuboid really) and back onto the street. It's cleared now, so it must be after kick-off. The only people around are the guard, three police officers, one woman and two men, Mrs Tabel and Mr Dhillon.

'Sorry, Sir,' I say, looking at the shopkeeper through bloodshot eyes.

'Why, Daniel?' asks Mrs Tabel, and I die for a split second. 'Stealing from this poor man.'

'I —'

'Enough,' says Mr Dhillon and I'm sure I see him wink at Mrs Tabel. 'Courtney's lad?'

I nod.

'Here,' he says, handing me the carrier bag. 'This lady has paid for the shopping, so no harm done.'

What?

A smile wobbles across Mrs Tabel's lips. 'I rang your dad,' she says. 'He told us you found your mum.'

'How long have you been there?' asks the female police officer with the blonde bobbed hair and tortoise shell glasses.

'A few days. She's not well. I needed to get her something decent to eat, but I haven't got any money.'

Shooting a concerned look over at Mr Dhillon, Mrs Tabel steps towards me.

'Daniel, your mum needs help.'

'Yes, that's why I'm here,' I say sharply. 'She needs food.'

'Daniel,' Mrs Tabel says with her hand on my shoulder 'You need to go home. Your proper home.'

'No. I'm not going back there. Mam needs me.'

'She —'

'It's ok,' says the police officer. 'We'll keep an eye on him. Daniel, this kind lady has paid for the shopping and an equally kind shopkeeper does not want to press charges.

Given the circumstances, you can apologise and get yourself away. Make sure you cook that chicken until the juices run clear.'

I proceed to skip home, in a bubble of confused success.

Back in the flat, I empty the bag of shopping onto the kitchen bench and choke on my own breath. This isn't the bag I nicked. It's an amazing array of fresh food that spills across the marble-effect melamine. Fresh, diced chicken breast and sirloin steaks. Garlic and herbs. Tortellini and passata. Garlic bread and parmesan. Broccoli, carrots, peas. Tea bags, coffee and a bottle of yellow OoGoo Joose. *They kept my ramen!*

With my eyes on stalks, I suck in the bleachy air and set about preparing a feast for my sick mam. She's listening to a pretty aggressive podcast, so she'll not hear me conjure up these delights, but she'll love the surprise. Using Keith's phone, I search for recipes and within half an hour, it's like "Ratatouille" in the kitchen, without the rat in the kitchen.

Aromas of sizzling garlic in olive oil dance with rosemary and fried chicken, while the pasta steams every window. Simmering passata, seasoned with cracked black pepper and basil, spits orange speckles onto yellowed tiles and twenty minutes later, I plate up two meals, laying slices of garlic bread on the side. Then, I shave parmesan over the top, adding more black pepper to taste and my delicious masterpiece is complete.

Throwing a teatowel over the shoulder, I then lock a plate along my forearm and scoop up the other in my hand. I knock loudly on Mam's door and anticipation swells inside as the lock clicks.

But she doesn't answer.

Instead, it's a skinny, greasy bloke with nothing but a towel wrapped around his waist. He's got a tab in his mouth, yellowing his wispy goatee, and the oil on his pigeon chest sticks clumps of hair to his nipples. It's rank.

'Who are you?' I say. 'Where's me mam?'

'Room service?' the stick insect splutters, leaning over to investigate my culinary skills. 'Smells decent, Room Service. Is it Chinese and spaghetti? Dees is bout time we had someone here to do the home-keeping.'

You what?

The vampire's about to get his garden sprinkled and I'm just about to slam the dish over Stick-Insect-Savile's head when Mam's door creeps open and my dreams are shattered.

No. My life is shattered.

My future is shattered.

Behind that door of deceit, is the most horrifying, disgusting thing I've ever seen and no matter how long my immortality lasts, I won't ever shake this image from my mind. Piles of knickers, condoms and used tampons lying on mouldy plates. A bucket is filled to spilling and there's no radio, or computer, for podcasts, unless it's under that mess. It was them. *They* were laughing at me. Stick-Insect Savile and her... the *thing* sitting on the stripped, stained mattress, zoned out, cross-legged and half-naked, her arms outstretched, spiked like a pin cushion.

She is not a diabetic.

'Out the way, Baby Boy,' says the dink with the foreign accent, shouldering me to take *both* plates of food into the room. He back-heels the door with his foot, relieving me of the vision, but incensing every morsel of anger from the centre of my soul.

That was my meal. For me and her.

I boot the plywood on the bottom of the door and punch

my fist clean through the top panel. It bursts the frail lock inside and swings the sharp edge into the head of the greaseball. The plates clatter to the floor as the door splits his brow in two, dropping him to his knees amongst dirty knickers and ragu.

'Do you know who I be?' the monster spits, wiping the blood streaming from into his mouth. '*Me be Diego Mare, Expert Educator.*'

'My Brazilian teacher,' the woman on the bed slurs, rolling her head back and forth.

'*Expert Educator,*' he snaps.

'A grafter isn't you, Diego?' Mam says, wedging herself up. 'Needs this job, don't you, Diego Mare? Promotion for Rat-trap if Diego stays. *Always to love, never to leave.*'

Diego Mare twists to kneel by the bed and slithers his slimy fingers along the mattress to her thigh. She moans and lays back, bracing for his abuse.

Ghost Soup screams in my head to get out.

Over and over.

Louder and louder.

Warning me.

Begging me to be a better person.

"Change the people around you."

Shut your face, Soup!

From top to toe, I glow sapphire blue. Sparks spray from every pore, encasing me in a furious, electric aura. Then it happens, like the rushed climax of the seediest action movie.

Diego Mare, naked bar a pair of sweat-soaked briefs and a vest of face-blood, mops the claret from his face with a pair of her knickers. He's talking to someone. He's talking to no one. He's talking to himself.

'Pretty Boy should swim in the sea like Diego do,' he says,

shaking his head so vigorously that it's opening the gash above the bridge of his nose. 'Be a man, like Diego. If Pretty Boy thinks he take Diego place, he need to read the contract. No competition, Pretty Boy. Diego send a lightning-fast team of lawyers, Pretty Boy. Diego has eyes and ears everywhere.'

Mental.

On the bed, a thick grey smoke swirls around the woman who gave birth to me. The woman who left us is enveloped until only glowing emerald eyes, within the whisking poison, are visible to burn deep into my soul.

'You *need* your mother, Daniel,' she whispers, saturated by reverb. 'Always to love, never to leave.'

A surge of adrenaline wells up like a bubble in my chest, as Diego Mare sneers amongst the filth.

My beautiful mother is right. I can always cook another meal. It was no big deal. Mam and I, we can make this work. We can —

Erm, give your head a shake, Daniel Lad. This is all kinds of wrong.

In an instant, a spark in my brain brings me right back into the moment. It splits my head like a nutcracker, lighting every corner of this vile room. Raging, I turn to leave as the flash of a silver steak knife lunges towards me and the warm blade plunges deep into my appendix.

'I am Diego Mare, saviour of young minds,' bellows my attacker, rising. 'You will not steal what is mine. *Always to love, never to leave.*'

I stumble back. Mare's momentum knocks me off balance into the front room, where, in the blink of an eye, I snatch the cricket bat and swing it to decorate the walls with haemoglobin and teeth.

'*I* am Daniel Ambrose,' I snarl at the unconscious slob laid before me. 'And I am going *home*.'

The thing on the bed begs for me to stay, but I step into the corridor, where the sunlight splits through the barred window and a small Hindu lady peeks out of her door. She looks terrified as she closes the door to phone the police.

I've got to nash and I've got to nash now.

24

Oh, You'll Never Get to Hebburn

Like a spider curled in the darkest corner of a busy cloakroom, I protect what is left of me with my arms around my knees and my head pushing through my thighs. I've not moved for two sunsets, thankful for the biting rain and high winds that keep families and dog walkers away from the brightly coloured play park at Roker. Fausto Coffee still gets a few in, but they're inside and then straight back to their cars.

Little shelter is provided by the wooden playhouse, but the mural, stone arch takes the brunt of the battering wind and waves. Only occasionally do the waves breach the barrier to shower me with saltwater that reminds me of Soup.

What have I done? In less than a fortnight, I might have killed *twice*. That's one a week; even the worst of mathematicians could work that out. Diego Mare... the image of his lifeless body, jaw detached, is surpassed only by the image of my mother, luring him in with some sort of sickening seduction. Nobody should witness that, especially a child.

'Daniel,' says a soft voice. 'Daniel, come on, Love. Let's get you home.'

Defying sheeting sands and bitter wind, Mrs Tabel has climbed the short rope ladder and has her head inside the playhouse.

'Come on,' she says, reaching in and slipping her fingers amongst my interlinked digits. 'We've got a funeral to attend.'

I forgot about that. I don't want to go.

Mrs Tabel separates my numb hands with gentle force and squeezes my palm with hers, pulling my arm towards her. Without resistance, I follow her onto the rubberised ground below.

'You're coming, aren't you?' she asks, linking our arms. 'To see Soup.'

'I can't. Everyone hates me.'

'Nobody hates you. This isn't about you. This is about paying your respects.'

Sirens soundtrack the sound of Sunderland. Blue flashing lights blur with yellowed streetlamps streaking into my retinas and hypnotising my brain, giving me the first respite from the vivid memories that torture me. I get scared about jail and despite the heaters in Mrs Tabel's Toyota Yaris, my body convulses uncontrollably. Increasing the volume, Mrs Tabel plays soothing music and I drift away.

At some point, I wake with a stiff neck that loosens in a hail of blue sparks. Through the hole in my hoodie, the stab wound has healed, but the crusted blood remains as a reminder of the horror.

Mrs Tabel has stopped for petrol and she comes back with

a hot chocolate for me. I sip at it, letting the sweet liquid burn my lips and the sparks prevent the blisters.

'How did you find me?' I ask.

'Your dad's phone,' Mrs Tabel says, not taking her eyes off the road or her hands from ten to two. 'Ken triangulated the signal.'

Dad was never going to manage that. He struggles with WhatsApp.

The phone!

With a surge of panic, I dig into my pocket. What if Mam messaged Dad about the Brazillian bloke, Diego Mare? I need to see Dad before the cops get me.

I open the app, but there's no message from Mam or calls from the police. There's hardly been any messages from mam, ever.

Scrolling through pages and pages of unread, unticked messages from Dad, I don't see the expected begging texts. Instead, I see hundreds of updates about me.

[Dan's been moved into
Penshaw Red! Can you believe it?
I bet you're as proud as I am]

[**Our Dan's mentor**
reckons he's going to be
a writer. Lol. Creative like
his dad and mam]
[**Any chance you could**
give Dan a ring?
He's a bit low after the
suspension]

[**Ha'way Courts. Let him**
know you love him. Don't
take our troubles out on

the lad]

These messages are splattered with messages of desperation spanning back to when she left.

**[I miss you, Courts. Please come
Home. Never to leave you said.]**

**[Listen, Courts. I will stop the
dreaming. Ha'way, Gorgeous. Giz
a chance]**

**[Courts, I'm sorry. Look, you
take your time and I'll
sort my life out. I can be
the man you want me to be]**

**[Right, I'm going to get a
solicitor. I'll make sure you
can't hurt Keith or
Dan any more. Bitch.
This is Jackie BTW]**

Then, as I reach the earliest texts, I see one from Mam that makes me wonder.

[Always to love, never to leave]

"Always to love, never to leave" That's what he said.

I relax a little when the Toyota takes us out of the city and up into the hills. The darkness of the countryside comforts me. Around the winding roads and then, the floodlit WOPPA building that pinpoints our destination. It's the only indication that a town exists out here. It is solitude and I crave solitude.

Pulling into Colliery Row, I'm shocked to see that there are no police cars outside. I thought they'd be here for me, waiting. The black paedo van is still parked across the road. It's a WOPPA van, but there's nobody in the driver's seat, so I reckon that Del and Owain might have grafted that and dumped it. It'll be burnt out soon enough.

Entering the door, I dip my head further as Jackie's frown contracts, pulling the muscles on her forehead tight. The split lip quivers. Her body language indicates vulnerability and pain. She's hurting inside and it's my doing, but the woman I blamed for my dad's misery and my "mother's" estrangement, steps forward, allowing me to see deep into her soul as her heart breaks right in front of me.

With a tilted head, she looks me in the eye and slowly opens her arms, pulling me to her chest, and embracing me with a love that I've never felt before. Rigid and shaking, I'm held tight against her. Her breathing calms me. I am no longer held in the wings of a devil. Jackie is an angel. Jackie is my protector.

'Let it out.' she tightens her hold on me. 'It's ok, Son. None of this is your fault.'

But it is. It's all my —

'It's *not* your fault.' Tears encased in sapphire sparks drench her shoulder and cascade down her back.

'It's all going to be ok,' she whispers. I can smell the cleanliness of her knitted jumper. Summer fresh linen.

'I... I...'

'Shhhhhh. It's ok.' Her own tears stream down my neck like rain down the VELUX window. Our hearts fight for the position of fastest and loudest, punching through our chests to meet in person. Her fingers hold my hair as she rests my head on her shoulder, rocking me like we're slow dancing.

'Let's get you all fixed up,' she says as Dad joins us,

surrounding us with strong, hero arms that pull us safe and I continue to cry real tears for what seems like forever…

Much later, Dad guides me upstairs, opening the door to a walled-off part of the master bedroom that's soundproofed with underlay. I've only ever heard dull tones coming from within, and I've never been allowed through the makeshift wardrobe door into the music room before.

Inside it's dim and sparsely furnished, with a two-tone armchair, a bookshelf and an old Dynacord sound system. The long, teak wooden beast could easily be mistaken for a coffee table sitting on the back wall of the sloped roof, directly opposite the VELUX window. Dad's record player — the one thing he takes care of.

Keith lowers the front panel of the Dynacord. A radio tuner and a metal plate with bass, mid and treble knobs line up next to a larger volume fader. At the other end, an oblong dial is marked 'on' and 'off', forty-five degrees apart.

My dad lifts the heavy teak cover, where two more hydraulics hiss and click-lock the lid above a dark-grey, rubber slip-mat, protecting a matt-silver disc. This plate is "belt-driven by the most important motor of all time" and from it, the air, which has lain dormant inside, smells of "lust, passion, dust and fashion".

After turning the dial, Keith steps back as the system powers up like a jet engine. The amp purrs to life and the belt on the turntable takes hold, dragging the slip-mat up to thirty-three rpm while I watch on, letting my eyes follow the raised rubber. It's hypnotic.

I scan racks of vinyl records on the wall adjacent to Dad's room. The narrow, indexed spines are sorted alphabetically, left to right. Keith strums his fingers along the top of each sleeve, caressing them like the strings of a guitar. He rocks the corner of a twelve-inch gatefold album, exposing enough to ease into his hands.

'Here,' he says, passing me the album. 'Here's a starter.'

"Now That's What I Call Music 11" is not what I expected. Dad's into some cool stuff, so I can't imagine him locking himself in this box and listening to cheesy Eighties synth-pop.

Keith makes me promise to wait until the sound system has warmed up properly before I lower the needle.

'Let it take you, Son,' he says. 'Marshmallow dreams reflect the futures of pomegranate stars and you will learn the secrets of our being.'

No wonder they locked him up.

Giving him the benefit of the doubt, with palms on either side of the sleeve, I apply gentle pressure, fattening the cover stars up. With a slight wobble board manoeuvre, the inner cover, protector of shiny wax within, slips out.

Carefully, I slide four fingers inside and hook them onto the central label. With my thumb on the edge of the disc, I remove the record from within.

'The sleeve holds time on the shelf,' Dad says. 'But the record contains the heart, soul, sweat and tears of an artist's entire lifetime.'

I'm expecting good things from, erm, whatever this is.

The record is heavy vinyl with a plain, white central label. I lay it onto the slip-mat, slotting the centre hole over the spindle, and I release a life story. The needle lifts easily from its cradle. I use a fingernail to pull away dust. The arm swings to the first groove and I lower it with a bassy thud. The stylus catches the run-in, the record crackles and then, as I settle back into the grey and mustard chair, I don't hear synth pop. Instead, I hear an acoustic guitar sounding like it was recorded in a field.

Then, a man sings a song that Jackie and Dad sing *all* of the time.

"Oh, you'll never get to Heaven," the voice sings, with confidence.

"Oh, you'll never get to Heaven," the crowd responds.

"As a human bean," the man calls.

"As a human bean."

"Coz a human bean."

"Coz a human bean."

"Soon won't be seen."

"Soon won't be seeeeeeeeeeen."

This is grim and hardly uplifting camp entertainment. It's sketchy rhyming at best and I prefer the famous "in a biscuit tin" version.

Dad lifts the needle, while Jackie pinches the record sleeve and gives the gatefold a little shake. There's something else inside. So, nipping the corner, I slip out a square insert with a photo on it. It's the same Scout and Guide Camp photo framed above Dad's bedroom door. The one that's in Soup's house too.

Jackie points to my dad and my mam in the centre of the picture and then, she slides her finger across to the other side of Dad, where, to his right, a pretty girl looks proud as punch in her beret and neckerchief.

'Recognise this little misfit?' Jackie says.

I look closely at the photo and then up at Jackie. It's her standing next to Dad in the picture... and they're holding hands.

'But that's not right,' I say. 'Dad fell in love with *Mam* at Scout Camp.'

'That's not *exactly* how it happened,' says Dad, grinning like Dirk Blaster, the bloke off the telly advert who cleans ovens. I can't quite put my finger on what has changed about him. Maybe it's coz I've seen his record collection. He's got his hands on his hips like he's extra proud.

Then, he takes his hands off his hips and looks a bit upset.

Jackie chuckles and folds all but my index finger into my palm. She moves it across the photograph, over the Scouts and Guides, Soup's folks and Molly's dad too. Eventually, she pushes my finger up to the blurred Arkela (Scout leader) at the top of the picture. There are four of them.

'Look *through* the picture,' Dad says. 'Like the Magic Eye book that I got you.'

By relaxing my eyes, blurring the whole photo and pushing my vision to the floor below, the Arkela drift slowly into focus as others blur away. For a moment, nothing happens. But then, just like the Magic Eye, the four leaders stand out in three dimensions, like holograms.

A loop plays over and over and the woman with white hair rocks her glasses on her nose. Next to her is a man with an apple who keeps offering it to me. Off-centre, there is a short man with a safari hat covering his face; he's doing nothing except hiding.

Then, I see the man standing to the far right and sparks rush to my brain before it bursts open.

No way!

The man on the right raises his hand to rub his beard. He is not one chin hair different from the last time I saw him. Not a day younger than the day he changed everything. There, at the back of the sepia picture, is the man responsible for all of this: *Dr Angelos Urielis. The Substitute...*

25

The Prisoner

In Cell Thirteen, **the prisoner** sat on a rough woollen sheet with their knees tucked up to the chest and arms wrapped around bent legs. It was eleven o'clock, according to the clock on the wall, but it was always eleven o'clock because the clock was broken. So, at eleven o'clock, **the guard** walked past and banged on the door. He laughed and strutted away only when he heard sobbing.

In the early afternoon, **the nurse** entered the cell with two guards. They unfolded a leather wallet and took out the needle, which they then stabbed into the prisoner's arm. Around five minutes later, there was nothing at all the prisoner could do except stare at the strip lights in the corridor as the guards tightened the straps and pushed the trolley to where the tests take place. The drugs made it impossible to cry.

The prisoner was returned to the cell after an hour or so. Within twenty minutes of returning, a pot of beige slop and a drink were pushed through a slot in the cell door. There was never a spoon with the slop.

The prisoner licked the last of the tasteless mush off the plastic and scraped the dried oats onto the floor for a hungry mouse. The plate went back into the slot and the guard tried to catch the prisoner's fingers as he slammed the hatch closed.

On the bed, the prisoner sat back and sobbed again and the mouse headed off to find **Oscar the Shapeshifter**.

26

The Potentials

'Arkela Urielis,' says Dad, nodding. 'You've met this man?'

'Yeah, he played Broken Telephone at school. That's how I'm —'

'Immortal,' Dad interrupts. 'We know.'

'How?'

Dad flashes a worried look at Jackie and the two unite to hold hands.

'You aren't the first and you won't be the last,' says Jackie. 'These people —'

'Beings,' Dad interrupts.

'Whatever they are,' Jackie continues, grinning. 'These beings have set you on a quest… a story… a journey.'

'Well it's not garna sell many copies,' I say, thickening my accent. 'Coz Soup's deed and I'm gonna find Urielis and knock his jaw to Hebburn.'

'Oh, I doubt you'll see him again, Daniel,' says Jackie. 'Once a story is started, he doesn't manifest again.'

'What do you mean he doesn't manifest? What story?'

'The Potentials,' says Dad. 'It's a long story. It's *many* stories.'

'Nope. Still don't understand.'

'*The Potentials*,' says Jackie, dropping the title of a future novel again. 'Just like our camp singalong, the Broken Telephone set The Potentials on a different quest. We have powers too.'

'What *the actual hell are you on about!*'

'Just what we said,' says Dad. 'They gave us powers around a campfire, just like you got yours in class. You and your friends are Potentials, as are we and ours.'

'Everyone at our Scout Camp ended up with a wish granted,' Jackie says, solemnly. 'But not everyone has a hero's journey. Someone like your mam for example.'

'What do you mean? What's she got to do with it?'

'She didn't want to sing,' says Dad. 'So I helped. Here, listen…'

The needle hits the record again and it's Dad singing with an unwilling, posh girl.

"*Oh, you'll never get to Hebburn.*" Both sing.

"*With snotty sleeves.*" Only Dad sings this bit.

"*Always to love,*" Mam spits out. "*Never to leave.*"

'Her spell,' Dad mumbles. 'Me and Mam. It wasn't real.'

The grey smoke and green eyes. Diego Mare. I heard him say that. "Always to love, never to leave."

'It's not all her fault,' says Jackie, sitting next to me. 'Your mum had a tough upbringing.'

'Haven't we all?' I say, semi-sarcastically.

'Ha. Yeah, we're poor,' says Dad. 'But money isn't the answer, Dan.'

'Your mum struggled with acceptance,' Jackie continues, 'because her parent's wealth and ambition led to unreasonable expectations of her. They were very critical and

Courtney grew up believing she was an underachiever. Worse, she believed she was unlovable.'

'They told her she'd never be good enough,' says Dad. 'That she'd always be alone.'

'So, your mum was determined *not* to live out her parent's prophecy,' says Jackie. 'She refused to spend her life alone and when she sang at the campfire, the lyrics cast her first spell.'

'She wished that any man of her choosing would *always* love her and *never* leave her,' says Dad. 'And because I had helped her, I think she kinda crushed on me.'

Do not ever say "crushed on me" again.

'Sorry,' says Dad. 'She became *attached*. Mam was well aware of Jackie and I but the spell was solid. Magic. You know how it works.'

Jackie was heartbroken. She didn't understand why Dad didn't want her, so she travelled and left them to it.

I was born and Dad set up the coffee shop. He tells me that customers came in to buy coffee, choose a vinyl record and put it on while they relaxed.

On an evening, he gigged for extra money. He reckons it was great fun being a loving, creative husband and father, but Mam wasn't happy. She wanted him to conform and work for the family business. She wanted him to be "good enough" for her parents. She wanted him to "termite".

Ashamed of him when speaking to her posh friends, Mam asked her parents to use their influence, so they caused the collapse of the coffee shop. Then, Dad's only income was from the few cover bands he played in, and while he clung desperately to what was left of his ambition, Mam left. He would never live up to the pedestal she placed her father on.

But when she went, the spell wasn't broken… and I know the rest — the drinking, the online stalking and the crisis team. Poor Dad.

'How come you came back then?' I ask Jackie, fighting tears. 'Even though Dad couldn't love you?'

'Keith's telepathy,' she says. 'He cried out from inside the spell to protect you, that day the hospital took him away.'

'And you've been here all along, despite all that?'

'Your dad may not love me, but I can love him. And I can love you…'

'I *couldn't* love her,' says Dad, stepping forward. 'Until you broke the spell today. Courtney has spent years not knowing if *any* man she meets truly loves her, or if it's the spell at work.'

'But by rejecting her today,' Jackie says. 'You've freed her from it. You've freed all of us.'

Wait a minute. Keith's telepathy? Erm… What?

'Yes, Dan,' says Dad. 'I can read minds.'

How much of my mind has he been bloody reading?

He tells me "a lot, but it's ok coz that's normal for a teenager".

If we had a carpet, I'd sink into it.

The needle bounces onto the vinyl again.

"Oh, you'll never get to Hebburn."

"If we cannot see,

"What is good for you,

Isn't good for me…"

'See,' says Dad. 'I sang about understanding people and I'm now telepathic.'

He steps back from the record player and pulls a face like he's modelling turned-up chinos and chest hair. He puts his fingers to his temple and seconds later, he's glowing sapphire blue, just like when I heal. He shakes out his greasy man-bun and I see his long, blonde hair for the first time. It's shining like a bloody shampoo advert. His skin clears of spots and broken veins and he has a properly chiselled jaw. With one raised eyebrow, Dad touches his temple again and tells me to chill out.

He absolutely shouldn't say "chill out". That's lame.

'Adults can say chill out too,' he says. 'Stop being ageist.'

'Stop reading my mind.'

'Ok.'

Get a carpet, Scruff bag.

'I will.'

'Oi!'

'Damn it.'

Gently stroking my hair and laughing, Jackie accepts my reciprocated smile. She tells me that Mrs Robinson casts masking spells because she struggles with her appearance.

Put the cake down Carol.

'Play nice, Dan,' says Brain Nonce. 'She's masked us for over a decade. I just asked her to remove the mask. I go by the moniker, *Loab — Master of Minds.*'

I prefer "Brain Nonce."

'It's Master. Of. Minds.'

Pack. It. In.

Standing, Jackie asks Dad's permission for something and he nods, strums his temple again, then steps back towards the door.

'You might wanna stand by the window,' Brain Nonce says. 'This is pretty special.'

Suddenly, the room glows like someone's turning up a light, or a candle is taking hold. Bending forward slightly, Jackie shakes out her thinning hair and when she lifts her head, she is glowing with a fiery aura just like Soup's. My eyes are almost on stalks as I watch her leathery skin smooth over. Her lip heals completely and her black eye disappears.

Stretching out her arms, Jackie snaps her fingers and instantaneously develops pro-swimmer muscles on her shoulders. She looks twenty years younger and saved three hundred benk on Botox. The weather-beaten hag that I've known for years simply vanishes and, well, she looks like a... a goddess.

Bloody hell, my dad's proper punching above his weight there.

'Oi.'

'Daniel,' says Jackie, in a voice that would dent cushions. 'I am Ardea, Princess of Fire.'

'Fiya,' I say and quickly change the subject. 'Were you messaging Mrs Robinson?' Dad nods and I ask, 'why do you need secret identities?'

'To protect you,' says Jackie, Fire Lass. 'With power comes great baddies. So we disappeared.'

'Everyone knows everyone's business in a small village like Hatley,' says Dad. 'That's why I fell out with *him*. Couldn't keep his gob shut.'

'Uncle Ken?'

'Yep.'

'So, you've pretended to be minging to save me from danger? Cheers, I guess.'

'Until you went to see your mam and decided upon a life of crime,' Jackie adds, stretching out her legs and taking a padded envelope from Dad. 'Kinda left us no choice. We can't let you wander down the wrong path.'

'Plus, the bloody squirrel left us no option,' says Dad.

'Eh?'

'Here,' says Jackie, handing me the envelope. 'This was meant for you, but you did a runner.'

Tentatively, I open the seal.

'So, all of you have powers?' I ask. 'From the same bloke that caused all of this?'

'Shurrup and open the bloody envelope,' Dad says. 'We haven't got time for a flashback. Maybe we'll do a prequel if sales slump.'

'Once you see what's inside,' says Jackie. 'Everything will happen very quickly, so you must be prepared.' She's still smiling, so I nod, nip something rubber between the index and middle finger and edge the contents out carefully.

What? That's not possible.

'This is Soup's glove,' I gasp. 'It's got a Wet Wipe stuffed in this hole. But it can't be. Noggin had — wait, is that blood? Is this… a bullet hole.'

'It is,' says Jackie, nodding to Dad. I feel sick. 'Tell him, Keith. Put the lad out of his misery.'

'Daniel,' Dad says with the cheesiest grin. 'Ralph Robinson… is alive.'

27

The Horse Botherer pt.1

My name is Hoshi Solo-Spock and my parents are divorced.

At around four o'clock this morning, I was awoken by my mother's new boyfriend standing at the bottom of my bed and asking me not to make a sound. For a moment, I was concerned, until a golden, frizzy-haired statue with a squirrel on his shoulder greeted me.

Fortunately, I have already deciphered the secret of Broken Telephone and therefore, I am not terrified by this ethereal presentation. I know that there are others like me and I surmise they are also in an advanced state of evolution.

Method: The secret to Broken Telephone is DNA — a molecule that carries genetic information in all living organisms.

Theory: During an impromptu lesson, Dr Angelos Urielis, a substitute teacher from another dimension, granted the

Broken Telephones.

Method: DNA is malleable, like putty. By heating and shifting molecular structure, Urielis moulded DNA into an advanced state.

Theory: The previous method is also theory.

Conclusion: Gareth the Golden Statue, Oscar the Squirrel and my mother's perv boyfriend, need my superior understanding of science.

After some persuasion, two of the invaders take me into Hatley Woods. They direct me to a sign at the back of the woods that reads 'INTROODERS BEWARE'. Someone has coloured the 'OO' to look like terrified eyes.

We follow a hidden path, knotted with thorns, to a clearing around the size of a tennis court. It has a neatly mown grass space, surrounded by trees.

Next to a twisted oak, a large door is embedded into a mound of mud and bush, partially obscured with Fern leaves. I recognise the entrance as one of the many bunkers within these woods, but, as we are in Haunted Hatley, this must be The Horse Botherer's residence.

The Horse Botherer is a crackpot conspiracy theorist who believes he can talk to animals. He could be a Peer-ee-Odd and looks like he could pretend to be fourteen online.

Gareth sits on a fallen log to tell me he thinks Oscar knows something about Ralph Robinson, a dead boy that keeps trying to engage me in conversation. Apologies — he has previously engaged me in conversation and no longer does because he was recently reported dead. I do not see dead people. This is not my supernatural ability.

'Ken's in,' Gareth announces. 'I smell farts.'

Oscar laughs, resembling a cartoon rodent with his exaggerated guffawing. I do not laugh.

A voice, distorted by a primitive changer, bellows from a giant speaker attached to the oak. All three of us jump.

'Halt. Who goes there?'

I suck on my inhaler once more, until the initial panic subsides. The voice changer has me excited that my favourite anti-hero will emerge from the trees with a laser-sword. Unfortunately, the fern door swings open and a shaded face hides beneath a Jedi bathrobe. Unofficial merchandise, for sure. Sadly, no Sith.

'I said not to come here, Squirrel.'

'Ken, it's Gaz Swift.' I notice Gareth has borrowed a tracksuit from an eighties fancy dress party that Mum attended last month. It is at least two sizes smaller than he requires.

'Brian's lad?' says Bath Jedi. 'What brings you here?'

The squirrel, Oscar, enters a heated debate with this madman. The call-and-response action between the pair suggests that this man can, indeed, speak to animals.

'Thou art *all* of mystical abilities?' he says.

Theory: This man recently began playing Dungeons and Dragons and only knows cliched phrases.

The squirrel nods.

'Come inside. If you must.'

'We interruptin' yer shower, like?' Gareth asks, nodding to the bathrobe that the man is wearing. The man apologises for his attire and begins removing the robe. I avert my eyes and peek through my fingers.

'It is ineffable how much bigger than you could possibly imagine imagining, this is,' he says, proving my earlier theory that this man has searched for "descriptive D&D words" online.

'It's alreet Hoshi,' says Gareth. 'Ye can look.'

Fortunately, underneath the robe, Bath Jedi is dressed as if he is on his way to Glastonbury with my mother and her boyfriend. He wears frayed-hem, purple flares — at least thirty-two inches — and an ill-fitting Hawaiian shirt with a lavender Palm tree print. He ushers us down a sloping, stone-walled corridor, towards a rusty door. The man types in a lengthy code and several hydraulic locks clunk open, revealing the interior decor of an old-fashioned static caravan, just like my grandmother's.

Inside the subterranean holiday home, an oblong sitting room leads to an open-plan kitchen, roughly ten metres by eight. Bland, vinyl-covered chip-board storage units, with toffee-coloured handles, line the kitchen. Benches made from varnished, reclaimed wood, rest unsecured, above various appliances.

In the sitting area, an old, battered sofa is dressed with cushions that are patterned with faded autumnal foliage clicked around the seams. Next to it is an acoustic guitar and a circular coffee table covered with varnished pages from a book. A Star Wars trivia book, I believe.

Walls of yellowed wallpaper are clumsily decorated with picture frames. Some are stock pictures of famous cities, while others are newspaper cutouts and they surround a familiar picture of Scout and Guide Camp just like my mother has at home.

There are no windows in the bunker, so the man has improvised with appropriately positioned landscape posters of farmland. This is unnecessary, as the scent of nature is already provided by mushrooms growing in the corners of the room.

'My name is Kenneth Ambrose.' The man scrunches his fingers into his wild hair. 'But you may call me Uncle Ken.'

No. I am not calling a stranger Uncle Ken. I reach for my

inhaler again.

Kenneth offers us a seat on his grubby sofa, so I find a bit that isn't stained.

'We need yer help,' Gareth says. 'Can ye translate Oscar for us?'

'I cannot be of assistance.' Kenneth stares at Oscar while he fills the kettle in the kitchen.

Having a basic understanding of this man's vulnerabilities, I wave my arm slowly from left to right. 'You c-can be of assistance.' I induce a trance-like state.

'Your mind games are powerless against me, Telepath,' says Kenneth through his voice changer.

'My mind g-games are not —'

'We dinnet have time for this, shite. Just translate the effin' rat, Ken,' says Gaz.

Oscar almost chokes on a nut.

Kenneth makes a cup of Earl Grey, dipping and raising the tea bag, then straining it and finally chucking it into a carrier bag tied to a kitchen cupboard. Gareth fidgets like he has threadworms and watches his cousin jabbering away in a foreign species language.

'In the absence of a p-proper adult, my mother's... t-temporary boyfriend,' I say to Ken, 'has entrusted the information within this squirrel t-t-to you,'

Method: Kenneth is a Star Wars nerd... too. 'Help us Uncle K-Ken. You're our only hope.'

This ignites Kenneth and he totters through to the sitting area with his tea and a soggy biscuit. He sits next to me on the sofa and nods before turning to the squirrel.

'Tell me all that you have learned and I, Kenneth Ambrose shall interpret.'

And so it comes to pass that a bizarre, mop-haired horse botherer translates "The Quest to Save a Flying Dink" by

Oscar Swift, a squirrel with a deformed paw... or a seagull with a dodgy leg.

28

The Quest to Save the Flying Dink

Disclaimer: everything I am about to tell you is true. Only the facts have been changed.

Spotting **Soup the Petrified** and his equally careless colleague, **the bravest seagull that ever lived** dropped below the jets and pulled alongside the amateurs.

Greeted like an old friend, the ginger gull tried to draw the idiotic pair's attention to their pursuers, but the morons attempted to engage in a Disney-style sky-dance.

Then, Silent Engine Mode disengaged forcing the gull to change tactics.

A flip allowed him to undercut the morons. The amazing bird let out an almighty screech before he attacked, hoping that fear would force a landing. Instead, **the buck-nuts** thrashed about in the air, rearing up, oblivious to real danger.

Moments later, **the immortal divvy** dropped to the choppy waves below. The **heroic ginger gull** was aware of the boy's immortality, so he fought on, focusing its attention on Soup the Bouncy, who begged the bird to let up.

But **the spectacular, brave gull** could not speak. He was powerless to tell Soup that he lay in the sights of two stealth jets with their guns locked on. The two solo-manned, futuristic assault craft approached the flying dink with red lasers spotted all over his wetsuit.

Unable to intervene, **the marvellous gull** watched on as **Soup, Beginner of the Skies**, lunged and straightened like a ruler. His flippers kicked hard. He sucked deep on the regulator, pushing out his arms to tear off through the syrupy air faster than ever before. But it was not enough.

The first bullet tore into his calf and Soup's body twisted in shock.

The second bullet grazed his cheek and he grabbed at his face.

The third tore through the right-hand goalie glove.

Soup spat out the regulator and ripped off his left glove with his teeth, dropping it to the sea and leaving a Wet Wipe in his mouth.

Tears filled the Scuba mask as he stuffed a Wet Wipe into the wound on his right hand, but a fourth shell cracked and ripped into Soup's left shoulder and he spun, uncontrollably.

The final bullet pierced the back of Soup's balaclava and **the ginger gull** watched his friend's lifeless body smash into the choppy waves below, cracking open the skin of the water and disappearing into the dark depths, as his blood marbled across the surface like an oil spill.

29

The Horse Botherer pt.2

Solo-Sock's Log. Stargate Bunker.

'Pahahaha,' spits Gareth. 'Yer "log".'

Shakespearian, to say the least, Oscar performs a prolonged death scene worthy of an Oscar (the award like Gareth, not the over-acting squirrel laid flat-out on the kitchen bench).

'So, he's dead then?' says Uncle Ken, pouring out his remaining tea. 'Nobody could have survived that.'

'Danny could have survived that,' Gareth says smugly.

'A standard wetsuit has high-quality rubber with five-millimetre-thick K-Kevlar lining incorporated within,' I theorise. 'The rubberised b-ber-balaclava and mask strap would direct a ber-bullet per-p-parallel to the flight p-p-path for the resistance t-to slow and alter its tr-trrr-trajectory into an upward curve.'

Oscar nods, clicking his claws and firing finger guns at me.

'Ye mean, it bounced off the back of his heed,' says Gareth, double smugly. Perhaps he is brighter than he looks, or acts.

Oscar chatters and informs the group that he has passed a rogue goalie glove, the one with the bullet hole, onto Daniel Ambrose. Mayor Noggin claimed to have both gloves, so something's amiss.

'The squirrel says your friend is locked in a holding cell underneath WOPPA headquarters.' Ken dips his head. 'He is not safe.'

'Reet, I'll gan gerrim then,' says Gareth. 'Two ticks.'

ZAP!

In a bright yellow flash, Gareth disappears, leaving his shell suit on the floor. Oscar shakes his head and rolls his little eyes. Squirrels look quite cute when they roll their little eyes.

ZAP!

Previously, my encounter with the golden one had been in a darkened room. Now, I retch and avert my gaze.

'Should really have warned him first,' Gareth says, looking dismayed. He is wearing nothing, but a pair of Speedos and he is spray painted with gold paint from the neck down. 'I might've just made things worse. He fully religious now.'

Kenneth grabs the Jedi bathrobe from the back of the settee and throws it over the naked one. Gareth explains he can teleport himself, but not anything else and wherever he goes, his clothes are left behind. My mother's short-term fling suggested super-glueing some swimming trunks to him and spraying him with gold paint.

'C-Clever,' I say.

'He'd seen a hanging snot teleport with iz,' Gareth says.

'You look like a b-b-battery.'

Kenneth and Gareth ask more about Ralph's capture. The squirrel continues his story.

'There is a lab,' he chatters (via Kenneth), 'I followed Soup and saw a map. WOPPA has pictures of a bus and a seagull and a speedometer in different places.'

'Danny and me,' says Gareth. 'I bet I'm the speedo.'

'You look like one,' I say. It is not a joke.

'*Very funny,*' Gaz sneers. 'S. S. S...peedo.'

'Where are you going?' I ask Kenneth, who is currently stuffing things into a bag.

'They know of my nephew's power.' Kenneth becomes very flustered. 'You are all in grave danger. I must inform Loab and Ardea.'

'Here, bell him. Ye got his number?' Gareth stands and reaches into his swimming trunks. After a short fumble, he pulls out a mini-mobile phone and the scene reminds me of a television show about a prison.

'Glued this *to* me arse,' he says, and I choke.

'Pass it here.' Kenneth says, pulling on a pair of Marigolds.

Pleased with his contribution, Gareth explains how to unlock the screen but he need not have wasted his time, because Kenneth begins pummelling the phone into a million pieces with a rolling pin.

Oscar, who has been drifting for the last five minutes, starts hopping around, pointing and chattering excitedly.

'No, Squirrel,' Kenneth shouts over the top of the bashing. 'We are not making *pies.*'

Finally, a sharp pair of scissors puts an end to the processors and memory card. Kenneth scoops it into a metal bin, dusts down the bench and pours lighter fluid over the container while Gareth's mouth hangs low. Seconds later the contents of the bin burn brightly in a compact shower room, next to the bedroom.

'I had to wesh fotty cars for that!' snaps Gaz.

Kenneth (rightfully) orders that, moving forward, we stay off grid. During the chaos, I slide my laptop under the sofa with my foot as I will need that to execute a plan I have devised.

Once Kenneth has filled a small rucksack with clothes, he opens the rolling pin drawer, for a pack of large batteries and a rectangular orange toy with letters on it. I wonder how big that drawer is, as he seems to have a lot in it. I'm thinking of a blue telephone box.

'That's for the squirrel to type on,' Kenneth says. 'It's a Speak and Spell.'

'I know what it is,' I say. 'I have seen E.T.'

'You've seen E.T.?' he yelps. 'Don't tell WOPPA.'

I might like Uncle Kenneth after all.

'We are safe here,' I ask. 'Aren't we?'

'For now,' Kenneth says, but there is an air of caution to his tone. 'But if they know who you are, they will find you. I will save my nephew, while you search the internet for the mole.'

PUFF!

'This is not the time for larking about, Mole. Search the internet.'

PUFF!

'We cannet search the internet for owt, *Kenneth*,' spits Gareth. 'Because ye've knackered me phone.'

'Use Raziel,' says Uncle Kenneth. 'She's in the oven.'

And with that, the hydraulic locks open. Uncle Kenneth disappears into the daylight leaving us to wonder who the madman has in the cooker…

30

After Maths

Like the meteor that rocked the dinosaurs, the door slams and the plasterboard walls of the music room rattle. Someone bounds up the stairs towards us, but Dad doesn't panic. Instead, he turns the handle calmly and skilfully and avoids being knocked out by his brother's forced entrance.

For a man who's spent the last fifteen years in hiding, Uncle Ken is hardly inconspicuous in his Hawaiian shirt. He's flustered and sweating heavily but I fling my arms around him. It's been an emotional few days and Uncle Ken is the tonic.

'Loab,' Uncle Ken says over my shoulder to Dad, soberly.

'Kenneth,' Dad says, equally sedate.

'Ardea,' Uncle Ken then says to Jackie, adding inflexion.

'Hiya, Ken,' Jackie says. 'What's up?'

'Daniel, my boy,' says Uncle Ken, ignoring her to demonstrate his ability to remember names.

'Uncle Ken,' I say, stepping back and shaking his hand

firmly. He looks at me with concern and Dad drains in colour.

'We're going to get you out of here,' he says, and Ken agrees.

'Indeed, they are coming, Nephew.'

Jackie spins on her heels and disappears towards my bedroom while Dad stuffs the folded sepia photo into my hand. Uncle Ken is already halfway down the stairs and seconds later, Jackie's chucked my full backpack at me and we're all heading towards the front door.

'Listen. I think I may have done something *really* bad.'

'We know,' says Dad. 'Psychic, remember.'

'I might have killed a man. At Mam's. I think I killed —'

'Oh for goodness sake,' says Jackie, frowning at Dad. 'Put the boy out of his misery again.'

'He's also alive' says Dad, with a smirk. 'But he'll have to stay off the wine gums until they've stapled his jaw back on. Top batting, Lad. One less drug dealer on the streets.'

'Dealer? Is that who's coming for me? The cartel?'

'Diego Mare doesn't work for a cartel,' Jackie snorts. 'He manages a dodgy company pretending unqualified teachers are better than trained ones. On a weekend he deals low-purity drugs from Bernie Rat-Trapperd's hot dog van.'

'Oh.'

'I'm afraid this is far more sinister, Danny Boy,' says Uncle Ken, sternly. '*WOPPA* are coming for you.'

'The alien museum?'

'The corrupt agency hunting down Potentials to strip them of their powers, kill them and end the world, you mean?'

'Oh,' I say. 'I preferred the cartel.'

We squash into the small entrance, like mad people in a phone booth. Jackie unzips my backpack, double-checking I've got two pairs of boxers and a bottle of shower gel amongst various all-weather-ready clothing.

'You've got your Haro top,' she says, looking at me like I'm about to be evacuated to Yorkshire and she's off to war. 'And there's twenty quid in the secret pocket for snacks and drinks. I've packed you a roll-up raincoat and some thick, warm socks.'

'Ardea,' snaps Dad. 'We haven't got time for this. Daniel, who else played Broken Telephone?'

'Gaz, Oscar, Hoshi, Soup and Molly and a couple of kids from Juniors.'

'Swift, Byrd and Solo-Spock are in the fortified bunker,' says Uncle Ken to Dad. 'Can you locate the Nell girl?'

With a fluttered sigh and puffed cheeks, Dad raises his hands to his temples. 'She's home, eating breakfast.'

'She'll be going to school this morning,' I say. 'Then the funeral this afternoon.'

'School should be safe' Dad says. 'Lots of people around. Were there any others in with Urielis?'

'Some kids from Hatley Juniors. Six of them.'

Once again, Dad fingers his temple. His aura glows as he strains like he's dropping a solid nutty one, but he just shakes his head. 'I can only see Nell.'

'Uriel wouldn't upgrade the juniors,' says Jackie. 'They're too young to be Potentials.'

'The wizard was pre-school,' says Uncle Ken. 'It would not be the first time.'

'Tea anyone?' says Mrs Tabel, holding a tray of steaming mugs. 'We have Sports Biscuits. They're lovely.'

Where the bloody Hell did she come from? Does the hippy have powers?

'The kitchen, Dan,' says Dad.

'Oooo, put it on the side,' says Uncle Ken with a glint in his eye. 'We can slurp the nectar over a chit chat.'

'Loab, further surveillance, please,' Jackie says to Dad

while she zips me up.

'Unmarked van in The Ivy car park,' he replies. 'Nell?'

'There's a black van parked outside ours too,' I say. 'I think it's empty, though. It's been there for days.'

All three look at each other, surprised and proud. Dad raises his fingers again, sucks his lips and flicks a tiny shake of the head to Jackie and Ken.

'Well spotted,' he says. 'Four in the back.'

'Daniel,' Jackie says placing her hands on my shoulders. She turns me towards her, stooping slightly and grabbing both of my biceps. 'Can you get to Molly Nell?'

'What for?' I ask. 'I don't know her. Or where she lives.'

Ok, now I know where she lives. Dad has two-way brain perv powers.

'Erm, that's not ok,' I say. '*Not* ok.'

'Sorry, Dan,' Dad says sheepishly. 'I thought it would save time.'

'Show Molly and Mr Nell the photograph,' Jackie says.

'Tell him Ardea and Loab sent you,' says Dad. 'Mr Nell has sacrificed *everything* for her before and he will do it again.'

'You'll need to run,' Jackie says, never breaking our locked eyes. 'Don't stop until you get to Mr Nell. Run as fast as you can.'

'As soon as we open this door, Danny Boy,' says Uncle Ken. 'They're going to come for you. The humans and the drained. They *are* coming for you, but you must run.'

Well, this sounds fun, doesn't it?

'You're running for your life,' says Jackie, placing a hopeful kiss on my forehead. 'You're running for *life*.'

'They'll catch me. There's this camera thing in the sky looking for "potential energy". I think WOPPA means us.'

Dad splutters a confident snigger and winks at Jackie.

'Nobody messes with *my* boy,' she says, turning towards the exit and gripping my shoulders one more time.

Uncle Ken twists the handle and whips open the door. 'Now, run, Daniel Ambrose. *Run.*'

I pull up my hood and put my head down. With all the power of a titanium spring, I recoil and pounce into the pink dawn that drenches the red brick street. Before I'm at the gate, the van bursts open and I see four figures running towards me, shouting my surname and telling me to stop.

Swiftly, I pogo the garden wall and my new trainers grip hard as I swerve left, straightening my body while I push back my shoulders, sprinting like I'm going for gold.

The shouting gets louder as I dodge a grab for my backpack, just to my right. With my pursuers behind me, I hot-foot it towards the back lane and get as far as the corner shop when I hear screams… but they're not from Jackie, Dad or Ken…

Woah there, Camel. I'm not missing this for anything.

Engulfed in a dome of flames two suited agents bend and twist to avoid the fire blasting from Jackie's fingertips. A burning wall surrounds them, while she glows with her fiery aura. Her face is as threatening as it is beautiful. Another WOPPA agent, in a black suit, flaps about horizontally, like when Soup was learning to fly. Dad's got his fingertips to his temple and his left hand is outstretched, flipping palm-side up and then down. The agent spins like a pig on a spit and he's screaming with terror while Mrs Tabel, in her long, multi-coloured cardigan, bats him with the handle of her brolly. Underneath the pancake agent is the last of the ground team and he's on the ground, kicking and screaming as hundreds of tiny bats pound him like heavy rain on a car window.

'Daniel,' Jackie shouts.

Aye, I know what they said to do, but that was worth the risk. I twist my heels, pushing into the insole and force my whole body to move faster than it's ever moved before.

Oh. My. Life. They're bloody brilliant.

Looking left and right after the corner shop, I'm over the road, hurdling the back lane obstacle course and I skid into the Tunnel of Trees. New voices join the hunt, calling my name but they've got no chance of getting me here. This is my territory and I know every single mud path and mountain bike route through Hatley Woods and the fields to the village.

I exit the Tunnel of Trees and continue over the country lane, vaulting the cattle gate into Farmer Ned's wheat field, where I grind the dusty mud for a quarter of a mile up to the back of Molly's house.

Panting hard I check behind, but I've lost them. Avoiding the van in The Ivy, I duck down behind Molly's bush and slip through her back gate, where I wait in the drive for her to leave for school. My sparks repair my lungs, calves and whatever else is bursting with adrenaline and I feel more alive than ever before.

'No,' Molly says, turning away and hurrying towards the car.

Buzzkill.

'Please Molly,' I beg.

'I want nothing to do with those stupid powers, now shut up.'

Molly's dad walks towards a silver Tesla with two BMX bikes strapped to a rack on the roof. The back door opens automatically and Mr Nell waves both of us over, asking Molly if she wants a lift. She says that she does, and I get cheeky.

'Thanks, Mr Nell,' I say, slipping into the back seat.

He'd have some nerve to refuse me after what I did for him.

Seeing this, Molly sits in the front, so she doesn't have to listen to me.

The journey is awkward and silent, but Mr Nell is doing his best to make conversation.

'Have you two fallen out?' he says, small talking.

'Don't think so.' I decide to push Molly to engage me in conversation so I can show them the photo. 'Have we?'

Molly slips her headphones into her ears, scrolls down and plays something. Her dad looks over his shoulder at me and then turns to his daughter.

'Molly? Can you hear me? Molly? Molly?'

Molly mumble-raps "The Magic Number" by De La Soul and stares out of the window while her dad surprises me with a darker tone in his voice. 'What are you doing here?'

'Ardea and Loab said to show you this.' I unfold the photo of the camp. Mr Nell acknowledges it and pauses momentarily.

'Adrea and Loab know that interventions are forbidden.'

'We're in danger,' I say. 'Soup's alive and we need to save him.'

'Kids,' he hisses, but it's not at us. 'Always kids.' Mr Nell ponders for a moment. '*Crap.*'

Screeching the car to a halt, I see what's got his attention. Molly does too but she ignores the limo and the WOPPA van blocking the road from the school. Behind us, another van rolls up with its hazards on and we're trapped.

'Listen carefully,' Mr Nell says. 'Do *not* say anything to Molly until you're safely in the school because she'll cause a ruck. She doesn't know subtle. Go into the school, show her the photo and take the fire escape down to the bike sheds. I'll put the bikes around the back. Do *not* scratch my Diamond Back.'

'Which one's that? It's just a bike.'

He's looking at me like I'm as dense as Jackie's homemade

bread.

I once drowned a duck at the pond with her sourdough. True story.

'Get to her to Ken,' Mr Nell says. 'I'll delay them.'

Not the giant duck! I didn't drown the giant duck! That's Pee Pants from Juniors!

Molly and I exit the Tesla, dodging around the bonnet while Mr Nell raises his voice, grabbing her attention.

'Your power doesn't define you,' he says. 'But don't write them off forever. Choose wisely.'

Molly shrugs and scuttles up the path towards the school doors. She waves at Sparky, who's grown a thick moustache over the summer, and he smiles through his top lip carpet. As I catch her up, he greets Molly and tells her to come and see him after Maths.

'I wasn't expecting either of you today,' Sparky says, not looking at Molly as he speaks. He's flicking worried eyes between me and the WOPPA vehicles parked by the school gates. 'Nobody would, under the circumstances. But well done for coming in.'

I'm grateful for the yard full of parents and kids. Nobody's kidnapping anyone in plain sight.

Maths is on the second floor, through the double doors. Molly makes it to the top of the stairs before I catch up and grab her bag. She spins around angrily to face me but stops herself short of knocking me on my arse when the school tannoy kicks in.

'Daniel Ambrose to the Head's office.'

Erm, I don't think so, like. I've been to Sparky's office enough times to know there's nowt good inside.

'Molly, we need to leave. WOPPA has taken Soup and

they're here for us too. We have to get to The Bunker at Uncle Ken's.'

'WOPPA? The Alien Museum? Are you mental, Daniel?' She snatches her shoulder away and turns her back to me.

'They're not what you think. They'll take us after Maths. Look out of the window. That van. It's them and they're here for us.'

Through the double windows on the stairwell, I see the limousine doors open. Sparky's on the phone and walking towards the gates. He's waving his free arm and keeps pointing back at the building. Molly turns away, but I grab her shoulders and look her dead in the eyes.

'Please, Molly.'

'My balloons hurt everyone. I am a child. I am *not* responsible enough to have this power.'

'You saved your dad,'

'*You* saved my dad. I only made things worse. Mum's off her head and Nan's in prison with the others I *healed*.'

'The Outlaw Oldies are healthy and famous,' I say. 'Nobody got hurt. Mr Wallace pretended his walking stick was a gun and they only got caught because the cashier noticed the rubber stopper on the end. They got two months for trying to steal a Victoria sponge and six lemon tarts. I bet she feels more alive than ever before. Molly, they're coming for us.'

'Del and Owain are in hospital and Stacy's lost her —' She drops her head. 'Oh, God, what have I done?'

'Del and Owain are total scum and deserved it, but there's nowt wrong with them. I saw them leave the hospital.'

'What?'

'*WOPPA* are outside,' I say, grabbing her shoulders. 'We *need* to leave now.'

'And you *need* to get off me.'

With a sharp step back, I raise my hands above my head.

'I'm sorry,' I say. 'I just need you to…'

'Grabbing me will not make me change my mind, Daniel. Is that how you treat women in your house?'

'I… I made mistakes.'

A blonde-haired girl barges up the stairs and bounds towards the landing. She gives me a snotty look and asks Molly if she's going to the Metro Centre after the funeral. Molly tells her she's not allowed out and I'm getting jittery coz outside, two massive gadgies get out of the limo. They're with the WOPPA agent who came to the hospital.

The girl says to Molly that "Ricky works on a Friday" and that "he'll be wearing his striped shirt". Molly blushes and I've had enough. I ask the stuck-up lass to give us a minute, sending her storming off in a proper huff. WOPPA walk towards school with Sparky. I need to get a move on.

'Hang with those rich dinks and drool over Ricky if you like,' I hiss. 'But I'm not going to let them take me like they did Soup.'

'Soup's dead,' she says. 'It's his funeral this afternoon.'

'He's alive. WOPPA have him.'

'Nonsense.'

'He is. I promise. Here, your dad said to show you this.'

I pull the sepia photo from my kangaroo pouch and unfold it. At first, she dismisses me, but I manage to persuade her.

'Look through the picture, like Magic Eye.'

Molly's staring at the photo like she's not hearing me. First, she points to her dad and mam and then she moves her finger up to the group leaders. WOPPA enter the building and I'm just about to leave Molly to them when she stuffs the photo into her satchel and shoves me out of the way.

'Did you see him?' I ask.

'I saw them all,' she responds, kicking the bar in the fire

escape. 'And I saw *her*.'

   'Who?'

   'Come on, we've got an appointment at the hospital.'

   'Atta girl,' says *Up-there Molly* and the mole pulses once more.

31

Dungeons and a Dragon 32

The Dragon 32 was white many years ago, but time has yellowed the long keyboard base unit and the monitor's vents are ingrained with the dust of forty years.

Gareth flicks the power button on the monitor and the screen powers up.

[Welcome to The Hub]
[Identify]

Gareth, who has an expert knowledge of IT, types:

[Gaz Ultra]

[Not recognised]

[Gareth Swift]

[Not recognised]

[KENNETH]

The Dragon 32 beeps:

[Password]

Gareth looks to be dissecting the information he has gathered in the short time since meeting the computer's owner. Next, he cracks his knuckles and types.

[Password]

[Not recognised]

[Password]

'Nar,' Gareth says. 'Got nee mare suggestions. I'm oot. Hoshi, got any ideas?'

I shove him out of the way and type:

[POTENTIALS87]

Gareth and the squirrel appear puzzled at my superior knowledge until I explain that there is a sticker on the monitor with the password written in biro.

The computer clicks and beeps.

[Access granted]

[Project — The Potentials]

[Welcome]

[Updates required. Installing update: 1 of 900]

Green block writing flashes and then the computer powers into a small spinning circle of doom at the centre of the black screen. Gareth huffs on the sofa and Oscar puts batteries into the Speak and Spell while I shed some light via an old, dusty lamp sitting on the side table. The Dragon 32 begins its slow process.

[1%]

'Knock, Knock' says Squeak and Spell.

I shrug my shoulders reluctantly.

'I eat map,' says Squeak and Spell. Gareth laughs excessively.

To my surprise, the Dragon 32 updates are rapid. The monitor beeps six times and the screen flickers from green to black.

[Welcome to The Hub] It shows in green block text.

[Identify]

I enter the details and correct password for the second time, but the Dragon 32 asks for an updated password. Before I think, Gareth has pushed me aside and is typing:

[KEN HAS SKIDDIES]

[Password updated]

[Project – The Potentials]

[Welcome back. I am Raziel]

[HELLO RAZIEL. I AM GAZ]

[I know who you are]

Theory: I suspect that Raziel is no ordinary Dragon 32.

[Shall I activate voice recognition?]

[A DRAGON 32 DOES NOT HAVE VOICE REC] Gareth types.

[I have modifications. Shall I activate voice recognition, or not?]

[YES]

[Activated: Say something]

'Alreet, Raz,' says Gareth.

'Clever, eh? Hello Gaz'

Conclusion: Raziel is *definitely* not an ordinary Dragon.

'Yer like Alexa, but not as aesthetically pleasing to the peepers,' Gareth chuckles.

'Perhaps. But can Alexa do this?'

A bolt of electricity fires from the back of Raziel's monitor and pings off Gareth's nose. His Jedi bathrobe falls to the floor as he disappears in a flash, returning a moment later in just his underwear. I cover my eyes again. It is not a pretty sight.

'Ow Man, Raz, that knacked. I've just give a lollipop lady a heart attack.'

I ask Raziel to adjust the monitor brightness because I have a headache and it informs me that it has an old copy of Windows XP from a position at the DWP last month.

[Updates required. 1 of 10000]

'Norr'again.' moans Gareth. I pull my laptop from my pack, ignoring warnings from the Speak and Spell about a rolling pin.

'Jokes. Is that better?'

'What is that *THING*?'

'My laptop?'

'Yes! That *THING*? That *SUPER COOL THING*'

Theory: I suspect that Raziel is not AI, but in fact, a hidden bedroom warrior with no understanding of the seriousness of our predicament.

Hmmmm, there are no cables to receive the internet.

Conclusion: Raziel is a supercomputer like nothing I have seen before, so I decide to give it a new coat. I snip the ends of Raziel's monitor lead with my multi-tool and fiddle with it.

'Oi! I can't see. Ooooo that tickles'

One by one, I push the coloured wires into the female connectors of my laptop.

'Oh, my… that feels goooooood'.

Seconds later, the Dragon 32 powers down, rebooting into a new outfit. I cannot help but feel smug about this as my laptop screen flickers.

[Searching…]

'OH, MY GOODNESS! The colour is so bright. I'm obsessed with this World Wide Web thing. What is this Twitter about? And TikTok? The dances are sooooo addictive. Soup. Who is that? Ahhh. Lovely. Wowzer. Hoshi, your browsing history is fun. It seems like you spend a lot of time on this short video site, Hoshi. You've been looking at Elvish Nak — OH MY! Hoshi! Has your mother seen this?!'

'Activate t-t-text mode,' I say.

[Meh. You can silence my voice but not my contribution, Hosh. I'm everywhere. I love this internet thing. I'm going to buy crypto, Hosh. Can I call you that? I feel we've

bonded. What about Spocky? I like that too]

'Pack it in, Raz,' says Gareth. 'We've gorra free Soup.'

Raziel continues its discovery of the wonders of modern technology but it does not take long to tire of silly dances and cute cats. Then, suddenly, Oscar becomes excited as he watches a cat chase a mouse that he says is his friend.

[This video is years old, Oscar. Your friend is fine]

'Raziel speaks Squirrel!' says Gareth.

[I speak everything, now]

'Raziel, c-can we modify the —'

[primitive electronics. Yes]

'Jealous?' says Squeak and Spell with failing batteries.

[Not at all. We used to date, but he's very predictable. I was always finishing his sentences]

[...]

[That was a computer joke]

[...]

[Billy Buzzkills. Hoshi, you will need some wires from that cable and your multi-tool]

Method: Intense work takes half an hour to complete and is not worthy of a montage scene. Fiddly twisting of wires proves dull and arduous, but the finished product is a technological advancement way ahead of anything I have been involved with before. The tiny speaker will translate Oscar's chit-chattering into a digitised text-to-speech voice.

[Glue it to the squirrel. There's Gorilla in the drawer by the microwave that's never been cleaned]

'Erm, no way,' snaps Oscar, holding the speaker that is speaking for him. It works perfectly. 'What if I become a tick? I'll be squashed.'

Theory: I explain quantum physics will come into play. The

speaker will be recognised as part of Oscar and when he shifts, it will also change size. It is all about neutrinos and that is why Gareth's revealing trunks and gold paint travel with him.

[Cool, eh? Snot face has advanced quantum technology]

'I have a question, Raziel,' I ask. 'Oscar thinks WOPPA are tracking us. Are they able to do that?'

[Searching... Blimp]

'Sorry?'

[Unlikely. There are 7251 reports of a miniature blimp on the day Ralph went missing. Hardly discreet. 10 YouTube videos, blurred — they always are. Debunked by WOPPA bots as fake.]

'Doesn't explain me, Oscar and Dan, though,' says Gareth.

[Where is Daniel Ambrose?]

'Colliery Row, probs. Ken's gone to get him.'

[Molly Nell?]

'Up her arn backside, mackin' everyone's life a misery.'

'Oi,' I snap. 'She will be at home g-g-getting ready for school. Raziel, search Biological Energy.'

[DNA]

'Search I.N.D.A.'

[The Interstellar Nebular Discovery Angel is a fourth-dimension camera system aimed towards the far reaches of space]

'Could WOPPA be using I.N.D.A. to search for us?'

[Without access to the central mainframe I am unable to confirm this]

'Fat Lips reckons it was searching for energy,' says Gareth. 'But why would a boring VR machine search the universe to find the energy to search the boring universe to find mare energy to search? That's like me dar gerrin' a kebab so he can jog to get another kebab.'

'I suspect they are p-planning to harvest our energy to p-p-p-power it. That's why they have Soup.'

'Errrr, nar,' says Gareth, twitching. 'I'm not being used as a flippin' battery like.'

Oscar and I look him up and down but say nothing.

[Perhaps you could rethink the outfit then, Gaz?]

The ancient computer has no filter. Nice one Raziel.

'We need to stop that camera,' buzzes Oscar.

'I can code a virus like, but they're not garna be hooked up to City Fibre,' Gareth suggests. 'We'll have to get to the mainframe.'

[Joke's on you. I had some pure killer viruses on the hard drive Hosh has just destroyed. WOPPA's mainframe is in the Labs below the building]

'Soup *and* the bad guys, all in the same place,' buzzes Oscar's Squeak and Spell. He pretends to look at a camera, winks and breaks a fourth wall. 'Convenient.'

[But WOPPA kidnapped Ralph, so it's not unlikely that he would be kept at WOPPA. I do like the fourth wall break though. If only this were a movie or a book. *Raziel turns to camera and winks ;)]

'You need a neck to break the fourth wall,' buzzes Oscar, leaping out of the way of Raziel's spark. 'No problemo, it's Soup's fake funeral. I can get us into WOPPA and down to the labs.'

'And out again?' I check.

'Dinnet worry, Jam Jar Binks,' says Gareth. 'Everybody will be sobbin' their eyes oot about Soup being not really deed, so they'll not see us sneaking in. Oscar's gorra plan to gerrus downstairs to upload the virus. Then, we free Soup and go home for free soup. Simples.'

I cannot see this working. Too many variables.

32

BMX Breakout

At the end of the road, the silver car flashes its lights and pulls away from the school. Molly and me launch down the fire escape and duck towards the bike racks by the Rec Room, as more WOPPA agents spill from the van. The female agent with a purple, highlighted crop-cut barks orders, instructing four to flank the building, while the first two follow Mr Sparks.

We bunk the front wheels from the rack, lifting the back wheels to stop the sprockets clicking and boule them to the science block, where we sneak a peek for an escape route. Two burly, suited agents approach, with one holding his hand to an earpiece, speaking low level into a lapel microphone.

'Get ready,' Molly says to me and I've never been more ready, squeezing the soft, rubber Mushroom grips on the Diamond Back BMX. I inhale the stench of bike grease and grin.

'Sorted?' asks Molly, her brow determined and furrowed as

her eyes lock onto the back lane.

'Back lane,' she orders. 'The Number 38 route.'

I place my foot onto the Beartrap pedal, tensing my thigh and wait for Molly's command.

'Three. Two. One. *Go.*'

My trainers ram down hard and the BMX breakout begins.

Molly pushes the Redline cranks on the Skyway TA and rocks the handlebars side to side, beckoning me to follow. We rip towards the agents in a blur of chrome and decals. Two bullets torpedo at them. One agent laughs out loud at the children's bikes until he's forced to swallow his mockery by our Trojan Horse. Molly levels her DX pedals and the Shimano freewheel stops the chain, skidding her back wheel. The two agents panic, unprepared to dodge as we split left and right, clipping both of the assailants with a skid and a spiked pedal to the shins. I hear the familiar crunch of metal on bone and watch my attacker drop to the deck in agony.

The *BMX Bandits* drive the pedals again, tearing between WOPPA vehicles, bunny-hopping high off the kerb and checking that we're both still rolling. I skid to a stop when Molly does. We clock Purple Vein yelling angry orders at her colleagues, but we're not sticking around, immediately blasting past The Tunnel of Trees into the back lane, weaving through the usual debris and banking left at the corner shop onto the Number 38 route to the outskirts of town.

Behind us, the van starts up as the agents slam the doors. Their only route will be the main street further up, where they'll emerge at the junction ahead of the bikes, like the best chase scenes in the best films.

Molly tilts the bike and drops her left foot, drifting the Skyway and dragging her Vans along the tarmac to keep her from falling. Then, she jolts into a forceful forward motion, rocking hard on the bars again. My thigh muscles burn and

I'm worried that I'm hallucinating because there's a ghost, or something, squealing with excitement above Molly's shoulder. My eyes are watering, so maybe I'm wrong.

Down the main road, we swerve through queued traffic and plough along the bus route leaving the WOPPA van stuck in the jam. It won't take long for the lights to release them and then we're in real trouble.

'It's half a mile of straight dual carriageway,' I warn Molly. 'They'll catch us, nee bother.'

'Downhill,' yells Molly, who's grinning, for a change. 'BMX versus BMW.'

My sparks are the only thing stopping my lungs from exploding as the WOPPA vehicles take full advantage of the straight stretch, closing fast on their target. But we're determined, and Molly's raced BMX before.

'Run from the cops,' she yells. 'Follow my lead.'

Molly's lungs suck in the air. 'Dad calls speed riding "Running from the cops",' she shouts. 'I won last year's X-Park Under Sixteens with it. Watch and learn.' She lowers her body to race position with her torso almost parallel to the bike's totally aerodynamic top tube and accelerates, leaving me to do the same.

With the gap between us depreciating slowly, Molly suddenly hits a sharp left, skipping up onto a kerb and off a raised grass mound that takes her high in the air. She tabletops the bike, landing right in front of me.

Then, a steep downhill section leads to the hospital, lying right off the roundabout, but queues of traffic form a solid blockade with no space for vans or bikes.

'Dead end,' I pant. 'There's no way through and *look*.'

Waiting at the first exit are three WOPPA four-by-four

vehicles, ready to join the chase as soon as the cars visiting the hospital give them space.

Undeterred, Molly drives harder on the cranks, speeding up as she nears the back of the queue.

'Up and over! Up and over!' Molly instructs, checking my skill level. 'Can you?'

What Molly is asking me to do is dangerous and stupid; it will probably result in a very painful pile of broken bones. But I've been through worse — several times in the last few weeks — so, I lean back, lifting the front wheel into a high manual wheelie and then, with a flick and a tuck, we jump the bikes high above the trunks of the first cars. We ride onto the roof and roll the back wheels down the windscreen onto the bonnet. An effortless hop onto the next car leaves doors open and furious drivers in our wake as Molly launches from the final automobile, high into the air, yelling "Phone Hoooooooommmmme."

I lean in, panting with pure exhilaration, landing the jump and cutting the roundabout to disappear into a crowded hospital car park.

At the bottom, we drop a ninety-degree skid into the hospital doors, where we crash the bikes to the floor and burst into the foyer, running, exhausted into Louis' Coffee Shop.

That was AMAZING!

"Leaving on a Jet Plane" chimes (with fresh batteries) as we dive into a booth in the raised area and sink low into the leather seats. Molly sits opposite, fixing her eyes on the double doors and I slump down to pull my hood up.

'Time is it?' says Molly.

'Nearly ten.'

The early morning coffee breaks fill the main street with

folk heading for a latte at Louis'. In a few minutes, the hospital staff will mob the machine outside, providing witnesses and just enough delay for the main attraction to get her ten o'clock caffeine hit.

Louis brings two shakes over to the panting pair and a confused Molly thanks him.

'I'va gotta gooda idea,' Louis says in his Italian accent, which everyone knows is as fake as my dad's trainers. 'Let's getta these curtains drawn, ey? The winter sun is awfullya lowa.'

The blind drops just as the door chimes and that nurse who was talking to Jackie skips in.

'Gabrielle,' Molly whispers to me, pointing at the sepia photo. 'Look.'

I thought I recognised her. She's one of the leaders!

Nurse Gabrielle shrugs her shoulders and playfully puts her fingers into her ears as the chime rings out. Louis pulls a funny face at her.

'Itsa gooda doorbella,' he cheers.

The Lego-haired Nurse tips her glasses, unconvinced, and then responds by sticking her tongue out and giggling. Louis heads back to his coffee machine to prepare a brew and Nurse Gabrielle spins on the spot until she's facing us. She drops her shoulders, smiles and then skips daintily from the doors, up to the booth.

'Hello, Molly and Daniel,' she says, straightening her glasses. 'I've been expecting you. You want another Malty?'

'No,' says Molly.

'I do. Can I have a banana one?'

And then it's there… in my hand, faster than a Maccie's.

'You're not a proper nurse,' hisses Molly. Her misery is seemingly unphased by magic milkshakes.

'Of course I'm a nurse. I don't save lives for a hobby, you know.'

'Whatever.'

'*Only kidding,*' the nurse says, doing a cutesy hop. 'I do save lives for a hobby and I love a uniform. You get away with blue murder in a uniform.'

'*This* is you with Urielis,' says Molly, pointing to the sepia photograph. 'You've not aged in over thirty years.'

'Are we doing the whole "serious" thing?'

Molly says nothing.

'Ok, ok, Grumpy Boots. My name is Gabriel… and I am a Celestial Entity often tagged as "Archangel Gabriel".'

'Get lost, man,' I splutter, spraying tiny globules of milkshake from my cheeks (some of which dot the Nurse's tortoiseshell glasses).

'Does oneth find attitude like that necessary?' says the nurse. 'Come with I and follow I to thine holy table of secrets.' A silent pause seems to last forever until Nurse Gabrielle raises her hand to her mouth and chuckles. 'Only kidding, Dafties. Who talks like that? Come on, follow me. You'll love this bit. My booth is quite an extraordinary booth.'

We stand to join the nurse on the steps and follow her toward an empty booth in the centre of the room where Molly says she's seen Mr Wallace and his son sitting many times before. I know Mr Wallace's son, the shopkeeper from the bottom of Colliery Lane.

The hustle of the other customers begins to fade and Nurse Gabrielle stops around a metre away, raising her palm to halt us. Then, she twirls around, taking a baby step backwards, holding out her hands for us to take hold. Her smile glows and her eyes glisten behind those big specs.

'Come on, Potentials. Let's get you all fixed up. That's a wonderful catchphrase, by the way, Molly,' she says gesturing for us to sit. She removes her glasses to reveal emerald eyes glistening like jewels and bends her abdomen as if to touch her toes. Then shimmies to standing, raising her hands high above her head and the uniform is gone, replaced by a long, white robe with an emerald trim.

'Tadaaaaa.'

Gentle and enigmatically, Gabrielle asks if we are ok. Molly glances nervously as WOPPA agents burst inside, looking around and under tables but Gabrielle smiles.

'Do not worry, Molly Mole. They can't see you. They see an empty table with a reserved sign.'

'But *I* see *you* when you're sitting here.'

'You are one of us, Darlings. Two of us? I dunno. Anyway, mi bootha es su bootha.'

Gabrielle raises a finger to the bruise under my eye and with a gentle rub, the yellowed crescent disappears. When she looks down at the scab on my wrist, I slap my hand down and pull my arm away.

Molly shakes her head to clear it. 'Nurse Gabrielle. What's going on?'

'That's a lot of question to answer without a brew,' she says, nodding over to Louis. 'Let me tell you all about Belinda.'

'Who?'

'Belinda... Belinda is a creator and her most beautiful creation is life...'

33

A Billion Stories for Belinda

'Like an artist colours paper or a musician soaks the air with sound, Belinda set to work, making nothing into something. All from her own imagination, she created this universe.

She started with a simple rock and smeared a layer of vegetation for sustenance. She added a dollop of pigmentation to brighten it up and splashed water all around.

Belinda nudged the rock closer to the sun, so it was warm sometimes. It rained — especially over Sunderland — so doing the global gardening was a lot easier. And, after a bit of tweaking and rubbing out, Belinda gave a weary stretch. She was done.

Observing her masterpiece with pride, she pulled a shaker from her drawer and sprinkled magic sparks called Biological Energy all over the place. Tiny cells became splodgy gloops and the gloops grew legs, flippers or tails, changing into remarkable creatures — some of which are extra-mega-remarkable.

For thousands of years, Belinda watched on, with genuine intrigue, as evolution played out like a reality TV show. But a creator's job involves more than binge-watching planets with a cuppa; before long, she was off, sharpening her pencils again. She didn't leave you to it though — that would be irresponsible — and with a twist of the wrist, Belinda whipped up a handful of clever souls to keep an eye on you. And ever since, we've recorded almost a billion stories of your achievements.'

'What about the dinosaurs?' I ask, unconvinced.

'I'll get to them later... Food was plentiful and luscious. The weather was glorious and humans lived in harmony with any species they didn't eat. Everybody frolicked in the sun, dressed in fig leaves, covering up only when they danced in showers or played in the snow. Earth was resplendent and enticing, so humans had nothing to do except make more humans.'

'Sounds like Colliery Row.'

''Talk of the town up there, you lot. But, unfortunately, insane population growth equals thirteen Celestials, mobbed by loads of you and stress levels went through the roof. Most of the Earth-based team quit, begging Belinda for a cushy job up in the office. But she wouldn't take us all back, so four of us remained. Uriel of Destiny, Michael of Reality, Raphael the Scribe and the best one, me... Gabriel the Protector.'

'Uriel? You mean Urielis?'

'Uriel. We like to use pen names on Earth.'

'Pen names lacking in creativity?'

'Whatever. It would have been disastrous had I not begged for a little help. So, with the enthusiasm of a hungover parent at a six-year-old's birthday party, she bestowed Uriel the ability to accelerate your Biological Energy. Humans with this advanced state of evolution became known as "The

Upgraded Humans".'.

'I'm sensing a theme here.'

'I was joking. You've heard the name bandied around. Biological Energy is DNA, which is potential energy, so, we named them The Potentials.'

'Sounds like a rubbish punk band.'

'You nearly got The Kinetics, so be careful what you wish for…'

'I think we've all learnt that lesson.'

'With the help of The original Potentials, your people evolved by making babies at a manageable rate and building amazing structures. You created art and roads and pyramids and stuff, while Raphael recorded your progression in "A Billion Stories for Belinda" — a compilation of human worthiness tales to spread hope and celebrate achievement amongst your species.'

'The Bible?'

'Sort of, but more like "The Big Bang of Books". It was the first of its kind that led to everything afterwards. It was, very simply, a completely accurate record of Humanity's evolution in Paradise. But sadly, "Paradise" means different things to different people and this was especially true of Raphael. Humans were a worthless waste of a soul that gave him nothing exciting to write about. It was Fifty Shades of Boring down here.'

'What about the amazing structures?'

'Just shapes. Hardly the flying cars and robots that Raphael dreamt of, so his boredom turned toxic, consuming his thoughts. He spent endless nights in the pub, where, drunk as a dodo, his loathing of people and love for fermented fruit gave him an idea to liven things up. Et voila: the introduction of a powerful antagonist — a massive flaming douche named Lucifer.'

'The Devil?'

'Not as such. The real Lucifer is delightful. He's charming, talented and very good-looking. Raphael despises him because he was allowed to return to the office and Belinda thinks the sun shines out of his bum — which it does because his job is to design stars.'

'Poor Lucifer.'

'Indeed. But Raphael's fictional stories stirred emotion amongst your kind. They gave you something to talk about, laugh about, cry over and hide from. Overnight, there was talk of evil snakes, plagues and locusts, sins and sacrifice, and everyone gobbled it up. Fear of this mythical super-villain spread like Somerset weeds and now, Lucifer gets the blame for everything — just like the bats.

But it was confusing for a simple species. Some humans believed in Lucifer and not Belinda. Others used Lucifer as a foundation for rule-making while idolising Belinda and chastising those who followed Lucifer. Some changed Belinda's name and some changed all the names. Earth's divides became cavernous, with religion, politics and greed leading to war and poverty. It was all because of a nightmarish narrative that depicted a fiery moron hell-bent on Hell. Raphael had invented "evil" and y'all loved it.'

'What did Belinda do?' I ask.

'She went ballistic. She stripped him of his powers but left him immortal. Banishment to Earth until the planet's last day. Banished with a permanently weird nose. Celestials, in their pure form, do not have noses. Furthermore, for a Celestial who hates humans, this is Raphael's worst nightmare, so this made him more determined. He wrote and wrote and wrote. He created more and more despicable characters, some of which were more despicable than Lucifer.

But, it was over; Raphael had made it to the bargain bin at the end of a supermarket aisle... because it turns out that word of mouth is a pretty rubbish way to sell a series. As "A

Billion Stories for Belinda" spread from its origins, the stories were misinterpreted, exaggerated and translated wrong. In no time at all — and no doubt inspired by the original Potentials — Raphael's bad guys were battling perfectly normal people with wildly exaggerated powers. And their adventures spread like… a Broken Telephone.'

'I knew it.'

'Yes, Uriel said you'd nailed that one. Mary the Weaver became "Wonder-Weaver". Jimmy the fisherman transformed into… erm… "Super Jimmy the … erm… Super-Fish" and so on. Davids were kicking Goliaths, Knights were slaying dragons and good pirates made peg legs walk the plank. They hailed Belinda and demonised Lucifer, banishing him to a fictional pit at the bottom of reality… and Earth settled.'

'Sound's farfetched.'

'Exactly. Humans aren't daft. Only the gullible believed in Jimmy Super-Fish, therefore, only the gullible believed in Lucifer and, as an unexpected side-effect, Belinda, too. The new version of "A Billion Stories for Belinda" was writing itself and working beyond all expectations — Peace for Belinda and peace for Mankind.

Now this bit is very important, so listen carefully…

While we all thought that Raphael was drowning in self-pity, he was far from procrastinating over a pint. He approached the original Potentials, one at a time, to inform them of their redundancy. With Earth settled, they were surplus to requirements and they would no longer need their advanced Biological Energy.'

'So he stole their powers?'

'He can't steal Biological Energy, but a Potential can relinquish their powers if requested by a Celest—'

'Take my powers.'

'At the cost of their soul —.'

'Don't take my powers.'

'So, armed with the Biological Energy of ninety-eight Potentials, Raphael dragged fantasy into reality. Beginning with a devilish approximation of Lucifer. Since then, he's recycled the energy to appear as countless abominable villains, reaping terror and striking fear into the hearts of children and adults alike.

Every time you take a relieved breath, he sends you another nightmare to deal with. Nobody can predict what Raphael will do next or who he will be. But one thing is for certain — regardless of costume, Raphael is stuck on Earth until Earth's last day, so he wants that last day to be yesterday. He's hoping she'll see the mess down here and press "reset". She's done it before and she'll do it again.'

'The dinosaurs.'

'Exactly. They were intelligent and funny, but now you've only got Barney left. However, because your fictional protagonists had managed to destroy Raphael's fictional villains in the past, Uriel figured you could do it in real life too. So, now, with a tweak of your Biological Energy:

A billion stories bring her joy, of quests assigned to girl and boy.
Three will set you on a path where choices lead to aftermath.
A journey lies ahead, torrential.
To mould a hero from Potential.

Like millions before you — the heroes and runners, wizards and warriors, laser-sword-wielding religious nuts, the lions in cupboards, water-walkers, and children in peaches, you will earn a chapter in history by banishing the demon back to the pages of a billion stories... Be they Orc or Goblin, or dork called Noggin.'

34

Mission Improbable

<u>THE PLAN:</u>

The tick will navigate a series of tunnels to the canteen, where he will steal **the security guard**'s badge while **the mouse** causes a distraction.

The Immortal, The Healer and The Telepath then enter the security code and sneak through to meet **The Teleporter** and the shapeshifter, take the lift down to **the lab** where they will upload the virus. Then, everyone sneaks past **The Smog Monsters**, behind the cylinder, to the secret door where the stairs lead down to the cells.

The Potentials rescue **Soup** and escape through a shutter to the rooftop car park, where Soup and Oscar carry Daniel and Hoshi to safety. The Healer will provide balloons and pop for the party.

Mission Successful!

<u>THE ACTUAL HEIST:</u>

'WHAT THE F-F-F— WHAT D-D-DO YOU MEAN SMOG MONSTERS?'

'Chill out,' said Oscar, the squirrel. 'It'll work.'

'T-T-Too many variables.'

The tick burrowed into the sock and resisted the overwhelming urge to dig its teeth into the security guard's calf. Dust mites busy-bodied like lunchtime shoppers, but the tick resisted the belly-rumbling temptation of Scrunch Face's blood.

PUFF!

The mouse recognised Jeremy immediately and asked for his autograph once this was over. He beckoned for the squirrel to come through a skirting board, into a corridor behind a security door marked 'STAFF ONLY'.

'4508,' squeaked the mouse. 'Entry code.'

The two friends waited in the walls for the woodworm's signal.

'Listen to this' sang Oscar/Jeremy. 'Too good to miss. Tra la la la la la.' And then he farted.

Five minutes later, they entered a staff training room on the corridor's left. Motivational messages covered the walls and Oscar's favourite was, "Enjoy Each Day, Because Tomorrow You Could Be Dead".

'One for Daniel,' said Oscar/Jeremy to Michael, the mouse.

'Ah, The Immortal.'

A locked cloakroom was accessible through a network of tunnels. Fading scents indicated the musty fur coats were long since abandoned and a slight twang of freshly chipped wood hung over a small hole in the skirting board.

Another network of perfectly chiselled tunnels ran from the cloakroom into a makeshift canteen next door. Stand-ups visited this room regularly as many scents stuck to the furniture.

Over by the fridge, a kettle and microwave rested on a shelf below an open cupboard displaying mugs with names written in marker. Another cupboard was jammed full of packets of porridge and plastic bowls.

Two spiders warned Jeremy/Oscar to hide, as 'Stink Finger' would prepare supper shortly.

As sure as cuckoo clocks cuckoo, Scrunch Face entered the canteen, sighed, farted, and filled the kettle (with water, not fart).

The kettle rumbled and Scrunch Face laid his badge on the bench — for the spiders to steal.

Sitting back on a plastic chair, Scrunch Face put his steel-toed boots on the table while Michael Mouse high-fived Oscar and introduced his family. His wife, Karen, said she was ecstatic to meet such a unique and powerful individual. Taken aback by the notoriety, but flattered as well, Oscar thanked the family and told them to take care on their distraction mission.

PUFF!

Seizing the day, the tick hopped onto a boot, up a leg and onto Scrunch Face's neck, narrowly avoiding the occasional slap. Michael the mouse's heart was in his mouth throughout the entire process.

In the final throes of the boiling kettle, Scrunch Face whistled and took the lid off a porridge pot. He opened the fridge, briefly turning his back on his badge, and placed a carton of OoGoo Joose on a tray. He poured boiled water into the oats and scratched his bum with his other hand. Finally, Scrunch Face waited for the porridge to cool and then stirred it with his finger. The stink finger.

Around five minutes later, an alarm sounded and Oscar headed up the guard's collar towards his sweaty neck. The dust mites chomped on Scrunch Face's dead skin, so the tick hopped up to the peak of the guard's hat, guiding like a ship's captain.

Oscar, the tick's, "tick sense" began tingling and one of the dust mites said she enjoyed this comic book reference.

'Easter eggs are important in superhero adventures,' she said. 'Dust mites spend munch-time around superhero nerds sitting on couches researching blockbuster movie references.'

And just in time, the tick leapt from a flattened palm and watched the guard burst through the door into the foyer, where Michael and his family terrified children and adults alike at the fake funeral…

35

Free Soup

The funeral procession is running late and it's just as well, coz without me, these three wouldn't get past the revolving door.

I flop down next to Gaz, keeping a decent gap between us. The kid's still not had a shower and his paint's beginning to flake. He looks, and smells, like a ten-year-old Ferrero Rocher.

'You do know it's a funeral, Gaz.' I say.

'Ye dee knar I can teleport?' he responds with a grin. 'Where's Molly?'

'Hospital.'

'Caught owt nasty?'

'Hopefully.'

Hoshi has her PE kit on and she's typing away on a laptop that she's named Raziel (…). Her face is covered with a black pandemic mask, repaired with a crude knot and her glasses are so massive they reflect the clouds in high-definition. Oh, and she's got a bag of marbles tied to her trackies.

'It's a funeral,' I say, again.

'It's c-c-cultural,' she responds, and I'm not going down that route.

Oscar's the only one who doesn't look like the leftover items at a car boot sale — he'd be snapped up before the gates open. Even the wonky leg and metallic neck growth don't stop a squirrel from being cute.

'It's a funeral,' I say to him, joking.

PUFF!

He's a penguin.

'Hey, Daniel,' the penguin buzzes, and I'm on edge, so my reflexes launch him the length of the coach park.

PUFF!

'Oscar can talk!'

'Aye,' says Gaz. 'Hoshi and Raz made him.'

I'm assuming that whatever has sunk its teeth into my earlobe, is Oscar in his current form, exacting his revenge for booting him into the fence. He'd better be careful or my sparks will pop him. We'll just see this tiny blue light and a mini mushroom cloud.

I get everyone up to speed with Nurse Gabrielle's craic, but they knew most of it thanks to Hoshi's science stuff and that computer, Raziel, who I'm sure is the beginning of humanity's downfall. Then Oscar bogs off to see his mouse friend and Gaz tells me he's been down to see Soup to let him know we're coming. Soup now thinks he's seen God... a golden god... in Speedos.... Gaz denies that his attire and sudden appearance may have caused Soup to go into shock and says it's because he's weak and hungry.

'Nothing new there then,' I say. 'I'll get him a cookie when we get him out. He'll be *Souper* again in no time.'

'Eh?' say Gaz and Hoshi together.

'Souper Soup.' I say, grinning and punching the air. 'Souper-hero.'

'Erm, Danny Lad,' says Gaz. 'Ye knar he's not called "Soup" coz he's into comics?'

'What? Then why's he called "Soup"?'

'Coz when he had Covid, me Dar and me made him some soup.'

'You what?'

'Like, aye, I took 'im some soup,' Gaz says. 'But he—.'

'You called the lad "Soup",' I say. 'Coz he ordered soup?'

'Sort of, aye. Soup. But —'

'Soup?' I ask.

'Aye. Soup.'

…

'But he thinks —'

'It's a p-private joke,' says Hoshi. 'They're in it t-t-together.'

'Joke?' I say, unconvinced. 'He doesn't get humour. You sound like you're just being mean.'

'Like Afro Gaz and Jam Jar?' says Gaz, making a point that I was unaware he knew about.

'Yeah, soz about that.'

'Nee bosh, Lad. All's good in the hood.'

And then, just in time to save my bacon, the funeral party arrives.

Hundreds of black ties and dresses disembark from coaches and cars to gather outside of WOPPA. Mark Barker and Doug are there, helping Sparky to organise the group. He's got his head up Noggin's backside and I've got no doubt he contributed to Sou— *Ralph's* disappearance. Doug will have revelled in telling his douche dad about Ralph flying.

As everyone filters in through the revolving door, Hoshi

drops her hood and together, we breeze past Scrunch Face, who seems lost without his fake metal detector and teenage girls.

Virgin families explore the tacky shop. Some gasp at the "falien artefacts" displayed on the wall, while others check watches and tissues. Mr Sparks spots me and Hoshi and heads over.

'I thought you would be at the cemetery,' he says. 'But I'm sure Ralph's parents would like to see you leading the procession. You were good friends to the boy.'

I nod and try to force fake tears when, on cue, a family of mice gets cheese deep in the middle of the crowd and it's pandemonium. Kids scream while Mams scream louder. Fathers stamp and some scream louder than the mams. Everyone runs around in a blind panic, bouncing into each other. It's a premeditated frenzy at its finest, with Scrunch Face in the middle being battered from side to side.

Seizing the moment, we sneak towards the door marked "STAFF" and I notice the Barkers are nowhere to be seen.

Scared of a bloody mouse... hilarious.

[4508]

We enter the security code and make it to the lift without issue. Above the doors is a lanyard with Scrunch Face's access badge in it. Oscar, the squirrel, tells us that when Scrunch Face was seasoning Soup's snack with arse sweat, the spiders nicked his badge and webbed it to the lift. Still hate spiders.

In the elevator, I hit a button labelled 'LAB' and we begin our descent. Hoshi pulls up her hood and hooks her mask across her face, causing her glasses to steam up momentarily until tiny wipers clear the lenses. Then, the doors open into the Biological Energy Lab, where, to the right of an ultra-violet corridor lies a computer room. Gaz zapped there and he's pointing enthusiastically to the vinyl acronym B.E.L. on the glass where he has scrawled 'END' in dry-wipe marker next to it.

Unimpressed, Hoshi's into the lab like a whippet, sliding under a desk like she's taking a Newcastle striker's legs off. She spins on her back and pushes under one computer, where she pulls out a multi-tool and sets to work. Flakey Gaz pulls a memory stick from his phone pouch and sticks it into a different type of base unit, while Oscar and I momentarily twiddle thumbs and claws.

'Ha'way,' I say. 'Let's scope out next door.'
PUFF!

PUFF!
Behind a metal cutlery cart, Oscar is a squirrel once more. Unnecessary. He was safer as a tick, but he tells me we're in it together and I need to wash behind my ears.

I take in huge gulps of an undead dankness that makes me retch. Oscar told me he had seen almost one hundred "Smog Monsters" who aren't human. The white lab coats sitting at these benches were once human; now, they slop food into their hoods, occasionally returning trays to the racks by the cutlery cart, and the one nearby makes my stomach flip.

Oscar takes a sharp breath as the creature puts its tray onto a trolley and then lifts back its hood. Grey clumps of patchy hair top a pockmarked, bald scalp. One solid eyebrow spans the forehead, highlighting piercing, bloodshot eyes. It has no nose, just two enormous, flesh-red nostrils. Wires run from its ears into a digital panel on the chest. When the Smog Monster opens its mucous-dripping mouth, it reveals two yellow fangs with a third, thicker tooth on the bottom and a bit of what looks like spinach stuck in the top gum line. They're horrific to look at and worse to smell.

Oscar skips behind another cart, freaking out like he's at a disco. He points to the energy cylinder surrounded by more lanky, rank-looking beasts with sharpened blades lining their abominable jawlines. In a panic, the squirrel returns just in time for a sliding Hoshi to boot him back where he came from (apparently, the grey squirrels will share that on their socials).

Hoshi tells us that Gaz is uploading the virus and once he's done, the lights will go out for about thirty seconds. Oscar's eyes widen with relief.

'Stealth,' he whispers. 'We can sneak past the Smog Monsters coz I can see in the dark. They'll not even know we're here.'

This would have been an excellent plan... if *the bloody squirrel could actually bloody whisper*. And just like that, Oscar's digital voice has announced our arrival to the whole of WOPPA's underworld.

Around one hundred hissing, heavy-metal-listening lampposts stop whatever they're doing, stand up, snap out their spines and turn to fix their monobrow-bordered eyes on three idiots sitting on the floor where a cutlery cart used to be.

Saliva splatters on my cheek, drooling from the gaping mandibles of the freakish abomination towering above me. And the lights go out.

Thank Gaz for that.

We scarper along the back wall, scrambling towards the cylinder, having not established if the Smog Monsters are nocturnal or not. In the darkness, the sound of their incoming, morbid meander rattles my spine with a chilling shudder and the black-blue glow of the energy tube tints the darkness where pinhole-red eyes block our path.

Oscar puffs into a tick, the wimp, and Hoshi skids to a halt, fumbling with her belt. I yell for her to hurry but realise what she's up to when I hear dozens of cracks like a bag of Fun Snaps hitting the deck. The ninja raises her hand and flicks her head — which probably won't go in my version of this story coz I'll get lawyer letters — and a diamond formation of marbles races across the floor, under elongated trotters and dropping Smog Monsters like skittles.

With floundering beasts seemingly terrible at standing up, the marbles float up into a sphere and re-pouch as I hop over writhing bodies and squeeze into the secret hole behind the tube. Then, as the emergency generator kicks in, a piercing siren wails and security doors slam shut like falling dominoes throughout the building.

This is the point of no return. This is it.

Leaping down the spiral staircase, I twist my feet to land each step, digging my toes into the insole of my trainer and gripping the mossy concrete. Dropping deep under the WOPPA building, the seemingly endless loop leaves behind the smell of undead and delivers the thickness of mildew, spore-filled, stale air.

Hoshi's hot on my trail, more nimble than I imagined her to be, being into martial arts, FIFA and Mortal Kombat. She's clipping my heels when we're spat out into a corridor lined with clunking copper pipes and crawling with slimy slugs. Puddles of stagnant water map a route to the end of the corridor, where Gaz hammers open bolts by a metal shutter. I walk cautiously towards him as he palms the last one, and the door creaks open. From within, a bright light radiates, highlighting fungal spores raining down like snow. Gaz looks at me and he's got a class grin all over his face that proper sets off goosebumps.

ZAP!

ZAP!

I thought he had done a legger, but as soon as he's back,

Gaz tells us that the dozy Smog Monsters are bottle-necking the door behind the cylinder.

'I'm not letting them bastards ruin the reunion, Lads and Lass.'

And I know what he's on about. With relief and excitement, I watch his foot, followed by the crash of a collapsing body into Gaz's arms. Ralph is still in his wetsuit, safe, and probably responsible for the smell. He grasps Gaz like a frail old man, without his Zimmer frame, and looks up in disbelief. Mould has formed around the seams of the rubber suit and infected scabs engulf a bullet hole in his shoulder. He sobs, confused and relieved, blinking away tears and sleep.

'Give ower ya daft get,' Gaz says, pulling Ralph up onto his feet. 'It's arnly been a month, Man. Yer legs still work.'

'Is it really you, Gareth?' Ralph splutters, releasing his embrace as soon as he realises Gaz is half-naked. 'Why are you a battery?'

He taps a few times and turns to Hoshi.

'Hi Hoshi,' he says, blushing. She bows.

'Get a room,' buzzes Oscar and Soup's eyes almost drop out.

'Hello Mr Squirrel,' he says.

PUFF!

'The ginger gull! You tried to save me.'

'Corrrrr,' says the gull. 'It's me. Oscar.'

Enough chit-chat. I need to get my mate back to his parents and be the hero for once. I step forward and he sees me for the first time. Then, before I know it, I'm in the air, about an inch from the rattling pipes above.

'Daniel, Fella,' he cheers, sobbing so much that my Haro top's already soaked. 'You came to save me, Fella. You are my hero, Fella.'

'Missed you, Lad,' I cheer back as we bounce from wall to wall with a bloody squirrel, a ninja and a television award all joining in the group hug. I tell them *all* they're my best mates and they say the same. It's an emotional, awesome moment. I love them all.

Obviously, that's not what really happened.

Ralph says his bit and I throw myself at him, flinging my arms around the fat dink and I'm squashing him like a stress ball, while he goes as rigid as three-day-old roadkill. He's muttering nonsense and doesn't stop until I let go. It's awkward and a complete anti-climax, but it gets the job done.

'Thank you, Fella,' he says, finally, and that's all the recognition that I need from my mate.

'Ho'way,' says Gaz. 'The demons will be down the stairs and this is gerrin' propa weird. Let's get oot of here.'

Hoshi dabs Scrunch Face's badge against the scanner and we wrench the shutter to peg it up another staircase at the back. Ralph flies up with Oscar behind him. Gaz zaps a flight at a time to check the coast is clear, while me and Hoshi push up the stairs. My adrenaline is pumping and my lungs are bad boys, so I'm on the top floor in no time. No bother.

We arrive at a massive fire exit by the car park, but it's padlocked. Everyone's looking at each other like we're stuffed and I'm thinking that there's no way back. We might as well book into the cells for a grim holiday and bonus prodding until the moment that Oscar buzzes.

'Oot the way, Boys and Girls'

PUFF!

A sturdy gorilla with massive shoulders, one wonky leg and git punchy fists, smashes the bar and the door swings open, saturating my lungs with the evening air and blinding my eyes with the glare of the spotlights.

'Proper unit, me,' Oscar buzzes with a gorilla grin.

'That'll dee,' says Gaz with a smirk. 'Ho'way then, Soup, gerra load of that Hatley goodness. Ye gan forst.'

I'm last to step into the warm, wet night and I sniff down petrichor like it's gravy granules. Up above, there are some stars visible and without the light of the pulsating cylinder, topped with its throbbing purple dome, this would be quite a view.

We did it. The Potentials saved Ralph Robinson.

'I told you, Barker. I told you they would come for him.'

A maniacal smile spreads across Mayor William Noggin's bloated face as he bares crooked teeth and projects the cackle of a madman. To his right stands Mark Barker, in his "gilet". And to the left, the broad frame of McKenzie Hilton — the school bully.

What?

No way. McKenzie Hilton? What? He looks terrified.

'So this one is surplus?' says Noggin to Barker.

'Yesh. It sheems sho.'

In the blink of an eye, McKenzie is cast across the open space to land at my feet. Lying limp, the school headcase gasps for breath amidst spluttered blood.

'He's not one of us,' I say, kneeling to lift McKenzie's head. 'He wasn't with Urielis.'

'Can't make an omelette without cracking a few innocents,' Noggin bellows, exaggerating his laugh even more. 'Hardly an innocent but a pest. Pest control just controlled your biggest pest, Barker. Step forward and take your rightful place on the throne.'

What's Mark Barker got to do with McKenzie Hilton?

Oh…

From out of the shadows, Doug Barker makes his entrance

with a smugness likened to that of a politician with a backhander from an iffy PPE contract.

'Number one,' he says to his father, with pride doused with desperation and disbelief.

'Yesh, Shon,' Mark Barker responds, faking acceptance. 'Rule the shchool.'

McKenzie coughs out a cupful of crimson blood and looks dead into my eyes, desperate and confused, while Doug revels in his deal with the devil. He must have told Noggin that McKenzie was a Potential. Doug Barker is the lowest of the low.

'He's dying,' I cry, baffled by the tragedy unfolding. 'He doesn't deserve this.'

McKenzie grips my hand and splutters, spitting spots of blood onto my Haro top. 'Barker. Our Zane. It was Barker,' he whispers.

Zane. McKenzie's cousin.

'Your mummy has gone missing,' Doug sings along with his father. 'And your best friend is a mouse…'

Doug told Zane to sing that song at me.

'Why?' I snarl.

'Oh you'll never get to Heaven,' sings Noggin with *the* most disgusting smirk imaginable.

'Oh you'll never get to Heaven,' sing Doug and Mark Barker in response.

'When you're third in line.'

'When you're third in line.'

'Take out number two.'

'And then take what's mine,' Doug chants gleefully, missing the call and response to look even more like a knob.

I look up, sucking in the realisation: Doug set this all up. The trouble at school, kicking off, punching Zane — I was his stooge in an increasingly elaborate plot to drive a wedge between me and the leader of The Fatfield Four. A twisted ploy to take the throne of a crappy gang.

What a dick.

Joining the congregation, dozens of Smog Monsters lurch between parked vehicles and into the floodlit arena of the WOPPA rooftop car park, hissing and spitting bile as their mono-brows dip centre to blood-red eyes and flapping nasal gills.

Carefully lifting McKenzie's unconscious body clear of the mob, Gaz and Oscar lay him down. A tear collects below Gaz's eye and I know this is serious coz that lad finds humour in even the most miserable of situations.

Fearless, the gorilla and teleporter stand by Ralph and Hoshi.

With not even the slightest sign of fear, Ralph beckons me forward to stand in front of the line. Inside, my bones shake, but I display a stoic resistance to Noggin's attempted terror because we are The Potentials — and we are mates.

'Ho'way then, Willy,' says Gaz, hopping from foot to foot like a boxer warming up. 'We're in the friend game now.'

36

Friend Game

It was over in minutes. What I'd expected to be a pitched battle, leading to a heroic victory, was a massacre that left two Potentials hiding behind a van, another rolling around the floor in agony, while a gorilla bleeds from his leathery pectoral.

We had no choice but to fight. My enhanced hearing picked up at least two craft in the skies and a high-pitched tinnitus-inducing tone suggested their targeting systems were powered up. Flight was not an option.

Slobbering Smog Monsters, or military-grade weapons… no-brainer.

I don't remember who charged first, but charge everyone did. Gaz landed the initial punch on the lower mandible of the niftiest Smog Monster. Despite his lankiness, the angle of his blow skimmed the drooling jaw and the trained boxer was swept aside like a reject on a dating app. I heard the familiar crunch of bone on metal and he collapsed behind the van.

Lesson learned: I went for the gut, landing several powerful punches that sent a shockwave of sparks up my forearms and biceps. Seconds later, I was lying next to Gaz and a WOPPA van with a dent roughly the size of my body. I'm grateful for the warm evening, as my sparks were fully operational.

Hoshi Solo-Spock hadn't moved. She slid behind the van and began rolling her marbles out along the floor. Then I heard the roar of Oscar's gorilla, so I dropped to the tarmac and from the gap behind the back wheel, I witnessed Oscar leap into the middle of a hoard of Smoggies and slam his humongous fists down onto one of their shoulders. Lime-green mucus spat from the ghoul's nasal sockets and for a moment, I thought we had a chance. But then, horror, as the Smog Monster pierced Oscar's fortified chest with its freakishly elongated, razor-sharp nails and the gorilla slumped to the ground. Blood oozed from his chest in strong, thick waves. My hearing picked up his heart rate doubling, as fountains spurted from his abdomen.

Now, the Smog Monsters shuffle, zombie-like, towards the van we are hiding behind. They're flanking either side and slobbering with excitement.

Oscar is dying. McKenzie is dying. Gaz won't survive another swipe.

I think we're done for.

But then, as the sun disappears and darkness falls, the Smog Monsters call an unexpected ceasefire. Louder than the baritone hum of the pulsing cylinder vibrating the vehicle walls, a thud rocks the van. My auditory senses pick up the squeaking of rubber. It's Souper-Ralph and he's landed directly above us.

'You won't take me again, Noggin,' Ralph says in his American accent.

'Resistance is futile. You're no match for my army and air assault, Fatso.'

'Maybe,' Ralph says, and I can hear a smirk in his voice. 'But *she* is.'

And the scales of justice tip our way.

'Let's get you all fixed up,' yells a voice and almost instantaneously, a ruby-red mist surrounds us, sucking Gaz and McKenzie into consciousness. Oscar rises instantly to a protective, quadruped stance, slamming down powerful fists and leaving knuckle imprints on the warm tarmac.

'Unit,' his unit buzzes. 'Proper unit.'

We all stand to watch the swirling mist whisk over the Smog Monsters, back to the shadowy figure of Molly standing on top of a WOPPA SUV and the spotlight swings around. She's wearing a black track top, black cargo pants and skate trainers, with her hair tied into several roped plaits. In her left hand, there's a cricket bat. Above her shoulder, more than a dozen balloons dart around like Medusa's snakes as three new ones inflate next to them. And Molly Nell is not alone...

To the left of the SUV, sharp flashes highlight the silhouette of a girl wearing a princess dress and a plastic Viking helmet. She carries a hammer fashioned from a rock and sticks bound to her tatty, old doll, Spindy. Billie, the scissor-cut Viking, steps into the smudged circumference of the spotlight.

'I am Princess Viking,' she warns, like a toddler pre-tantrum, 'I like Princesses and Vikings — oooooo, is that a monkey? I hope Nog Nog and his silly doctors did not hurt you, Mr Monkey.'

The little radgie makes a sprint for Oscar, who grabs her backpack and swings her up onto his shoulders, where she twirls Spindy the doll-hammer, and tiny thunderclouds strike spark-lightning into it.

Molly joins us too, passing me the cricket bat and nodding with respect.

'Where'd you get that?'

'Your step-mum's been to Sunderland. Handle's a bit burnt.'

'She's mad cool, isn't she?'

'Awesome.'

'What's in your balloons?'

'Pick and Mix.'

'Sweet.'

Noggin steps forward with Mark and Doug Barker on either side. The twisted grin from his weather-beaten face has withered away, replaced by a staid projection of internal monologue.

'You're late, Nell. Just like your father. Never on time.'

Molly strums the threads of her balloons like a harp. 'What did you do to my dad?'

A twitch at the side of Noggin's mouth suggests he is suppressing malevolence, but he refrains from answering. Instead, exhaling forcefully into the night sky, he raises his left hand and all hell breaks loose.

As if flicking on the power, the Smog Monsters come to life, swarming around us like kids when the ice cream truck chimes. They're almost on top of us before we know it and it's probably going to go belly-up again. But before punches are thrown, everyone is distracted by Billie's thunderclouds. They splatter tiny white lightning sparks that fill the sky like a vigorously shaken snow globe. Billie whirls Spindy the hammer, faster and faster, sucking the air and lighting into a mini tornado, that is uncoiled towards a Smoggie's nose-hole. Then, just as contact is about to take place, Oscar's wonky foot sends them sideways and the hammerhead sinks into the side of its head instead.

The monster is stunned momentarily, looking to be bracing a finger-slash at the child, but it deflates, hissing and blinking like it wants to sneeze. One of the earpieces attached to the chest plate pops out, so Oscar grabs the wire, yanking it from the chest and unceremoniously crunches it onto the tarmac with a wonky gorilla foot. The vile cretin rears up, piercing red eyes widening, and then it drops both spindly arms by its side. Like a teenager off to college, the docile monster turns and stumbles towards the throbbing purple dome.

Raziel beeps and Hoshi yells, 'mind control.'

'Pull out the headphones,' instructs American Ralph from above.

And finally, we get to have a bit of fun…

Clearing a path to Noggin, Molly pops balloons on Smog Monsters like she's firing a Tommy Gun. She's got her Bluetooth headphones in and she's popping in rhythm.

With a golden flash, Gaz zaps behind the mob nearest me and whips their plugs like he's picking blackberries.

One by one, the Smog Monsters snap out of their funk, turn, and walk away.

One Smoggie is right on top of me, scratching with its lethal claws and I recoil the bat, just as Ralph swoops down to yank the earpiece out. Full contact below the temple takes the monster's head clean off.

Overkill, I think. The headless body stumbles around in its lab coat looking for the cranium that has landed right by the dome, which now glows pink. The head twitches, unaware of its detachment, trying to edge towards the colourful display by its ears.

Hungry Sticklebacks dart around. Gaz and Ralph flick off the Smog Monsters' kill switches while I hit them for six and

Oscar and Billie have major fun playing "Whack a Smog". Oscar's foot is making him so unpredictable that none of the monsters know where to slash.

'Bopped him with a goodun there, Mr Monkey,' shouts Billie with glee. 'Quick, bonk that one.'

Hoshi's nowhere to be seen, but her marbles are shattering the plastic headphones like tiny sniper bullets and it's not long before the power struggle is well and truly over. An increasing number of Smoggies become preoccupied with an ever-changing light show at the top of the cylinder, while we sense victory and up our game to finish them off. Although I try to knock out the earphones and not knock off their noggins, coz I feel a bit shan about the first one.

Pushing through dopey demons, I emerge to a line of upchucking beasts fallen foul to Hoshi's marbles and the contents of Molly's balloons. She's humming "Ninety-Nine Red Balloons" and stepping over a carpet of bile and I arrive just in time to see her pop a balloon on Mark Barker.

I'm looking forward to this one.

Almost instantly, when the churning and bubbling begins, the scrawny conman's squished face drains like an emptying sink. A single bead of sweat appears on his forehead, followed by a heavy shower of droplets that cascade down over his swollen eyes and onto his *body warmer*. I jam the tip of the cricket bat down on the toe of a remaining Smog Pest while Barker mewls a hollow groan, clenches both cheeks and grabs his bottom. Penguin-like, he waddles towards the scoop of a yellow digger, with a mustard-coloured slipstream lingering behind. And, seconds later, the scoop echoes with the abysmal fart of a desperate man.

Trala lala la la…

Lost, like he's *literally* fallen into a hungry lions' den, Doug twitches, backing towards the escape route, with as little regard for his father's wellbeing as he has for anyone other than himself. But, just as he's about to leg it, his backtracking is brought to an abrupt halt by the one person on this rooftop who hates him more than me.

'Alreet, Fake-oh Malfoy,' says McKenzie Hilton, pinching the cartilage at the top of Doug's ear.

'McKenzie,' Doug chokes. 'It's Ambrose's fault. It was his idea.'

'Your dad's a slimy douchebag,' says McKenzie Hilton, cracking his knuckles. 'And you've got a massive house.' Doug spins and stumbles back towards us. 'Yer ma steals kiddies ice cream and ye… yer a slimy woodlouse.'

Give the lad a break. He's failing English.

Three cracks, as loud as thunder, fill the night sky. The first, a punch. The second and third are the bits of the nose that I see is now in three pieces when the blow twists his torso and drops Doug to his knees. Blood masks his face like he's wolfed a Ninety-Nine and a signal from Oscar sends his mouse mates scurrying from every corner to engulf the scummy twerp in a blanket of gnawing and squeaking. Doug rises to his feet, stumbling, squealing and lashing his arms around to rid himself of his attackers, but spiders and ants join the show and I still don't feel sorry for him as he disappears towards the car park.

I nod to McKenzie. It's a nod of respect that is returned immediately.

'Get safe, Fella,' I say. 'We've got this…'

McKenzie Hilton is not the sort of person who'd normally dodge a scrap, but he's not stupid either. So, he clenches his fists to follow Doug down the spiral exit and out to freedom.

'You didn't answer my question, *Raphael*,' says Molly.

'*What did you do to my dad*?'

Raphael's not paying attention — too busy watching the fall of his soldier *things*. But when she asks again, increasing the volume and aggression of her delivery, he turns with a sinister grin.

'I made him suffer.'

Molly's waited for this excuse.

POP!

'Molly, no.' Hoshi skids out from behind the van nearest me. She's got Raziel cradled in one arm and the laptop is beeping like a Saturday afternoon supermarket cash register.

Raphael lowers to one knee.

'Potentials with power inside,' he says, rhythmically.

POP!

'Will set a demon's soul free.' The tiny mayor grabs his gut.

POP!

'Potentials giving their brief lives.' Noggin grimaces but no balloons remain.

'Are bags of En-Er-Geeeeeeeeeee.'

The slimy mayor bows his head to the floor as ruby flashes race across his immaculate suit. He clutches swollen, throbbing temples and collapses to the floor, howling a deathly howl. Molly looks around at us with a victorious expression, but the look on Hoshi's face and the warning alarms from Raziel, tell us she's made a terrible mistake.

'Your b-b-balloons c-contain your DNA. Your B-Biological Energy.'

Noggin's writhing around in agony, bleeding, sneezing and trying to kneel with a buckled hip. My oesophagus clicks and I can hardly breathe at the realisation that, when Molly popped her balloon on Noggin, she didn't just give him a dodgy hip and the runs — she gave him her power too and it's *really, really* bad news.

'Belinda took Raphael's powers,' I say, spluttering. 'But you've just given him three doses.'

'So?' Molly says. 'I want to watch him suffer like he did my dad.'

'He's immortal. It won't last.'

'And?'

'Noggin can't steal powers,' I say, pointing to the cylinder. 'The Potentials relinquished theirs.'

Gaz arrives with his fingers linked above his flattened Afro Fade. 'Is that what's in the penis dome?'

'Yeah,' I confirm. 'But with Molly's power, Raphael can take as much Biological Energy as he likes. He can't be defeated.'

Molly lowers her head.

'Excellently deduced,' says Mayor William Noggin, dusting himself down. He raises his hands above his head and flattens his palms, singing in the drawn-out style of an overconfident club act, goading his audience to take part.

'Oh, you'll never get to Heaven...'

CLAP!

With a deafening slam, Noggin lights the evening skies and Molly crumples to the deck. An enormous balloon inflates rapidly from her shoulder, bursting and sending a swirl of ruby-red mist across the car park, where Noggin sucks it down like cranberry juice.

'As a human bean...'

CLAP!

Thunder clouds crackle, firing lightning bolts as Princess Viking lets out a war cry and boots Noggin as hard as she can on the shins. He barely flinches, looking down at the girl with a single, muffled chuckle and picks the little warrior up by her hair. Billie's body falls limp. Tiny lightning sparks rain from Spindy, the hammer, into Raphael's acceptant nostrils, snorting them down with immense satisfaction. He looks pitifully at the lifeless child and casts her to one side like a rag doll.

'Coz a human bean...' Noggin sings, cracking his neck.

CLAP!

Ralph slams onto the sticky tarmac like a bag of cement. The bullet hole stitches burst with ribbons of twisting amber mist. The sparks sketch the outline of a glowing butterfly, which whips up, twirls and darts into Noggin's awaiting mouth.

'Soon won't be seen...'

CLAP!

Gaz's knees buckle and he stumbles backwards, almost hitting his head on the concrete base of a floodlight. Just in time, I push my trainer under, cushioning his fall as Noggin's screech reverberates across the car park and golden sparks burn at the back of his throat.

'Oh, you'll never get to Heaven as a human bean, coz a human bean soon won't be seen...'

I've heard this one before somewhere...

CLAP!

Oscar, the mighty gorilla, makes his final PUFF! and transforms back into the little lad with a wonky leg. Cradling the unconscious Billie, Oscar's speaker falls from his ginger curls, bouncing under a car and Noggin shrieks again. Smoky green energy leaves Oscar, disappearing into Noggin's ears while the boy lies down on the tarmac next to his little warrior.

Hoshi's pegged it again. Pure ninja style, she's vanished into the night and I can't blame her. My unconscious mates lie in a heap, dying, and I'm next, surely. Noggin raises his menacing eyes to me and sings,

'I ain't gonna grieve-eye-eee-eye-eve... *my lord*, no more, more, *more*.'

Squeezing my eyes tight and bracing for the handclap, I hear sickening cracks, tearing and ripping. Through squinted lids, I see giant wings, with scorched feathers, split his blazer and spread wide from the shoulders.

'I will not grieve,' the winged mayor howls, glowing ruby-red and roaring into the darkness. 'I will not grieve for one second more.'

Tearing off his shirt reveals a body engulfed in flames. White hot muscles swell with energised power and Raphael raises an eyebrow, spitting a few embers into the night. Then, suddenly, he's gone, leaving only some crumpled, burning clothes and shoes below where he once hovered.

'Oh my, I wasn't expecting that,' the monstrous, flying nudist bellows by the entrance to the car park. He glows bright yellow above a van and has nowt to brag about. He wants to get himself covered up before his Smog Monsters snap out of it and have a good laugh at him.

'Let me change into something more appropriate,' he chortles, drawing his wings around him like a personal changing room and his outline fades from yellow to green.

PUFF!

The wings spread wide and his shoulders arch. Raphael's veins swell with rivulets of molten lava. His pale skin crusts over into volcanic rock and flames spill out of cracks that cover his ever-growing frame.

Soon, twice the size of the human form that had stood before me, a maniacal grin cracks molten rock from his cheeks. He slaps a hand to his burning head and fondles two ribbed horns that crack out, curling upwards as the thick bases squeeze through scorched skin.

With his wings spread wide, the demonic beast of darkness

rises above the van and howls into the night. The transformation is complete. The Devil is here on Earth. And, as the beast rises, the penis dome back-lights the ominous villain looking down at me with malice. I brace, tightening my grip on the cricket bat, while Raphael draws his hands to his face, observing his nails as they stretch and sharpen.

'Belinda created life, blah, blah, blah…' he spits. 'And she sprinkled molecules, double, treble blah. So, Belinda created Celestials, quadruple blah and Earth became Paradise. But you were worthless, thoughtless, selfish termites… and nothing more. Evolution? You barely left the mound.'

'You made us who we are.'

'*She* wanted worthiness, and *you* wanted action and adventure.' Raphael teleports so close that I see the reflection of a floodlight sparkle on his claw as he raises it to slash down. 'We created legends.'

'You ruined a good thing, that's what you did.'

'I only struck the match,' he whispers venomously. 'Your species used it to burn the place down.'

I prepare for an immortal scrap that won't end well for me. He can't kill me, but he will see me suffer. He wants *everyone* to suffer, just as he suffers, trapped here until the planet's dying day… Hatley for life.

Towering above me, the monster raises his other claw and spreads wide his charred wings. His grin stretches from lug to lug and molten lava dribbles from the corners. His eyes glow white hot and I am reflected in them. I feel the heat of the beast, singe my skin. My nostrils spasm with the smell of burnt hair.

The penis dome shines brighter and fractal patterns graffiti the walls of the car park, tarnishing the brickwork with neon pinks, blues and purples. It looks just like the mosaic entity I saw alongside the four jesters before my respawn.

Something drifts towards us, like weightless ash from burning paper. It dances with the Devil, gracefully dipping left and right as it glides to the floor between us. It is the sepia photo of Dad's camp, with our parents.

And like seagulls on dropped chips, I'm engulfed by pecking realisations.

"Oh, you'll never get to Heaven as a human bean" — Dad's record.

'It's *you*,' I spit. 'In the picture with *them*.'

Raphael says nothing, choosing instead to tilt his head with momentary intrigue.

'It's you in the hat,' I say, pointing to the photo. 'Standing next to Uriel, Gabriel and Michael at camp.'

'Coz a human bean soon won't be seen,' he sneers dismissively, setting off my sparks with his fire spit.

'But you're the bad guy. Why would you be in a picture with your enemies?'

Again, he remains silent, but I see hurt amidst the flaming barbecue's lumpy embers.

'"A Billion Stories for Belinda" isn't a tale of Human worth,' I gasp. 'It's your siblings being mean to you.' Raphael isn't a maniacal villain seeking the end of Humanity; Raphael is the stooge in a twisted game of Broken Telephone. It's the only explanation.

'No,' Raphael yells, shaking his head as it registers. 'No, they would not —'

'Who suggested the name?' I ask. 'Which Celestial named you *Willy Noggin*?'

'Gabriel,' he mumbles. 'She said it sounded very English.'

'They're making fun of you, Raphael.'

Raphael spits flames and rewinds his neck, spasming in confusion. A chunk of rock cracks from his thigh, exposing fresh, pink skin. It drops to the tarmac, but instead of melting through, it dissipates into a ruby-red mist and floats towards

Molly.

'Think about it,' I continue. 'When I had my vision, I saw Smashed-Plate-Face and she said *"four* will set you on a path", but Gabrielle said *"three"* coz they don't see you as part of the gang. The jester was curled up. They see you like they see us… as pitiful entertainment.'

The devil wrinkles his brow and I watch my words register. His charcoal snaps at the shoulder and the limb twitches, evaporating into a green smoke that floats towards Oscar.

'Doug Barker made a proper mug out of me because McKenzie preferred my craic,' I say. 'My *mate* fooled me into believing kids like Ralph, Gaz, Hoshi, Oscar and Molly were nerds, geeks and freaks, so I avoided them or made fun of them.'

Bewildered, the flaming beast snatches his head back and hollers, but his jaw falls off and bursts into a flash of white lightning.

'Humans devoured your creativity and admired you for it, but you couldn't see it coz your *mates* have been stirring the pot.'

Half of Raphael's molten mask bursts into Soup's amber sparks, revealing Noggin's despondent expression. Behind him, I see a sphere of marbles float towards the pulsating cylinder, so I hold his attention, allowing his flames to cool and another lump of eyebrow to disintegrate.

'My step-mam has lived with a man still in love with his ex, but she's stepped in and never faltered as a parent or partner. She's fed Dad, held him, held me, clothed me, turned up at school, worked and has remained consistent throughout. In return, all I have given back is hatred when all she's done is show me love. I have been a complete pain in the arse. I'm judgmental, angry and rude. I have been awful to be around ever since life chucked a laborious ball I couldn't catch. I wanted the world to feel *my* pain, Raphael. I wanted *everyone* to suffer, because...'

I pause and give it a moment, long enough for him to register and reflect, while the marbles form a larger dome above the WOPPA energy cylinder. Then, with my chest puffed out in acceptance, I lower the cricket bat, release my grip and let it fall to the floor. Bewildered, Raphael snatches his head back and gives me just enough time to look the Devil dead in his eyes. Just enough time, with a heavy heart, to brace for pain... and let her go.

I ain't gonna grieve my lord no more.

'Because *my* mam abandoned me, too,' I say, releasing my breath.

Raphael drops to his knees, spewing chunks of volcanic rock across the car park and lighting the corners with a rainbow of superpowers. I'm smashing him with a monologue worthy of Tennyson, but I'm about to sweep the leg.

'Your VR machine isn't looking for energy or planets,' I say. 'It's searching for Belinda. You're looking for your mam.'

'Biological Energy Labs Interstellar Nebula Discovery Angel: B.E.L.I.N.D.A.' Hoshi says, without a single stutter. Raphael lowers his molten face, and lumps of ashen rock scatter into the auras of my friends.

'Did the others tell you that they still see her?' I ask.

Raphael nods.

'They don't,' I reveal. 'She's gone. She's got so many demons, so much stuff consuming her thoughts, that we're not even on their radar. They're just shit parents, Fella.'

Powerless, his exterior crumbles and the Celestial doesn't look surprised by my reveal. Scorched feathers fall like blossom and his body slowly withers to normal size. As Gaz returns, Raphael curls onto the tarmac, crying, naked and shivering as Hoshi unzips her bag and pulls the Jedi robe from within. The final molecules of light separate in the air and are swallowed down by the respective members. Over by the van, I hear Oscar and Billie giggling. I think they're telling Knock-Knock jokes.

'B-Biological Energy is unique to the individual,' Hoshi says, wrapping the robe around the defeated man. 'Our immune systems reject foreign b-b-bodies. Foreign B-Biological Energy b-b-belongs to the owner, not the thief.'

'You never had a prayer, Sunshine,' I say, nodding to Raphael. 'Doesn't matter how much Biological Energy you've got in the penis dome, you can't do much with it. It wants to go home.'

'Superheroes will always win if the villain's power is temporary' says Sou— Ralph. 'That is not a paradox, Daniel Fella. Rigged fight.'

'Aye, get some better mates, Raffer Lad,' says Gaz, who probably should have brought his own bathrobe. 'Give the ugly bunch their energy back. I bet they forgive ya coz they're propa marras. Lerdsa potential.'

'I'll be your friend, Mr Nog Nog,' says Billie, arriving with Oscar. 'Spindy needs a prince.'

'Here,' says Hoshi, resting her hand on the sobbing man's head. 'Let me help.' With her other hand outstretched and fingers spread, Hoshi looks up, below her wrinkled brow. The marble dome expands and then implodes, shattering the glass cupola that caps the pulsating cylinder. Multi-coloured Biological Energy snakes out of the tube, separating into individual colours that wrap around the Smog Monsters one by one. They gulp down every drop and thrust their heads back as the years of slavery are finally over.

Oh, the headless one has a head now too.

The colourful congregation removes their lab coats to reveal unblemished white robes, from shoulder to floor, trimmed with various colours. There is something beautiful about these featureless beings. While their heads are similar in structure to ours, they're a mishmash of pastel shades, blurred into each other and over the edges like a child has coloured them in. These creatures radiate peace and love. They're the first Potentials. They are evolution. They are you and I… if we learn.

The OG Potentials drift over, surrounding Raphael, singing a cacophony of choir harmonies. They stoop to lift him to his feet and support him as he hobbles towards the broken fire door, cloaked like James Brown.

'There ya gan, Raffer,' says Gaz (I can tell he's getting a bit chilly). 'They'll look after ya. Mack sure ye get them some chocolates or summat decent to mack up for nicking their souls and that.'

'Hatley for life isn't that bad if you're not a Willy Noggin to everyone,' I say to the Celestial as he disappears. 'Oscar *and* Sou— *Ralph* know some cracking chippies that make Heaven a place on Earth.'

'Daniel, Fella,' Ralph says, tapping his face typewriter. 'My name is "Soup".'

'Aye, coz Gaz was taking the pi —'

'No, Daniel, Fella. Gareth calls me "Soup" because when I had COVID, Gareth and his daddy brought me some homemade soup but it was mushroom.'

'And you hate mushrooms.'

'Yes, so I told them there was "mush-room for improvement" and I made them laugh. We have been friends ever since.'

'Eh? Are you kidding me? I thought you didn't get jokes?'

'Ye've gotta watch this one, Danny Lad,' says Gaz, as Soup's mischievous cucumber bursts each cheek. 'He's gorra wicked sense of humour.'

THE END

Credits

Starring (in no particular order):
Isaac Woodland, Colin Woodland, Lukas Miley, Helen and Neil Miley. In loving memory of Dianne Woodland. To all of my extended family, thank you all. To Sharon, Margaret, Bailey and Joseph. To my friends who have somehow kept me sane: Will Crosby and Vicki Colborn, Kenny Sanger, Erin Elliott, Daniel John Lowes, Andy Nic, Tony George (rest easy, Brother), Ben Alpin, Dave 73, Peter Riddell, Steve and Tracey Paterson, Wendy Telfer (uber fan), Kat Yeats (super fan), Adam and Grace Crozier, Andy Baker, Ange and Shem, Ian Butler, Frank Styles, Daniel Coggins, David Younger, Simon Ainsworth, Lucas Renney, Ian Barnes, Beak, MC Moose, Suzanne Johnson, Steve Harrison, Sinead Florence Livingston, Waffle, Tomma, Neil Turner, Smoove, Gillian Humphreys, Daniel Smithson, Darrin Forse and Amy Linsley. To members of The Good Child, Mooch and Station to Station. To Paul Lomax (R.I.P.), Matt Robinson, Jim Maynard, Skelly, Oggy, Mark, Scotty and Slamber, Baz Crosby, Jacob, Katie and Becky Dodds, Christine Whitworth, Sharon Thomas, Jamie and Monica, Paul Oyston, Lindsey Tennant-Williams, Dave Camlin, Bex Mather and Tony Williams — thank you.
Thanks to all of the BMX Massive, young and old. The South Shields Old School and North East Vintage BMX. Keep it RAD.

Mid Credits Scene

Hoshi helped light the last of seven flaming torches outside of the bunker entrance, while her mum and Brian served up steaming mugs of broth.

In between hugs and handshakes, The Potentials fought to ask questions and tell the story to the adults.

Mr Nell chatted with Molly. It cheered her up enough to manage a smile when she saw Eric and Lil. They hovered over by the trees with Uncle Alex and Aunt Stacy, and when Billie saw them, she ran up for cuddles.

After a minute, Alex headed off, leaving the Nell family to discuss the events of the day.

Gaz ran straight through the bramble and into the bunker, passing a laughing Brian. 'Giz a jumper or summit, Ken,' Gaz said. 'I'm brass monkeys.' He emerged later in his ill-fitting shell suit.

The Robinsons sandwiched Soup and Daniel between them while Mrs Robinson stuffed sandwiches into Soup's pockets. Daniel had to fight his way out of the family squeeze to find his dad and step-mam.

Jackie and Keith were talking to Uncle Ken, Brian, and Hoshi's mum, but as soon as Daniel arrived they made their excuses and grabbed their boy with love and pride. Daniel wished the embrace would never end.

Raziel beeped from inside Hoshi's backpack.

[Lemme out, Hoshi. Lolz. IDC]

'Where's my Raz?' asked Uncle Ken, taking the laptop and opening it. 'I love the new outfit.'

[It's a bit bling for me, Darling. Take me indoors. I want

to get changed into something for the occasion. LMAO]

Soup cucumber-grinned when he saw Daniel holding Jackie's hand, while Oscar sat quietly on the fallen log.

Suddenly, Uncle Ken made an announcement.

'Ladies and Gentlemen. Let me introduce my beautiful angel — Raziel.'

Like dry ice, a sparkling mist spilt from the doorway of Uncle Ken's bunker. A beautiful golden glow from inside caused Hoshi to worry that the laptop had burst into flames. She need not have been concerned, when, from amidst the mystical mess, stepped a pretty, petite lady in a flowing, flowery dress, and Adidas Superstar trainers. Her long dark hair was crowned with a golden hairband and she curtsied as all the children gasped.

'Sorry I'm late,' said Raziel. 'I couldn't decide what to wear.'

Ken blushed.

'Where did you get those trainers?' asked Molly curiously. 'They're mint.'

Oscar sipped his broth, occasionally wiggling his wonky leg. He stared into the woods and sighed as an owl hooted and Raziel explained that she had refused to relinquish her Biological Energy to Raphael. It was a lot easier to wipe a computer's memory than a Potential's. And so she hid in a microchip. Daniel wondered if this was tenuous and possibly an afterthought to fix a plot hole.

After her brief introduction, Raziel tip-toed through the wet grass, over to Oscar and placed her hand on his curly hair. She pinched his cheek gently with the other and nodded to his wonky leg.

'Want me to fix the little fella?' she said.

Oscar pondered for a moment. 'No thanks, Raziel,' he said. 'Great White Sharks and all that.'

'Okie dokie. Then let me fix this instead.'

And with a wave of her hand across the little lad's face, she said, 'Boy to beastie and back to boy. Now you can see your friends, on both sides.'

'Thank you, Raziel,' said Oscar. 'But that's not what I'm worried about.'

'Tomorrow has space for concerns,' said Raziel. 'For now, Ken and I have a little surprise for you.'

She turned to Ken, who was engrossed in hugs and handshakes with his brother.

'Kenneth!' Raziel said sharply and Ken flung his hands to his head. 'The heroic squirrel awaits.'

'Oscar! Of course. Quiet as a mouse over there,' Uncle Ken said. 'Gladys! Gladys!' He spun on his heels and disappeared into the bunker, returning moments later to help a little old lady, unsure on her feet these days, to take one step at a time into the clearing.

Nanna Byrd leant on her walking stick and hobbled carefully towards her grandson. Oscar threw down his mug of broth and skipped towards her, squeezing her as tight as he dared.

She squeezed him back, shaking and shedding a tear or two.

Then, Nanna Byrd took a step, holding her grandson's cheeks with delicate fingers.

'I've missed you, Nanna,' said Oscar.

'And I, you, Sweetheart,' said Nanna Byrd. Her eyelids were translucent and watery.

'Don't cry, Nan. I'm ok.'

'Oscar, I'm afraid I've got some terrible news.'

Oscar's heart sank. 'What is it, Nan?' he said.

'It's just… that I can't seem to find the cat…'

Credits Continued

To Prince and Kate Bush for your music.
To music.
To Northumbria University for setting me on this journey with knowledge and encouragement. To Teesside University for your support, guidance and kindness. To the University of Sunderland (BA Community Music), for opening more doors than children in December. To the staff and students of Stockton Riverside College, thank you for accepting me. To the staff of Silksworth Community Pool, thank you for everything you do for community wellbeing. To Charlie, Millie and Karen for coffee and life in the fast lane. To Billy Kelly, Caroline Mundy, Luke Duffy, Emma Farrell, Alex Waterson, Rebecca Baty, Katy Sylvester, Tabitha Lines, Lauren Dilbo, Ben Wellstood, and Eileen Wharton, thank you for the critiques, beta reads and support. To Garron Noone for cracking me up and keeping me smiling during the long days: Follow him, he's delicious. To New Writing North, Fausto Coffee, Seven Stories, Sunderland College, Southmoor Academy, Barnes Junior School, The Saulty Cow, Wild-Fire Pizza, Mick and Daughters, The Ivy House, Chaplins, The Bunker Sunderland, Woodie's Invisible Guitar Hanger, OF Bell, Sandy Bay Caravan Park and every other business/charity and human who kept me going on this five-year journey. To authors everywhere… keep on keepin' on. Extra-Special thanks to Helen Tabel, who never doubted that The Potentials would one day see the light. I am eternally grateful for your effort, support and the split infinitive. And last, but by no means least, thank you, the reader. You are all proof that magic, miracles and superpowers do exist.

Post Credits Scene

The Office

FADE IN:
INT. A CLINICAL OFFICE — NIGHT
BOSS sits at a desk, video calling UNKNOWN

BOSS
How did it go?
UNKNOWN (V.O.)
Should have done a quest for a ring.
BOSS
They're remaking it. The wizard too.
UNKNOWN (V.O.)
So? We've had to delete the Kate Bush Walkman bit and we
did that first.
"I'm cloud-bursting, Daddy" would have sold millions.
I'll have to speak to floor five, I reckon they've read my notes.
BOSS
So you've not seen the naked teleporter on "The Boys" then?
UNKNOWN (V.O.)
Are you kidding me? I Googled that to check. We were first.
BOSS
So, what happened with these Potentials?
UNKNOWN (V.O.)
Erm, well, there's a problem.
BOSS
Go on, I'm all ears, without any ears.
UNKNOWN (V.O.)
The immortal one. He… talks to *them*.
BOSS

(looking around)
What? That's not possible. It'll be a fourth wall thing for entertainment.
UNKNOWN (V.O.)
No, he's been talking to them from the start.
(Pause)
Boss? Are you ok?
BOSS
Uriel must have told him. He's always had a massive gob.
UNKNOWN (V.O.)
Nope. It started before him. Can't you feel them?
BOSS
Feel who?
UNKNOWN (V.O.)
Them. There's one here now.
BOSS
There's always one.
UNKNOWN (V.O.)
They're not watching the humans. They're watching *us.*
BOSS
How? They can't. Pull the plug. Shut it dow—

FADE OUT.
THE REAL END

THE POTENTIALS WILL RETURN

About the Author

Adrian Woodland is a novelist, English teacher, musician, inventor (really) and BMX enthusiast with a love for 80s movies. In 2019, he graduated from Northumbria University with a Master's degree in Creative Writing and spent four years plotting, developing, writing, and changing The Potentials (over and over again). He promises that the next one will not take as long because he has ironed out most of the plotholes that would see him torn to shreds by his nerdy friends.

Born in Durham, Adrian lives in Sunderland and is about to close the laptop to get some sleep.

Web: www.adrianwoodland.co.uk
Facey: www.facebook.com/adrianwoodlandwriter/
Insta: @adrianwoodland
TikTok: @woodies_creative

Printed in Great Britain
by Amazon

51960827R00169